Vincent Briton

Some Account of Amyot Brough

Captain in His Majesty's 20th Regiment of Foot

Vincent Briton

Some Account of Amyot Brough
Captain in His Majesty's 20th Regiment of Foot

ISBN/EAN: 9783337196424

Printed in Europe, USA, Canada, Australia, Japan

Cover: Foto ©Raphael Reischuk / pixelio.de

More available books at **www.hansebooks.com**

Some Account of

Amyot Brough

Captain *in* His Majefty's 20*th Regiment of Foot, who fought (but with no great glory) under* H.R.H. *the* Duke of Cumberland *in the* Low Countries, *and had the honour to be wounded in the left fhoulder under the eyes of* General Wolfe *at the taking of* Quebec.

By E. Vincent Briton

Volume I.

LONDON
SEELEY & CO., 46, 47 & 48, ESSEX STREET, STRAND
(*Late of* 54, FLEET STREET)
1885

PREFACE.

In relating, at some unnecessary length, perhaps, the plain and unvarnished history of Captain Amyot Brough, my mind has been entirely at ease on one important point—none will ask whether it be true or false. It is a pleasing reflection, and my pen has much enjoyed the liberty thereby secured.

But another name is found in these pages—a name which all men honour, and concerning which I have not felt a like freedom.

In treating of the doings and sayings of Captain Brough, I needed to take council of no one; but in dealing with the character and deeds of the hero of Quebec, I was constrained to seek aid from other writers. I trust they have not misled me.

My chief aim, however, has been to paint the man as I read his mind in his letters, of which a sufficient number are given in the biography by the Rev. R. Wright (1864) ; and I am bound to say that a careful study of these letters has constrained me to follow Mr. Wright in doubting the accuracy of the story told by Lord Stanhope of Wolfe's extravagant behaviour in his interview with Pitt.

E. V. B.

October, 1884.

CONTENTS OF VOL. I.

CHAPTER		PAGE
I.	CONCERNING A DIREFUL EVENT	1
II.	IN WHICH AN IMPORTANT LETTER IS WRITTEN	23
III.	TORY MAKES FREE WITH OTHER PEOPLE'S TAILS	43
IV.	A RIVAL GODDESS	62
V.	IN WHICH WE TAKE A JOURNEY	87
VI.	WHEN TORY FINDS HIS LITTLE MISTRESS	115
VII.	FINDING HIS LEVEL	135
VIII.	ADMIRAL HOSIER'S GHOST STORY	151
IX.	A GLANCE AT LONDON LIFE	177
X.	WHEREIN AMYOT BROUGH BETAKES HIMSELF TO THE NORTH	192
XI.	REBEL OR NO?	207
XII.	CONCERNING THE AFFAIR OF CLIFTON BRIDGE	227
XIII.	OF EVENTS AFTER CULLODEN	250
XIV.	WHEREIN TWO LETTERS ARE RECEIVED	267
XV.	CONCERNING A CHRISTMAS ROUT	286
XVI.	HUMILIATION	312
XVII.	YEA OR NAY?	329
XVIII.	CAPTAIN GUY	345

AMYOT BROUGH.

CHAPTER I.

Concerning a Direful Event.

' You are right, madam ; I'd have been wiser if I had stayed by my own fireside in such weather as this ; but, you see, I had business to see to, and an old sailor is loath to show the white feather, though all the spirits of evil in the shape of sharp winds be abroad and adoing — which same evil spirits, as it seems to me, do as much mischief on land as on sea. But, as I said, it was business that brought me out, though if I'd had two grains of good sense I'd have stayed at home.'

So said Captain Brough, late of his Majesty's

Navy, as he stood at the door of the Griffin in Penrith town, and looked forth into the fast gathering darkness. It was barely three o'clock, but the snow had been falling for some hours, and dense black clouds were coming up, presaging a still increasing fall. The mistress of the inn shivered, and drew her shawl around her, remarking that her guest would have to stay the night in the town—the road must be blocked by the snow-drifts by this time. But that was of no matter; the captain would find company in the parlour, and a warm chimney corner, at any rate.

The captain smiled and shook his head.

'A warm fireside and a hearty welcome you never fail to offer, Mistress Thwaites,' he said; 'but if your boy will bring round my cob before the weather worsens, I make no doubt but I'll cast anchor in my own port before night; for though I can't deny that my eyes are fair dazed with staring at the white blanket all around me, I'd trust old Jonah to find his way home to Broughbarrow were it as dark as pitch; and I've my bits of bairns at home expecting me.'

And with these words, waiting only till the stout horse had been made ready, the captain bade her a courteous good-night, and set out on his homeward way. Those in the inn-parlour gazed after him with some wonder and not a little anxiety, while the stable-boy shook his head ruefully, saying :

'A rakkan he'll niver dew it ; lang afooar he gits heeam, he an' t' nag 'll be lost in this terble girt snaa, sooa thae will, sewer an' sartan.'

But the captain had no such misgivings. The distance was not great, old Jonah was stout and willing, and with the thought of the warm stable to allure him would breast the storm bravely, and scoff at the snow-drifts ; and in imagination his rider fancied himself already past all danger, and snugly ensconced in his high-backed chair by his own chimney-corner.

We will leave him to his battle with the snow, and let the wind carry us straight over hedges and ditches to that same fireside in the old parlour of Broughbarrow Farm, and make our own observations unconstrained by his presence. And in truth, reader, I had as lief trust myself to the guidance of the wind as to aught else, for when I looked for Broughbarrow Farm a while since, though it seemed to me I knew

exactly where it used to stand, I could not find
it ; and well I know that in days of yore the
captain used to say the wind and the old house
were well acquainted. So on the wings of the
wind we'll travel, and whether it pleases to put
us in at the front-door, or drop us down the
chimney, is small matter on such a night as
this, so long as we find ourselves safe sheltered
from storm and snow at last.

And the old parlour, with its high wainscoting
and faded curtains, its polished floor, its bright
log-fire, is a comfortable sight ; aye, and full of
the cheerful sound of children's play and children's voices, that best of all music to the heart
of him who loves God's creatures. The light
has nearly gone ; the room would be dark, but
for the glow on the hearth ; the lad who was
reading by the window has thrown down his
book, the little sister has deserted the task of
sewing which has made her fingers ache for the
last half-hour, and they are playing a wondrous
game of their own invention, which has no name
in books of sports, but is glorious fun for all
that, not only in their opinion, but in that of
Tory, the dog, and Whig, the cat. It leads to
many a clamber over chairs and tables, many a
scamper out at one door and in at the other,

many a spring from stool to chair, many a rush behind the curtains.

'If only I could creep as Whig does,' sighs little Joan, quite out of breath, 'you'd never catch me, brother.'

'I never can catch Whig,' replied the boy. 'It's not fair of him; he won't let himself be caught. Tory often thinks he's got him, but he's always just too late.'

And as he spoke the white poodle, having caught sight of the cat, made a bounce at him from the shining oak table on which he had been keeping guard, and, as usual, just missed his aim, but was unlucky enough to descend with unusual weight on little Joan's dearest treasure, a waxen baby, which its mistress had just put to sleep on a footstool. Her cry of alarm checked the game. Whig abandoned the idea of rushing up the curtains, and Tory, much terrified, came timidly to discover how much mischief he had done. The waxen beauty was tenderly picked up by its mistress, who seated herself on the floor to examine into the misadventure. Tory's paw had fallen too heavily on the doll's head, and the result was a serious crack across the crown.

'It's bad—very bad,' said the child. 'I

doubt if Cleopatra will recover.   I do, indeed, Tory.'

'O-o-oh !' said Tory mournfully.

'You see, her head is cracked, and that's a mortal injury.   No human being can recover when the head is cracked.'

'O-o-o-oh !' said Tory in despair.

'It's of no use to say "Oh !" in that doleful way.   You should not be so clumsy, Tory ; I often tell you so.'

Tory hung down his head, and heaved a deep sigh, whereupon Whig, who had been rubbing himself against Joan's anxious little face, seeing that Tory was in disgrace, thought it fitting to deal him a smart box on the ear.

Tory looked piteous, but was too depressed to avenge himself, feeling that, considering the crime he had committed, even Whig might be at liberty to punish him ; but Joan's sense of justice was offended.

'Whig, I wonder at you ! Have you no feelings at all ? When you see the trouble I am in, must you, too, begin to vex me ?   Tory is not your kitten, that you should beat him.   Do mind your own business for once in your life ! My precious darling, does your head ache ? Do you think you are going to die ?'

' Joan,' said her brother, ' you are a goose.
Who ever heard of a wax doll dying ?   You are
making Tory wretched—he didn't mean to hurt
the stupid thing.'

' He is careless, and thoughtless, and clumsy.
You know you are, Tory.'

Tory whined a piteous assent.   He did know
he was a wretch, a brute, a monster, the greatest
villain that ever breathed—but he adored his
little mistress : he could not live if she would
not forgive him, and he continued to utter short
ejaculations of distress in such tones of lamen-
tation, that at length Joan condescended to
say :

' There, that will do, I see you are sorry ; we
will hope the child will get better, and the crack
will not show much if I make her a pretty cap
to cover it. Shake hands, Tory, and make your
bow.'

Whereupon Tory wiped his eyes with
his paws, rose gracefully on his hind legs,
and laying one paw on his heart, extended the
other to his little mistress, and then, feeling
quite himself again, gave Whig to understand it
might be advisable to flee up the curtains if he
did not desire some return for his ill-natured
treatment.

Joan continued to lavish tender attentions on her baby, and Amyot, seeing that the romp was at an end, picked up his book and tried to pursue his reading by the firelight. But the flame was so flickering and uncertain that he soon desisted, with the remark :

'It's very hard we mayn't have a light till father comes in. There's nothing on earth to do.'

'But candle-light costs a deal,' was the sage reply of the eight-year-old maiden, 'and you can think as well in the dark, and talk as well in the dark—and I don't think it's good manners to sit mum and silent when you're not alone in the room. Deborah says book-learning makes men-folk dull and poor company—and I think so, too.'

'And I think,' said Amyot vehemently, 'that a man that can't read can have nothing to say worth hearing ; and so he'd better be mum, as you call it, Joan.'

'You are rude,' was the little maiden's calm reply ; 'why speak so loud, Amyot ? I am not deaf.'

'No ; but you aggravate me, Joan. I can't tell why—but you do.'

The little sister looked at him with the same quiet gaze of dignified surprise with which she had subdued the dog Tory. She was a soft, gentle little creature, but wondrous staid and managing for her years. Her blue eyes were serious and earnest; she could laugh a good ringing laugh, but she never smiled. Sometimes Amyot felt subdued by her air of unconscious authority, but not unfrequently his temper, naturally somewhat hasty, was ruffled by her very quietness. Being a year older than she was, it seemed to him that he ought to be able to consider himself older and wiser; but instead of being able to enjoy any such feeling, he was continually conscious of her superiority in every respect but that of physical strength. He not unfrequently lost his temper, she never did; he was often idle and careless, she was ever occupied and busy; he was constantly reproved for his short and uncourteous speeches, she could always say just the right word to everybody; and thus, from one cause or another, Amyot could scarcely fail to have an idea that his little sister was his superior. Happily he could not accuse her of anything like conceit, and consequently his love for her was as real as his respect. True, as he had said, her calmness aggravated him, but he hated himself that so it was.

She was a pretty thing to gaze at, this little maiden, with her fairy-like figure, clear skin, and long fair hair. Amyot's hair, too, was long, and both children wore it low upon their foreheads; but Amyot's hair and skin had a darker tinge, his shoulders were broad, and he had little grace of movement. Tory and Whig took liberties with him which their sense of propriety would never have permitted them to attempt with their little mistress. He was their playfellow, *she* was their goddess. They would turn a deaf ear to his commands when such commands were not entirely to their minds; her voice, never raised above the gentlest tones, brought them to her feet in a moment.

The sudden cessation of the noisy game in the oak-parlour had brought on the scene one of the inmates of the kitchen—the afore-named Deborah, a stout, elderly country-woman, who, ever since the death of the captain's wife, four years before, had, to use her own expression, ' kept things going ' at the farm. Her husband, Michael Jephson, was hind, or managing man, out of doors; for the captain was, in their opinion, a mere babe about farm matters—and how could he be aught else, seeing that ploughs and harrows, spades and pitchforks, are of no

account on board ship? No doubt he might be
well enough at driving a ship; but it took a
wiser man than he to keep a farm going, and
that wiser man, in his own and his wife's
opinion, was honest Michael Jephson.

But though they did not think highly of their
master's wisdom, both husband and wife were
truly attached to him and his children; and
Deborah's usually cheery face wore an expression of anxiety as she opened the door of the
parlour to see how the children were amusing
themselves, and, in reply to Amyot's exclamation, 'I wish father would come home!' remarked:

'It'll be lang afooar he'll git heeam t' neet.
Only heear what a terble storm's cumman;
t' hoose an' t' trees can scarce bide wheer thae
bea. Mappen he's stoppin' in Peerith,
Michael says. Sewer, he'd niver bother to
cum heeam sick a neet as thisan.'

'Not come home!' cried Amyot. 'Father's
been a sailor; he cares naught for wind and snow.
Oh, he'll come home, I make no doubt at all!'

'Whist, lad, ya ivver fur thinkin' yasell
reet. We'll see. I'd be terble glad to knaa
as t' maester, top-cooart, pipe, an' a', be safe in
Peerith this varra minute.'

'And I'd be glad to know he was coming down the lane, as I dare say he is,' responded Amyot. 'I'll ask Mike to come with me to meet him.'

'Nae, that ta wilna. Mike an' his rheumatic to gang oot in t' snaa !'

'Then I'll go by myself.'

'Nae, I tell ya; sit still in t' hoose, an' hooap all's reet sae lang as ya can.'

And she turned back into the kitchen, leaving the children gazing at each other with awe-struck faces. Joan was the first to speak.

'Deborah is frighted,' she said; 'but father is never afraid of the wind and the rain. He will come home, Amyot.'

'If he can,' said Amyot. 'Mike told me one day that he remembered a storm which blocked up all the roads about here in a few hours, and it has been snowing all day. He said several men were lost in snow-drifts.'

'To-day ?'

'No, not to-day; that time years ago that Mike was telling me about.'

'Years ago the roads, I dare say, were very bad,' suggested Joan. 'I do hope father will get safe home. The wind does howl terribly.'

There was something unusually sad in the little girl's voice. Tory's ear caught it, and fearing doubtless that she was still fretting over the mischance of her waxen baby, he came to her side with a sympathetic and regretful whine.

'Yes, Tory,' his little mistress said, 'we are thinking of your master, and the storm, and we are very unhappy about him.'

Tory sighed deeply, and went to the window to gaze out into the darkness. After a few minutes he pricked up his ears and seemed to listen. The children noticed this movement, and ran to the window to discover what was to be seen. But all was dark as pitch ; the wind howled, the snow beat against the pane ; and though Tory evidently heard something more, the children strained their ears in vain to catch the much - desired sound of horse's hoofs.

'I shall go and tell Mike and Deborah,' Amyot exclaimed. 'Tory thinks he hears something—that's plain enough.'

Mike and Deborah were sitting at their supper with the two lasses who formed the kitchen staff, when Amyot burst into the room exclaiming :

' Tory thinks he hears father coming ; but we can see nothing. Do, Mike, bring a light and come and see !'

He rose slowly, but willingly enough ; for he, too, had had misgivings, though it was not his way to talk about them. Suddenly he stopped.

' A heears summat tew,' he said, ' bet it'll no be at t' hoose-dooar, Amyot, lad. A heears a scratchin' loike at t' shippen ; sewer t' maester's beean and rooad rin theear ;' and he went down a long flagged passage, and opened a door that led into the back-yard.

' It isn't like father to do that,' murmured Joan, as the two children followed down the dark, cold passage, shivering as they met the keen blast that rushed in at the open door.

Mike had disappeared ; but ere they reached the open air, they heard him utter an exclamation of astonishment and dismay, and at the same minute Tory rushed past them, barking furiously.

' Amyot, lad, bid yan o' t' women fooak ta git es a leet ; yan can see nowt,' called Michael in a voice which was full of fear ; and in a few minutes Deborah and both the lasses were out

in the yard, she holding a lantern, by the light
of which Michael was to be seen holding by its
bridle a poor drenched horse, in as sorry a
plight as horse could well be.

'Whist, whist!' said Deborah, as the girls
began to utter cries of alarm. 'Joan, my lamb,
rin in t' hoose; t' wind will blaa ya reet awa'.
Yer fadther mun a tummelt aff in t' snaa. Mike
'll ga a bit o' t' rooad, and he'll be sartan
to meet wi' him, if bet t' mooan wud cum
oot.'

'Let me come too, Mike,' pleaded Amyot,
with white lips and eyes wide open with terror;
'let me get up on Jonah, and come with you.
Oh, I must go and find father!'

Mike looked at his wife. She had pulled off
her shawl, and was wrapping it round the
boy as he scrambled on to the weary horse's
back.

'Ya mun let him ga,' was her reply; and
Mike took the bridle and turned the horse's
head back the way he had just come.

It was not easy to make Jonah stir : he was
almost spent. Every hair on his body, as well
as the saddle, was wet as possible. What could
have happened to the master? Where could
he be at that moment?

This was the question in Deborah's mind; but as Mike and the lantern disappeared, and the court was left in darkness, she turned to the trembling child beside her, and drawing her into her arms, carried her back into the warm kitchen, soothing her as best she might. Joan did not speak, but some quiet tears were falling; and Deborah wished she would talk, and be for once, as she said to herself, like other bairns. There was a long silence, only broken by the one question from Joan, 'Did Tory go with them?' and in answer to the assurance that the dog had followed close in the horse's steps, she sighed, 'That is right; it was his duty,' and said no more.

An hour passed in this quiet suspense; then the same muffled sound of trampling in the snow was heard, and Joan slipped down from Deborah's knee and darted to the door. The three women were following, but before they could lift the latch, it was opened from outside, and Amyot, panting, wet, and utterly worn out with battling against the wind, stumbled into the room.

Joan shrank back in alarm. Amyot's eyes stared at her, but did not seem to see her. Great sobs shook his whole body, and his breath came in deep gasps ; his face was as white as ashes, his long dark hair hung over his face.

'Ya mun teeak aff hes claes, and git him summat warm ta drink, Deborah,' said Mike, who followed closely ; 'and a mun teeak Jonah t' shippen, and then I'll ga call oot t' lads, and we'll ga tagither and leeak in t' river and ivverywhaars, an' mebbe we'll find him teean side o' tuther. Bet git t' barns t' bed, an' mak' 'em teeak summat to it.'

He swung the heavy door behind him as he spoke, and was gone.

Amyot had sunk down on the hearth before the fire, and, deaf to all Joan's entreaties that he would tell her where he had been, did nothing but cry and sob, till the little sister fell into her wonted manner, and said :

'You will never be a man. I thought boys were ashamed to cry and moan like babies. I am surprised at you, Amyot—Mike was right to say that Deborah should put you to bed.'

' Deborah will not put me to bed, and I am not a baby. But you do not care, Joan. I suppose it is nothing to you that father is drowned, and will never come home again—never !' and Amyot burst out into a piteous wail which brought tears into Deborah's kind eyes, and made the two strong country lasses sob and cry.

But Joan did not cry. Her little face grew very pale and almost old in its intense anxiety, as she clasped her small hands together, and gazed earnestly at her weeping brother.

'It is not true, Amyot—you love to frighten me, but I will not believe it is true. Deborah, it isn't true ; he is frightened and doesn't know what he is saying. Jonah came safely home. Father may have fallen off and hurt himself, but he can't be drowned—can he ?'

'Nae, nae, ma lamb. He sud a gaan roond be t' rooad ; bet mebbe he cudna find t' naarest rooad. Speeak ta her, Amyot, and tell her wot Mike telled ya, and whya ya are sae sewer es yer fadther's lost.'

Amyot, thus urged, made an effort to control himself, sat up, and in a choking voice told his tale.

'We went exactly the way Jonah had come. It was easy to find it, because he had struggled along through the snow ; he had come straight down the lane, but before that he must have lost himself, for the track led into the little meadow, and right down to the river-side, and

there, Mike says, he must have stumbled and
lost his footing, and Mike believes they both
fell into the water ; and, oh, it is deep there,
and goes rushing and foaming along, and we
could see nothing—nothing at all—neither in
the river nor along the bank, and Jonah
wouldn't stay; he was so frightened Mike
couldn't hold him—he broke away, and would
come home, and carried me with him.'

'An' a varra gude thing tew,' said Deborah
soothingly ; ' fer ya cuddent hae deen nae gude.
Mike 'll dew better by hissel. An' noo, ma
bairn, ya mun coom ta bed, an' Joan 'll cum
tew, loike a gude lile barn.'

' I'll come and sit by Amyot, but I cannot go
to bed,' was Joan's resolute rejoinder. ' If they
bring father home all wet and cold, there will
be a deal to do, and he will want me.'

Amyot's heavy eyes were closing before he
was laid in his little bed. Was it the shock or
the cold that had so crushed the strong spirited
lad ? Deborah feared it was both, and fears for
her master, anxious thoughts for her husband
out in the storm, and great misgivings for the
little lad, together made up a burden, the like of
which she had seldom known.

She paced restlessly to and fro, upstairs and

down—now listening at the back door, now gazing out into the darkness from an upper window,
now returning to the room where the dark head
was nestled in the pillow in an uneasy slumber,
while the brighter head of the little girl lay back
in a rocking-chair, as she kept her weary watch
by the bedside ; anon returning to the kitchen
to see that the fire was good and the kettle was
boiling, that when the master came all might be
in readiness.

When he came! Ah, if ever he should
come !

The long hours crept on slowly—oh, how
slowly! Only those who have watched for the
morning can guess how slowly it came at last.
Deborah had listened to each hour as it struck,
had struggled against the drowsiness which as-
sailed her at the darkest, stillest hour of all, had
wrapped herself in her warmest shawl as the
night grew colder and colder, had built up the
logs on the hearth, had seen her candle burn
down in the socket, and had lighted a fresh one,
and still no sound was heard outside the farm.
She had seen with relief that Amyot's sleep had
grown more peaceful and natural, and had rejoiced to find, on one of her visits to his room,
that the little sister's eyes had closed, and her

bright head had sunk down on the pillow by his side—the fears, the sense of responsibility at last forgotten, and the children were both fast asleep.

How the good woman dreaded their awakening! Long before sunrise the beasts would be astir, the lasses would be at work, and then the children would awake. And what should she say to them? How tell them to hope, when all hope had died in her breast? 'But children are children,' she thought; 'they'll not die of grief, though Amyot has a warm heart, and the lassie is not quite like other bairns.'

A footstep in the snow, a hand softly lifting the latch, and her husband stood within the door. A miserable figure, drenched and battered, dejection in every line of his usually cheery face, utter weariness and exhaustion in every movement—and behind him, looking, if possible, still more a picture of despair, was the dog Tory.

Michael spoke no word as he put down his lantern and stout stick, and spread his hands to the blazing log.

Deborah gazed at him, and uttered the one word:

'The maester?'

He shook his head.

'Ase nowt to tell.' Then, turning to the dog, who was making for the stairs, ' Nae, Tory, lad,' he said, 'thoo munna gang to t' bairns. Let the lile things be, thae'll knaa sune enoo.'

The dog hesitated a minute, then, convinced apparently against his will, he returned to the hearth, stretched himself wearily down and waited—waited for the day to come and all that it might bring.

CHAPTER II.

In which an Important Letter is Written.

Ah, me! that waiting time!—that weary waiting time, how long it lasted! People were, methinks, more patient in those days than they are now. This century has ushered in the demon haste, and we can wait for nothing, bear nothing, put up with nothing, as in days gone by our forefathers could. Uncertainty is unbearable ; delay not to be tolerated. Last century events moved more slowly, and, perhaps, it seemed more natural to have to wait. I know not, but it seems to me that in the bustle and hurry of life of these days many of the virtues of our race have become extinct. We have no time for the genial courtesies of life ; scarce time to enjoy our pleasures ; may it not sometimes be said, scarce time to mourn our dead ?

But in Amyot Brough's childhood there was

time enough and to spare. No telegraph called
friends to his help ; no railway brought them in
a few hours to his door. Not that sympathizing
friends were wanting. Neighbours came in
plenty ; stout farmers waded through snow-
drifts to help in the search, and more than one
kindhearted motherly woman came to comfort
the poor children ; but so long as the snow continued to fall, no trace of the lost father could
be found. Day after day Amyot roamed restlessly about the house, and Joan sat silent by
the window. Mike and other men came and
went with never a word to say, and Deborah
and the maids whispered together, and wondered
how it all would end. And in the evening the
children would crouch in the chimney-corner,
silent still, but ever listening, with Tory and
Whig beside them, full of comprehending sympathy.

How long those days of uncertainty seemed !
But the certainty came at last, when the snow
melted, and the river grew less troubled, and
the skies cleared, and the snowdrops peeped
above the ground. Then the doubt—if doubt
it had been—passed away. The good old
captain, who had many a time braved the wildest
tempests on far-off seas, had met his death not

far from his own house-door, in that stream which looks so harmless as it rushes over its rocky bed, in bright summer weather. The certainty had come—the certainty that a grave in the old churchyard was all that the captain now needed; the certainty that the children were alone in the world, and must now live for each other—Amyot for Joan, and Joan for Amyot.

Looking back, in after-years, on those long days of waiting, Amyot. once said, ' They seem to me as long as any year of my life ; and Joan grew paler and more still every day.'

She was very still and silent for many a week after the father had been hidden from her sight under the sod behind the church. Amyot longed to make her talk ; but in those dreadful days he had made many a firm resolve, and one was that never again would he speak sharply to that little sister who was now his one and only possession—he would be to her a real elder brother, knight, and protector. But why—oh, why would she not talk to him ? At last she did. It was a bright day at the beginning of February. The church bells had been sounding in the morning ; but it was long since any one had taken them to church, and the idea of

going had not occurred to either of the children
when suddenly Amyot spoke.

'There are lots of snowdrops under the apple-
trees in the orchard, Joan. I have heard of
people putting flowers on graves. Shall we go
to the town and take some? It would be something to do.'

Joan woke as if from a dream, and said somewhat listlessly, 'If you like.'

Amyot remembered his good resolution, and
replied, 'It is as *you* like, Joan dearie.'

'It *is* hard for a lad to have nought to do,'
reflected the little girl; 'but about the snowdrops, Amyot—I scarcely know why we should
take them. Why do people do such things?
But I'll come; we can think about it as we go.'

'Shall we take Tory?' asked her brother,
when she had arrayed herself in her cloak and
hood for the walk, and was standing by his
side in the orchard. The dog had followed
her, and was earnestly seeking leave to go with
them.

'Take Tory to the churchyard! it wouldn't
be right—he might tread on the grave.'

'Oh no, indeed he wouldn't; he went the
other day, you know.'

'Well, he can come; and the flowers—I wish

I knew about them ; there are so many things we don't know, Amyot.'

'Yes, indeed,'—it was delightful to have a talk once more. Amyot determined to encourage her to continue—' But if people put flowers on graves it must be the right thing to do.'

'That is just like a boy,' Joan replied, in quite her old tone ; ' you speak without thinking ; but, Amyot, people always say that those who are buried know nothing about it. So why we should put flowers on their graves, I cannot see.'

' It's the only thing we can do for father now, at any rate.'

' No, indeed !' Joan's pale face grew animated and earnest. 'We can do just the same things now that we used to do. I don't mean to make the least difference.'

' Don't you ! but he won't know !'

' How can you tell, Amyot ?'

' Well, I can't tell, that's just about it. We know nothing about him now, Joan ; people say that he is alive, gone to heaven, and such things, but I don't know what they mean, do you ?'

' I don't know what heaven means, so I can't

think about that; but I've been thinking, Amyot, about father and us, and it seems to me it's like this. When father went to market, or to Carlisle, and was away a day or two, we did just as we should have done if he'd been at home. I helped Deborah, I read my books and sewed my seam just as usual, and you did your lessons and worked in the garden; sometimes father asked what we'd been doing, and sometimes he didn't; but we went on just the same. Well, why should things be different now? Father's gone somewhere, perhaps further than Carlisle, perhaps not so far; he's away, but if we're honest folks, we shall treat him just the same as if he was here.'

'Have you been thinking this lately, Joan, while you've been so quiet?' asked Amyot, with admiration; but as she did not reply, he continued, 'But father's gone further than Carlisle, it seems to me.'

'Does it? Well, to me it doesn't, and I'll tell you why. Some time ago, I forget when it was, I was sitting in the kitchen one evening— you were in the parlour with father, looking at his maps—well, I was undressing Cleopatra, and Tory was waiting to rock the child to sleep, when I heard Deborah reading to Mattie and

Sue while they ironed the clothes in the laundry. She read about a number of different people. I can't remember half their names, but I know they were dead, and some had died very hard, starved with cold, and famished, out on the mountains, some had been murdered. I felt very sorry for them, but I wished Deborah would not read such doleful stories, and I was trying not to listen, when she stopped a minute and then went on; she was still reading about the same people, but the book called them a cloud of witnesses, and said they encompassed us, and that *as* they were watching us, we ought to run our race well. It was like poetry, but it wasn't poetry. I am not quite sure I know what the race meant, but if the book spoke the truth, those who are dead are not so far off as Carlisle.'

'It was a fairy tale, I suspect; you always did like to hear about fairies and ghosts, and sometimes, I believe, you fancy you see them; don't you, Joan?'

Joan avoided the question. 'I like to think that father is not very far off—that part of him. I mean, that thinks and loves; the best part of him, that is.'

'*I* don't believe he is; you believe so easily,

Joan, and you imagine so much ; but look here, if father should be able to see us now, he can't be happy, because you know he'd see how dull we are without him, and people say folks are always happy when they go to heaven.'

' I've thought of that, too,' Joan replied, with hesitation ; ' but if he isn't as happy as he will be some day, I believe he's satisfied, and that's a kind of happiness. Of course, he's glad to have mother again ; and as for us, perhaps as they say it's good for us to have to manage for ourselves. Mother and he might have taken too much care of us if they'd stayed with us—who knows ?'

She stopped with a sob, and Amyot felt a great lump rise in his throat ; something within him seemed to say that that slight, fairy-like creature needed a good deal of care, and that any-one would say it was hard for her to have to do without both father's and mother's guardianship.

They trudged along in silence for some time, Joan choking down her sobs, and struggling to be as calm as it seemed to her she ought to be, and Amyot fighting with the angry sorrow that was clamouring to know the why of it all. Neither spoke till Penrith town was reached, and they crossed the market-place, and passed under the old church-tower to the new-made

grave on the north side of the churchyard.
There was a sound of music from within the
church, and when they had laid the snowdrops
in order on the grave, they stood and listened.
Joan loved music, and thought the sounds very
sweet and pleasant.

Penrith Church.

'Shall we go to church sometimes?' Amyot
suggested. 'I should like to hear the singing.'

'Yes; we'll go *sometimes*,' Joan said; 'just as
we did when father was alive; and when we
grow up, we'll go every Sunday. I heard him
say to Mike once, "It isn't well for the children

to see too much of the parsons; they're a breed
that don't improve, Mike."   I don't know what
he meant—do you?'

'Not quite; but, Joan, last time I went to the
church with father it made me feel as if we'd
all been doing something wrong, and I didn't
want to go again at all.'

'When was it, Amyot; and what happened?'

'It was just before the cold weather—the
roads were bad, and father wouldn't let you
come.   That Sunday when Tory ran after us,
and came into church.   Don't you remember?
—I told you about it.'

'Yes; he didn't behave well.   You said he
sat and groaned.'

'But I've often thought of it since, and I
think I know why he groaned.   You know he
always groans when he has been taken-in—when
he thinks a bone is meant for him and Whig
gets it; or anything like that.   Well, I'd had
a notion till that Sunday that church was a
solemn sort of place, and that decent, respectable
sort of folks went there; but that day it
seemed to me that it was all make-believe and
play-acting.   Of course, I like the singing, and
I like the stories one hears read; but I didn't
like the rest of it.   The parson wasn't our

parson that Sunday—not Parson Morland—but
a man from the Fells somewhere. I know all
about him, but I can't remember his name. He
made a great talk about folks denying themselves,
and working hard, and doing their duties, and
not drinking and eating too much, or wasting
their time going to cock-fights, and the like. He
said it quite solemn, as if he meant it; but it
was all make-believe, because I know, Joan,
that that man himself drinks hard, spends all
his time playing bowls or skittles at the public-
house, and never does any work at all.'

'Oh, Amyot! you must be mistaken. You
can't have seen him, so how can you know?'

'Never mind—I do know. But that wasn't
all. Before he began to preach I'd been wondering about some other things. The parson
had read out a long list of things that people
ought to do, or oughtn't to do. He said folks
mustn't steal; and there was that bad lad, Nick
Bowles, that Deborah says she can't keep from
stealing the eggs and pulling up the cabbages,
looking quite good and honest, and saying very
loud—as loud as the parson—that he hoped he
never should steal, or something of the sort.
And there was Jem Sykes, who beats his old
mother, who's bedridden, praying as loud as

loud could be that he might honour his father and mother; and Farmer White, who makes his men work on a Sunday, saying the prayer about keeping the Sabbath. Oh! it was play-acting, every bit of it—that's why Tory groaned. And, do you know, Joan, that crusty old doctor was sitting in front who always swears at Tory, and when the parson said folks oughtn't to swear, Tory gave a grunt and caught his coat-tails in his mouth, as if he would say, " There, listen ; that's meant for you." But if he could have got up in the pulpit, Tory would have made a better sermon than the parson, I believe —for he likes things honest and straight-for-ward, Tory does ; and it's my belief he won't go there again in a hurry.'

Amyot looked very hot as he ended this long speech, and his little sister's ' Hush, they're coming out of church,' scarcely availed to silence him, so excited had he become.

They mingled with the departing congrega-tion, and received a great deal of compassionate notice from many who were sorry for the poor captain's children. Just as they were passing through the little iron gate, they were overtaken by the vicar—Parson Morland, as he was generally called. Joan looked with reverence

at the tall figure in gown and bands, and laid a
warning hand on Tory's head, as she fancied
she caught the sound of a low growl beside her.
Amyot pretended not to see the clergyman, lest
as he said to himself, he should have to listen
to some good advice which would be all sham
and tomfoolery. But he was too well-bred not
to answer when he heard his name called, and,
as it happened, the vicar's mind was not just
then set on giving good advice—perhaps he had
exhausted his supply in church.

'I've been thinking of you children many
times,' the parson said. 'If the roads hadn't
been so bad, I should have come out to see
you. But I want to know what is going to
happen to you. You can't go on living at the
farm by yourselves. Have you written to your
father's relatives to tell them of his sad death?'

No such thought had occurred to either of the
children, and they said so, Amyot adding that
they knew none of their relations, and couldn't
write to them. They meant to go on living at
the farm, he said; they were not alone—
Deborah and Michael lived there, and were
very good to them.

'Oh, yes; I know. All very well for the
present. But your friends ought to know, my

lad; you must write to them and ask their advice—or if you don't I must. What relations have you ?'

'Father had neither brother nor sister,' Joan replied, for her brother did not like the vicar's peremptory way of speaking, and was not in-clined to reply. 'He often said he had nought but distant cousins—and mother's family lived in the South : grandmother lives in Kent, and I've an uncle and aunt in London. Father used to write to them sometimes. Mother was half French, and father said Aunt Aimée was like her.'

'Do you know where they live, these people ?' inquired the vicar.

'There are some of aunt's letters, and grand-mother's too, in father's desk,' answered Amyot, rather sullenly. 'I can write to them if you like, sir. But we do very well as we are.'

'Amyot, the vicar knows best,' suggested Joan timidly. 'Yes, sir, we will write. Amyot can write a nice letter if he tries.'

'Then try, by all means, and do it quickly, Amyot ; business is business, and should always be attended to without loss of time.'

He patted the children on the head and strode rapidly away, feeling glad to have thus discharged his duty towards the lambs of his flock.

Amyot was inclined to be very angry at what he called the vicar's meddling, but Joan's decided ' I am sure it was kind of him to trouble his head at all about us,' quieted him, and he began to wonder what he should say in this important business-letter, and what the result of it would be.

' I hope they won't say that we can't go on living by ourselves, as the vicar did,' sighed little Joan. ' I shouldn't like to leave Brough-barrow at all, and Mike and Deborah, and the cows and all.'

' It is my farm,' said Amyot ; ' I couldn't leave it ; everything would go wrong if I did ; people should always live on their property.'

Joan's demure little face relaxed a little. ' Deborah said our uncle and aunt would be our guardians, whatever that means. I suppose we shall have to do what they say. But I hope they'll say we may stay here.'

The composition of that letter was a most serious business, so serious that Joan was inclined to think it ought to be put off till the next day, Sunday not being the day to transact business ; but when Amyot protested that he would not have the vicar say that he neglected business, she gave way, and consented to ask Deborah to light the candles for them in the oak parlour that evening, that they might be quiet while they wrote their letter.

'Now, if you really want to help me, Joan,' her brother remarked as he seated himself before the old desk which had been his father's, 'you must put Cleopatra to bed, and not allow Whig to jump on my back, and you had better have a cloth ready, in case I should upset the ink.' Joan did most truly wish to help him, so these little arrangements were soon made, a chair drawn to Amyot's side, and all was in readiness.

The name of Broughbarrow Farm was carefully written at the top of the page, then Amyot paused.

'I shall write to grandmother,' he said ; 'I have seen her picture, and know what she is like. I can't write to this stranger man, my uncle ;' and Joan assenting, the letter began—

'To Mistress Darley.
'Honoured Madam, my Grandmother,—
    'You will marvel why it is I, Amyot Brough, who Write and not my Honoured

Father, but a Terrible sad thing has come to pass, and I am forced to write you word of it.'

'You know that is quite true, Joan. I am forced—I would not do it otherwise.'

'Yes—but never mind, go on.'

'I am not going to hurry, Joan, or I shall make mistakes. I don't know what to do. Must I tell all about it—about the snow, and the long time that we didn't know what had happened? I can't tell that.'

'No, there's no need; all that does not matter now, you know; just tell that father's dead, and that we are living here just as usual!'

'And that we want to stay—I shall say that too, Joan.'

'Shall you?—will it be respectful, do you think?'

'Of course it will, if I write it neatly and put plenty of capital letters—that's the difficult part of a letter, to know just when to put capitals.'

'And the spelling!' suggested Joan; 'but you'd better go on, Amyot, it's getting late.'

So the letter proceeded :—

'It is a verry Sad thing for Us, Joan and me, and I make no dowt that you will be much disconsolate too when you hear that our dear

Father is dead. People tell Us that He is bettre off, but we think He was quite content here, and We wish He had stayed with Us, that is, Joan and Me We are verry lonelie without Him, but bye-and-bye We shall be youst to it perhaps. The vicar bade Me write You this sad news, so We hope you will excuse this short letter, which is writ by me in great trouble.

' Your dutiful grandson,
' Amyot Brough.'

'I have heard people say,' remarked Joan, who had watched every word with deep interest and much admiration, 'that a letter ought to have a postscript—do you know what a post-script is ?'

'Yes, it's a piece written on at the end after the name of the writer—any important thing which has been forgotten; it should be something very important, and I've written all there is to write.'

'Well, I hope it's all right; it looks quite beautiful. Do you know how to fold it up and fasten it ? You must be sure to write the address very large, because when Mike has taken it to Penrith and paid for it, and sent it off, we shall not have the least idea what sort of people take care of it : they mayn't be able to read well, or they may be blind, or very old and stupid, and it is such an important letter, you know.'

Thus cautioned, Amyot wrote the address in very large letters, and added, by way of additional security, ' Kent is in the south of England, a long way off.' A remark which Mike thought extremely prudent. ' If ya nobbet sewer, Amyot, as it beant in t' Noarth.' But on this point both the children were confident. Father had so often spoken of their relations in the South, that there could be no doubt about it ; and it would doubtless be a help to the people at the post to know, otherwise, of course, they might have to look it out on the map, and then, if they chanced to get the map wrong side upwards, the letter would certainly go right away over the border.

' An' I've heeard es they be sick a set o' feckless fooak tuther side o' t' Tweed, like es not ya letter would be liggin in a ditch, if so be es thay git hoald on it,' was Mike's opinion of his Scottish neighbours ; ' bet mebbe fooak in t' South are a gae bit daft. I's heeard nowt sae verra good aboot them.'

'Father was fond of Aunt Aimée,' Joan remarked with a sigh. 'He always hoped that I should be like her, and like my mother; and they both lived in the South, Mike.'

'Na doot; and I's verra sewer es ya cuddent dew better than be loike ya mudther, my lile lassie. She wes es bonny an' es blithe es a bird, and a reet good wife to t' fadther; ay, she wer ower good fur this warld. Bet, hawivver, theear beeant mickle fooak loike her; an' Londoneers, es I've heeard tell, are pooar feckless things, a-gossippin' an' a-bodderin' wi' udther fooaks' consarns; a-rinnin' off a feytin' in forran parts, an' leavin' t' wife an' t' bairns ta fash for 'emselves.'

'But grandmother doesn't live in London. She lives in Kent; still further off than London. Father said it was.'

'I rakkan it meaks lile differ; somewheears int' South; tudther side o' t' Atlantic, beant it?'

'The Atlantic!—oh, no, Mike. The Atlantic Ocean is on the west of England,' cried both children at once. 'Father sailed across more than once.'

'Ay, ay—all reet. I thowt as 'twer a river. Bet river or ocean, it meeaks na matter, call it which ya wull.'

CHAPTER III.

Tory makes free with Other People's Tails.

IT is impossible at this distance of time to follow, even in imagination, the career of that important letter: whether it went south or whether it went north ; whether it crossed the Atlantic, or contented itself with a trip to Ireland, we do not pretend to say ; one thing only seems certain—its travels must have been tedious.   More than once had the vicar, who was not an impatient man, expressed the belief that it must have miscarried.   More than once had Mike vowed that next time a letter needed to travel so far, he should have to go with it, and see it a bit on its way ; and many times more than once had the children wondered whether the people at the post troubled themselves to send children's letters at all, before anything seemed likely to happen in consequence of the epistle composed with so much care on that Sunday evening.

'Not that it matters much,' Amyot would say; 'we did our duty by them, and if grandfather and my uncle don't care that father is dead, we cannot help that.'

But Joan was not so easy about the matter. Perhaps she felt more desolate than he did, and had a yearning in her heart for these far-off relatives, who, though strangers, were still her own flesh and blood.

She believed in them. Father had always spoken with much affection of her mother's sister, her Aunt Aimée, and as she lay in her bed at night, weeping those tears which were never seen in the daytime—tears that came from her very heart, so desolate and hungry— she wondered what that Aunt Aimée was like, who was her own mother's sister—her own mother's! Joan could but faintly remember that mother; but the picture that memory when sorely taxed would still occasionally call up was a very sweet one, and Joan could not but long to see one who was said to be like that dear mother, gone far away.

And yet she scarcely knew what she hoped would happen. Aunt Aimée was not likely to

come and live at Broughbarrow, and Joan did
not wish to leave it, not even to go to see that
wonderful place called London. Still, she
wanted something to happen, and when Amyot
said every day, ' You see, Joan, they don't want
to be troubled about us. They think we can
look after our own affairs ; and they're quite
right, so we can,' she did not echo his words, or
seem cheered by them.

She was sitting one day in the deep window
of the oak parlour, pondering over the uncertain-
ties of the future. Her seam had been forgotten ; Cleopatra, too, was unnoticed, though
seated close beside her, and Whig, after trying
in vain to attract some attention, had curled
himself up and gone to sleep, when she was roused
from her reverie by Amyot's voice calling her
in impatient tones from the garden. There was
something in the sound of his voice that made
little Joan's heart beat more quickly, and a
flush mount to her pale face. ' Joan, where are
you ? Joan, Joan !' and by the time she had
reached the lawn in front of the house, her
brother, breathless and panting, came rushing
up the slope from the rocky stream which flowed
below the farm.

' Joan, Joan, Mike says——' was all he could

gasp out; then, stopping to recover breath: 'Mike says that Tom, the carter, told him this morning that a post-chaise from London has brought company—that he saw a gentleman from London at the Griffin Inn yesterday evening; and the landlord told him he was a real gentleman, and no mistake.'

Joan drew her head up, and looking at her brother, said:

'If the gentleman is our uncle, Amyot, he will not say the same of you; he would think you a cowboy, if he saw you now.'

'Why?—because I've been fishing, and the bank is all red mud, and it sticks to my clothes, and my hat has gone somewhere down the stream, and it's useless to wear shoes and stockings when one's after trout? If he's a real gentleman, and if he's my uncle, he won't judge me by my clothes. Hey, Tory, what's the matter?'

'Oh, Amyot, run—hide yourself!' cried his sister in dismay, as, turning to ascertain the cause of Tory's bark, she saw a tall gentleman in wondrous trim attire coming towards them.

Such an elegant coat, such perfect small-clothes, such lovely shoe-buckles little Joan had never seen. She gazed in speechless admiration, and so, alas! did Amyot, totally forgetful of his rough hair, red face, and dirty clothes.

'Hush! down, down, my good fellow!' were the stranger's first words, addressed to Tory, who had his own good reasons for wishing to ascertain the character of the visitor. Then, as Joan moved shyly to meet him, making the prettiest courtsey she could accomplish, he added :

'So this is Broughbarrow Farm, and you two are my niece and nephew. I am glad I have found you at last, for I thought once that I should verily have been lost in the mud, and had to go back to London without seeing you, and that would have been a pity, seeing that I have been travelling nigh upon fourteen days for that very purpose. My little maid, will you lead me into your house and let me rest awhile ?'

Joan promptly complied, while her brother, somewhat abashed that his sister was receiving more notice than he, ran off to wash his face at the pump, repeating to himself, with a pertinacity not unusual with him, that he should not change his clothes, since a man could be worth nothing who would judge another man by his garments. But in this resolution he was over-ruled. Deborah caught him as he was coming in by the yard-door, and, turning a deaf ear to all his arguments, fairly dragged him to his room, where she did not leave him until she had seen him attired in what he called his Sunday-best.

But a change for the better in the outward man is not always accompanied by a corresponding improvement in the mind and temper. Amyot's disposition had not improved during the last few months. His was a character that greatly needed control. He had been his own master of late, and the least attempt at dictation roused a spirit of opposition and defiance which was apt to break forth in surly speech.

Joan's little face grew anxious as she turned it towards him as he entered the parlour. She knew the look on his face, and her heart misgave her.

She had been trying to act the hostess, feeling terribly shy and timid, and longing that Amyot, who was never shy, would come to help her; but when she saw that scowl on his face, she repented of her wish most sincerely.

' And you are fond of your old home ?' their uncle was saying as he entered ; 'you love Broughbarrow, you say ; but, nevertheless, my little mountain fairy, you must say good-bye to it for a while--only a while perhaps. Aunt Aimée wants you, and your grandmother too.'

Joan's lip quivered, and she glanced at the gathering cloud on Amyot's face. Did her uncle see it, she wondered ? She half thought he did, for he was watching Amyot with a strange smile lurking round the corners of his mouth. His face was grave; not exactly severe, but Joan felt that, whatever her brother might say, she at least could never dare to question her stranger uncle's will. He was so different from the only man she had every known inti-mately—her father—that though he held her hand and his arm was round her waist, she knew she should never feel inclined to lean her head against his shoulder, or nestle into his arms, as with her father she loved to do.

' Yes, your grandmother says you will be a great comfort to her, and when your letter arrived, she was greatly distressed that it was impossible for me to start at once to fetch you ; but I was busy, and it is a long way to these mountain wilds.　And Amyot is growing a big lad; we must find a school for him.'

'There's a school here—that is, at Penrith. Father always said I should go there,' Amyot broke in suddenly; then, so far remembering himself as to reflect that a man may fairly be judged by his manners, if not by his raiment, he added, 'I beg your pardon, sir, but that was my father's wish.'

'Oh, Amyot!' exclaimed his sister, 'but if I go away, you could not stay here—you will not separate us, will you, sir?'

'My uncle said I was to go to school, Joan; you could not go with me there.' There was a quiver in the boy's voice, but he tried to make it sound hard and indifferent.

Joan's head drooped: this was a trouble she had not anticipated, and the future was instantly shrouded in the deepest gloom. Tory, sitting at her feet, threw his head back and set up a most dismal howl.

'Come, come,' said their uncle, 'we must not be so doleful; why, even the dog thinks something terrible is going to happen.'

'Oh, Tory always knows what we think,' Amyot replied hastily, upon which his uncle laughed, and, getting up, said:

'Well, well, we will talk more of this by-and-by. I shall call upon your vicar, and consult him about you; and in the meanwhile let me see this house of yours, and the man who manages the farm—I must have some talk with him; and then you must show me where your father kept his papers, my little maid.'

Again that preference for Joan. Amyot felt much aggrieved; and it was with a swelling heart and a strong sense of ill-usage that he accompanied Mr. Pomfret about the premises. Was he not master of the farm?—had not even the men learned to understand that, and to treat him with something like a proper degree of respect?—while this stranger-uncle looked down upon him as a mere child, who would of course have no will of his own!

During the next two or three days Mr. Pomfret stayed at Broughbarrow, looking over papers and settling many matters of business which had fallen into confusion since the death of Captain Brough; and one day he had old Jonah saddled and rode into Penrith to see the vicar.

Parson Morland was always glad to see a new-comer, and such a distinguished-looking visitor as this was doubly welcome, and the more so because he did not call to patronize, but to seek advice 'about those poor little orphans at Broughbarrow,' as he expressed it.

'Oh yes; such a sad case—the captain a most worthy man—a little rough, but a real old English gentleman, all the same. The lad takes after him, but the little lass is a sweet winsome maiden. But how can I help you, my good sir?'

'Well, I am much perplexed. I came here fully intending to carry both the children home with me. Mrs. Darley, their grandmother, has set her heart upon having little Joan, and my wife, too, would gladly have found her a home. She is, as you say, a comely little lass, but needs gentle training to make her what a lady ought to be. The boy we thought to put to school, for the old lady, my wife's mother, cannot be troubled with lads; and mine being now grown up—my two sons, I mean—I have no call to keep a tutor; and, after all, a school is the best place for a boy.'

He paused, and the vicar cordially agreed, adding, 'For this lad, unquestionably.'

'You think so? Well, I own the boy looks as if he had that in him which would not be easily contended with—and I like peace. I am ready enough to do my duty by my brother-in-law's child, but I shall be glad if that doesn't mean taking him into my house. People say I'm not altogether pleasant to deal with when my blood is up, and that boy has a look in his eyes which means mischief, or I'm much mistaken. But I am wandering from the point which led me here. Amyot tells me that there is a good school in Penrith, and that his father always meant to send him there. Is it true that your little town can undertake to furnish a gentleman's son with the learning necessary to fit him to hold his own when he goes out into the world to try his strength? It seems to me scarcely likely.'

'There's the Grammar School—Queen Elizabeth's Grammar School—that's what the boy meant; the teaching is said to be good. I am no judge of such matters; but if you mean to leave him here, he could doubtless attend the school for a while. A little knocking about will do him no harm,' and the vicar laughed maliciously: poor Amyot had evidently not won for himself a very warm place in the heart of either of these two gentlemen.

Mr. Pomfret mused. 'It seems hard to part them,' he said, 'but partings must come sooner or later—it makes little difference at which period of our existence they occur; and having inquired his way to Queen Elizabeth's Grammar School, the conversation was changed from the subject of the children's prospects to the more interesting topics of crops, weather, and the prospects of the war just declared with Spain. Parson Morland gathered much intelligence on this last head from the traveller fresh from the fountain of all news, and grew taller and broader as he reflected how welcome a guest he should be in certain houses, for a week at least—that is, until his draught of news and gossip should have been drained to the last drop.

An invitation to dine with Mr. Pomfret at Broughbarrow, which was eagerly accepted by the parson, closed the interview, and, after a short inspection of the Grammar School, Jonah's head was once more turned towards his stable, and Mr. Pomfret returned to the farm pretty well resolved in his own mind what course he would pursue.

Not to linger over this period—rather a melancholy period in my story—I must pass over the succeeding days, during which the children by degrees discovered that their Uncle Godfrey had determined that, as he said, ' Amyot should

have his will—for a while at least—and that the
mountain nymph,' as he called little Joan, ' must
pack up her baggage, and come with him to the
South.'

'You'll be separated for a year or two, of
course,' he said, ' but don't let's have any crying
or fuss about that ; your father's children ought
to be brave, and I hate tears, and so does your
aunt.'

And he saw none—rather to his surprise
I think. Joan squeezed Cleopatra tight to her
heart, to still the wild beating there, but she
said nothing, and kept her tears for those dark
hours when she alone lay awake in the old farm-
house. Deborah wept, but Joan never cried,
merely because others did ; I think the sight of
tears rather served to dry up hers than to cause
them to flow—it *is* thus with some natures.
Joan's natural reserve made her constantly remember her uncle's words, and they served
effectually to keep her calm.

And Amyot ? Pride kept back his tears.

' It was quite right,' he said ; ' Joan should be
with ladies, he had no doubt ; but a farmer
should always stick to his land, and a farmer he
meant to be.'

Joan knew that there was a great lump in his

throat which made his voice so strained and odd. If she had not known it, I believe her heart would quite have broken.

It was a very pale little face, and very still quiet little person that Uncle Godfrey saw by his side as they stood on the high-road waiting for the heavy post-chaise which was to carry them to London. Until that morning dawned, Joan had cherished a secret hope that Amyot's courage would give way, and he would beg to be allowed to go too ; but no such request had been preferred, and the last moment had come.

Deborah and Mike were rubbing their eyes, but the children's cheeks were dry. Uncle Godfrey was proud of them, and much relieved also, for he had dreaded the parting above all things.

'We shall get off without any scenes,' he said, and he mentally rubbed his hands with satisfaction. But, alas! he had forgotten one person, and that one, no insignificant part of Joan's world.

'You will be very good, Tory, will you not ?' Joan had said to her humble slave that morning. 'You will not whine, or cry, or even groan, because you know my trouble is big enough, and if you forget yourself, I may too.' And Tory

had promised ; nay, more, he had given her his
hand upon it. 'Two years will soon pass away.
Tory, and then Amyot will come to see me, and
bring you with him ; so you see we need not
cry!' Tory agreed, but he went away and told
Whig, and they both declared that it was a
scandalous shame, and that under the circumstances it was clearly impossible to eat any
breakfast.

'Tory never breaks his word,' Joan said to
herself, as she watched the downcast mien of
her favourite, and read in his mournful eyes the
tale of his bitter grief ; 'he will do as he has
promised.'

And so he did. But Joan's compact had not
been as comprehensive as she had fancied.
Tory received her parting caress with every
symptom of subdued sorrow, and made no
attempt to follow her into the chaise ; but his
pain could not be controlled—it must have a vent
—and as Mr. Pomfret was following his niece
into the chaise he found his stiff coat-flaps
seized from behind! There was a crack and a
rent—and Tory's pent-up rage was let loose in
full fury over a large piece of rich silk, which
his teeth had torn away, and were now dragging
about in the dusty road. The chaise rolled off ;

little Joan's face, as it was last seen, was a strange mixture of amusement and consternation. Tory's fit of frantic revenge was not wholly misjudged, for it had the effect, at least, of changing the current of his little mistress's sad thoughts, and if, as in duty bound, she made his excuses to her much-incensed uncle, I think her favourite's parting demonstration of affection, though unbecoming in the highest degree, did her sore heart good.

The chaise had entirely disappeared from view ere Tory had satisfied himself that his spoil was torn to shreds ; until then, Amyot's stern orders to him to let that thing alone and come home fell on perfectly unheeding ears. At last, groaning bitterly, he obeyed; but Amyot marked that one shred of the rag was carried home between his clenched teeth and taken straight to Whig, and then the two, who had forgotten many grudges in their mutual hatred of the departed guest, united to make an entire end of this unfortunate fragment of his dress.

'I suspect Whig put him up to that piece of mischief,' Amyot thought to himself ; 'it is like Whig's spiteful ways.'

I believe that in his heart the boy felt

jealous of these two dumb animals ; they had each other's society, and he, why—he was all alone. It was very selfish of Joan to have gone away and left him ; no doubt it was fine to travel up to London in *a three-horse chaise* with Uncle Godfrey ; no doubt, when he saw her next, she would be a fine young lady, ready to laugh at her clownish brother ; no doubt she meant to forget all about him, and be happy and all the rest of it ! Well, he could not help it : he had done what was right ; for a man should live on his property—everyone said that —and if he was miserable there, why, he supposed it couldn't be helped ; only if Joan had stayed all would have been right.

Then he went out to look at his property— the fields, the haystacks, the farm-horses, the cows, the sheep ; they all looked just as usual, and paid no special regard to him, their owner and master ; had Joan been with him, the cows at least would have turned their heads to look at her.

Then he went into the house again, and finding nothing to do, he fetched the book which Uncle Godfrey had given him on parting, and stretched himself on the window-seat to read it.

It was by that wonderful man who wrote 'The History of the Plague,' and it was a real boy's book; more than once Captain Brough had promised that he would buy 'Robinson Crusoe' for his boy, but the purchase had been put off from time to time, and this was Amyot's first experience of the delights of that wondrous tale.

Tory, sitting in hopeless grief at a little distance, wondered much at his absorption, and gave it afterwards as his fixed opinion to Whig that boys were but poor creatures, had no feeling, were stupid, senseless beings; in which decision Whig fully concurred, being much aggrieved because Amyot had read his book while he ate his dinner, and consequently had quite forgotten Whig's customary portion.

'Girls for ever!' he had said, pushing his saucer of milk towards Tory, who, though he had no heart to eat, could not refuse so loyal a toast, and drank long and deep.

But although 'Robinson Crusoe' was a great solace, that day was terribly long and dreary, and as he went to bed, Amyot was not sorry to think that a new life was to begin for him on the morrow.

He was to become a grammar-school boy.

His uncle had settled *that* before he went away; every day, wet or fine, he had told his nephew he was to go to Penrith without fail: there was to be no shirking, no unpunctuality; only on those conditions had Mr. Pomfret deemed it right to allow his nephew to remain at Broughbarrow.

And Amyot had promised, thinking this injunction very uncalled-for and interfering, and with difficulty repressing a haughty answer. True, it was a long walk, but what of that? It would wile away the long days, and at school he should have some friends.

CHAPTER IV.

A Rival Goddess.

AMYOT, as we have seen, had not improved in temper or disposition during the months which had elapsed since his father's death ; a strong will, somewhat hasty temper, and dislike to submit to authority, had always characterized the lad, and his uncle had not been slow to discover these peculiarities. He had shrunk from the task of putting himself into the lost parent's place, being by nature averse to trouble, and not specially fond of children. The boy must, by-and-by, go to a good school, but for the present, perhaps, a somewhat rough one would do well enough. If the boys were rather uncouth in manner, and of very different grades of social rank, as Mr. Pomfret deemed likely, they would do Amyot little harm, since he, in his uncle's opinion, had no manners at all ; if they were rough and knocked him about, it might take the conceit out of him, which was much to be desired.

But in this last respect Mr. Pomfret's hopes were not destined to be realized. With many of the little fellows who frequented Queen Elizabeth's Grammar School, the son of Captain Brough, who had a right to call himself owner of a good-sized farm, who could ride into Penrith on his own nag, and who, moreover, was as good a scholar as the other boys of his age—I say, such a new pupil was decidedly worthy of consideration—in fact, rather a great man.

' I loike him verra weel, for all he's a gentle-mon, es ya can hear by his talk,' said a sunburnt, white-haired laddie, who came from the Fellside, and could give Amyot no further address, but was very desirous to place himself on a footing of something like intimacy, because, ' ya see, when t' weather be dirty, twa could ride on t' beeast es well es yan, and t' wud be sae con-vanient loike.'

But something, I scarce know what, made Amyot rather shy of the Fellside laddie, and be much more disposed to make friends with some of the town boys, whose conversation was more interesting, inasmuch as they heard ' if anything was stirring, and brought word to school with them.'

Three of these, brothers of the name of Kirkbride, were not slow in responding to his advances ; they lived at a very short distance from the school, in a square dark-red house, with their mother, who had been a widow for the last ten years. The eldest, Lance, was fifteen years old, and the head boy of the school, and Amyot looked up to him accordingly with great respect ; the other two were younger, and worked in the same class with Amyot—and Jasper and Percy were neither very clever nor very fond of books, so that their new class-mate received them with quite different feelings ; they were his peers, in no sense at all demanding respect. Jasper, it is true, declared that he could lick Amyot in a fair fight whenever he liked, but as yet no fitting cause for a fight had presented itself, and Lance set his face against fighting for nothing. ' But we'll have a bout before long, let Lance say what he likes,' Jasper assured Amyot ; ' but I'll not fight you when that poodle of yours is by—he'd be a dangerous sort of second, I warrant you.'

That poodle, as Tory was so irreverently

termed, was very frequently by. The farm was dull without either of the children, and Whig had been driven by despair to take to poaching, so Tory was fain to follow his young master's example, and spend much of his time in the town. Of course he was too sensible to spend hours shut up in a close room staring at books; he had a much greater variety of resources than Amyot, and carried on inquiries of many kinds: there was a weekly fair which afforded him much amusement; there were rats by the river side to be hunted; there were cats who, unlike Whig, ran away when he came near; there were others who rushed up trees, and at a safe distance spat at him—very amusing creatures, they were. Then there was an old woman who spent much time cleaning and dusting the church. Tory made friends with her, and wiled away many a half hour running up and down the gallery stairs, or watching her from the gallery or from the pulpit itself. The church was so conveniently near to the school that Tory felt always safe, when there, that he should not miss the happy moment when Amyot came out free to go home. Among Amyot's school-fellows he had also many friends: the white-haired laddie, whose

pockets often produced some dainty for him ; the
three brothers, who loved to teach him new
tricks ; and sundry others, who capered and
shouted around him whenever they saw him.
But in Tory's faithful bosom there was still a
terrible blank. 'The days were well enough,'
as he told Whig, 'but the evenings were fearfully tiresome ; no games now, no helping to put
Cleopatra to bed, none of that sweet society
without which a dog feels himself sinking to
the level of the brutes ;' and Whig condoled
and suggested that he should try poaching, but
to this proposal Tory turned a deaf ear.

But one warm afternoon towards the close of
August, on coming out of school, Amyot found
that his dog had made a new friend.   The gate
into the churchyard stood open, and there,
walking round and round the quaint stones
called the Giant's Grave, Amyot saw Tory in
company with a little girl whom the three
Kirkbride lads at once hailed as Primrose.

'Hilloa, little one ! hilloa, Primrose ! how
came you here ?'

'Come to take you home, if you's been good
little lads,' was the little maiden's prompt reply ;
'mother's left me here to wait for you—she's
gone to see Goody Greenaway.'

'And you've found a friend while you've been waiting; you're a rare one for making friends.'

'Such a funny dog! such a dear dog!' said

The Giant's Grave.

the child, seating herself on the stones and taking Tory's head in her arms; whereupon

Amyot, though feeling shy, came up and stood by his dog's side. 'Is he yours?' asked little Primrose, lifting up her face and looking at him.

It was such a lovely little face that Amyot's whole thoughts were given up to considering it, and he quite forgot to answer her. Eyes of the deepest violet blue, with long dark fringes; a rosy budding mouth, and skin as white and soft as milk. It was a face that rippled all over with smiles; there was the merriest laughter in the eyes, the gleefulest quiver about the lips, while the tiny feet seemed rather to dance than walk.

'Of course, this is Tory, and he belongs to Amyot Brough. We've told you about him many a time, Primrose,' said Lance, taking the child's hand to lead her away; but she stopped him.

'Wait a minute, I am not ready yet; he has been very agreeable to me—I must give him something that he may not forget me. Have none of you lads something nice in your pockets?' and she looked round at the three boys, who searched, but in vain.

'Oh, Tory needs nothing, Miss Primrose; he would be hurt, if he thought you wanted to pay him,' said Amyot, blushing up to the roots of his hair.

'How stupid of me,' he thought, 'to grow red as a turkey-cock because a little girl speaks to me; what a fool she will think me!'

But if she did, she did not say so, though she gazed at him very earnestly as she said:

'I like your dog; I almost love him. I wish he could come and spend the day with me sometimes, while you are at school and do not want him. I like gentlemanly dogs!'

'Tory will be very pleased,' Amyot said, feeling much the bitterness of the fate which cut him off from such a privilege. 'If we may walk home with you now, Tory will know where to come; and I too should like to know where you live.'

He said this with another blush, and the little maiden laughed.

'You are almost as gentlemanly as your dog,' she said, as she allowed him to take her left hand, the right resting in Lance's large palm; and in this order they went down the narrow path towards the street where the Kirkbrides lived.

They parted on the steps, Primrose laying her soft hand on Tory's head, and saying:

'Do you understand, you dear dog, that I want you to come and spend the day with me on Friday—not to-morrow, because I shall be busy, but the day after—Friday; shall you remember, Tory?'

'Trust him—he'll remember!' Amyot answered; and Tory made his very best bow and departed.

What an evening that was! Whig wondered what had come over his master and Tory; but he was left to wonder, for no one enlightened him.

The evenings were very long just then, and Amyot usually spent them in poring over 'Robinson Crusoe,' and another tale by the same fascinating author, which had lately come to him from London, called the 'Memoirs of a Cavalier.'

How Tory and Whig hated those books; but on this particular evening, though the book was open before him, Amyot lay on the grass and stared absently at the blue sky, though I doubt whether he saw the sky at all, or the trees either; the fairy vision which had crossed his path that afternoon was still before his eyes. It had made him think of Joan, and long more than he had ever yet done that she would come back, and things would be as in days of yore. And Tory, he too sat staring straight in front, only starting up occasionally to rush round the garden and then return to his seat, with an air of great contentment—'Just for all the world,' Whig said to himself, 'as if the little mistress had come back.'

Had Tory been the hero of my tale, as I am half inclined to wish he were, dogs being for the most part more easily comprehended than men and women—I say, had Tory been my hero, it would be my duty, as it would also be my pleasure, to follow him on that eventful day when he found himself introduced into the new world of Blencathara House, and go with him through the many excitements that awaited him, as his new friend showed him her many treasures, her family of waxen babies — all whose virtues and faults she detailed to him as he sat sedately before her, and listened with eyes wide open and full of interest; we would follow them into the old garden and see the jackdaws, whose chattering almost turned Tory's brain; we would sit under the old cedar and listen to Primrose's tales of the fairies that lived under every bush, until we longed, as Tory did, that our eyes could see all hers saw from under those wondrous long lashes. To be appreciated once more was balm to

Tory's spirit; to be talked to, as Joan had talked to him; to be the trusted recipient of many secrets; to be assured finally, 'I have told you all this, Tory, because you are so gentle and polite, and because I see that you understand all my feelings,' was simply enchanting; and the good dog became on the spot her devout adorer, a slave once more to beauty and virtue.

But we must not be led away from the straight path of duty by the bright eyes or witching wiles of this wee damsel, but return to the plain unvarnished history of Amyot Brough. And truth compels us to admit that the day which was so bright to Tory was but a sorry one with his young master. Never had school been so fruitful in woes to him; never had lessons seemed so hateful, or the master so stern a tyrant. Unhappily his thoughts had gone after his dog. The master grimly assured him that he was daft, or little short of it, and when that observation failed to bring him to his senses, recourse was had to a bunch of twigs from the tree created, as the master assured him, for the special benefit of children. Proud as he was, Amyot had no doubt of the soundness of this reasoning: his father had held the same views, and acted upon them, and even when most uplifted by the idea that he was master of Broughbarrow, he had never failed to recognise the fact that as long as he was young enough to be whipped, he must not expect exemption from that most necessary part of education.

Nay, had fate so willed it, that Amyot had escaped correction, far from respecting himself the more for such exemption, I suspect that he would have felt in after-years that he had missed something which might have made him a wiser and a stronger man. His education would have been in some sort imperfect ; his childhood would have been a childhood of neglect.

Nevertheless, it was a sorry day, and this Tory was not slow in perceiving when, full of bounding glee, he met hi · master coming out of school, and found his rapture at once checked and chilled by an almost unnoticing reception. There was no need to tell the wise dog what had happened : he had been young himself, and knew well the consequences of youthful folly ; perhaps he wondered whether Amyot had been drinking the cream, or tearing up the flowers in the garden ; but he wisely refrained from inquiries, and showed his sympathy by respectful silence, and by walking quietly by his master's side all the way home, instead of rushing wildly backwards and forwards, as was his usual practice.

But the darkest days in our lives have an end, and the sun that sets in a storm often shines its fairest on the morrow; and so it proved on the morrow of that gloomy day. It was a half-holiday, and the Kirkbride lads, full of good-natured remorse for having laughed at Amyot's afflictions on the previous day, had resolved to make their peace with him by inviting him to go for a long walk with them in the afternoon, and Amyot, who in his bitter trouble had vowed that he would never speak to them again, was readily appeased, and gladly agreed to their proposal.

'We are going to take some cakes with us, and stay till the little one's bed-time,' Lance said; and both Amyot and Tory were rejoiced to find that Primrose was to be of the party.

'The little madam, did you think she would let us leave her at home?' Lance exclaimed; 'no, indeed, wherever we go she goes, to keep us out of mischief, she always says, and my mother says she is right. But we shall have to carry

her, for we want to go right up to the Beacon,
and that is too far for her.'

'Lance,' said Amyot, with some hesitation, as
they started for Blencathara House, 'is Primrose your sister? I thought she was, but the
boys say no.'

'She's our sister, and she is not,' Lance
replied. 'That is, my mother has adopted her,
but by-and-by she will be my wife,' and the lad
blushed with an air of pride and some defiance.
'Didst never hear how she came to us?'

'No, indeed, tell me.'

'It's more than three years ago—we think she
is about six now, she may be more, but we
cannot tell; I was sauntering about in the
woods, trying to shoot wood-pigeons with a
bow I had made, when I heard a strange
sobbing sound. At first I thought it was a
bird, and then I feared it was a pixie, for there
are queer creatures in some of these woods, but
I could see nothing. I looked all around me,
and grew more scared every moment, for the
wood was still and silent, and no living thing
seemed stirring, and yet ever and anon I heard
this sobbing noise. Folks tell of uneasy ghosts
that cannot rest, but wander about crying and
lamenting their wicked lives, and it seemed to

me that this sound might come from some such wretched being. But while I was wondering and listening, a tiny child came tottering from among a quantity of bushes and bracken, holding up the skirt of her little petticoat, which was full of primroses. Her pretty face was all swollen with crying, and when I asked her who she was and what she was doing in the wood alone, she only sobbed and cried most pitifully, and kept repeating, "Nanny dorn away." And then I could just remember that before I heard that sound of crying, I had caught sight of a woman's figure just disappearing along a distant path. I had thought little about it, and could never call to mind in the least what she was like.'

'And you do not know any more than that? You have no idea whether Primrose was born in Penrith, or had been brought here by that horrid woman?'

'My mother did all she could to find out something about her, but all we could learn was this: some travellers had stopped for a few hours at "The Two Lions," a tall gentleman, a little girl, a man and a maid; they only waited to have a meal and bait their horses, and then they rode away. The landlord of the inn thought little Primrose was like the little girl, but he had not asked their names, nor heard anything about them. So my mother took the little lass and said she should be our sister; but, I say that she is mine, and when she grows up I mean to wed her, and then, Amyot Brough, what say you, shall I not have the fairest bride in old England?'

'She is right bonny,' said Amyot warmly; 'but how did you know her name was Primrose —did she tell you?'

'Nay, I say she could tell us nothing; we called her Primrose because I found her among the primroses. My mother chose the name, and we all liked it well. But here is the child, all ready and waiting, you see.'

It was a blithesome afternoon, something too sultry perhaps, but as they had nought to do but amuse themselves, the heat was no great matter; the two younger lads were very intent just then on an insect collection which they were making, and had little thought or attention to bestow on aught else. Lance and Amyot sauntered along, now talking to Primrose, now conversing with each other. 'You need not mind me,' the little maid had graciously remarked; 'Tory is quite as interesting to me as

any boy can be—he has more sense than many
boys.'

'Has he?—how does he show his superior
sense?' asked Lance, much amused.

'He takes no pains to show it, that is why
he is so charming,' Primrose observed. 'Now
you, and Master Brough, you talk in fine long
words, just to make me think you are wiser
than I.'

'Well, Tory does not do that, certainly.'
Amyot answered, laughing; 'but as he does not
talk at all, Miss Primrose, how do you know he
is so wise?'

'He understands,' the child replied, 'and he
believes, that is why I like him. You boys
believe nothing.'

'Indeed. Miss Primrose, I believe everything
you say, every single word.'

'I will not try you,' the child replied, shaking
her head doubtfully; 'boys believe nothing.'

'What is it she wishes us to believe?' Amyot
asked, much perplexed.

Lance smiled. 'Her little head is ever
running on fairies, pixies, and such like, and we
laugh at her; it is stupid of us, for her fancies
are pretty ones enough. I will take a run
down the hill and see what Jasper is after, and

perhaps she will tell you some of her visions if
you are very docile and teachable.'

He ran off, and Primrose looked after him
in some alarm; then, laying her hand on Tory's
head, she seemed satisfied that she was well
protected, and sat down on the mossy trunk of
an old fir tree, and began tying up a bunch of

Penrith Beacon.

blue harebells, to make a posy to adorn the side
of his head.

'If you were my very own dog, you should
wear a bright knot of ribbon every day,' she
said; 'do you love flowers, my Tory dear? The
little fays do: they take such care of the flowers,
and are so sorry when they are all withered and

dead; what will they do, now all the foxgloves are dropping? They ring their tunes of joy on them; these pretty little bells are so feeble, they give scarcely any sound at all, that is why everything seems so still and quiet to-day.'

' Where do the fairies go in the winter time, Miss Primrose ?' inquired Amyot in a humble tone of meek inquiry.

The large violet eyes rested on him with a look of strange wonderment, then, with a tone of calm assurance, she said, ' The flowers' fairies must have some rest, I suppose, like other people. Why, they sleep while the flowers are sleeping, and then the others come out.'

' What others, Miss Primrose ?'

' Poor boy, he goes to school, and yet he asks such simple questions ! Why, the wind fairies, and the water fairies, and the ice and snow fairies. Oh! Tory, such a lovely ice fairy stayed in our garden last winter—he was there for ever so long. The jackdaws saw him, and they took care never to hu.. him, he was so beautiful—all bright and clear and shining—and he had such a sweet little face. I got up one moonlight night to look at him, and he was standing on the edge of the stone fountain looking into the water.'

'Do they do any good, these fairies, think you, Miss Primrose?'

'Oh! I wish,' said the child fervently, 'that I might ever do half as much. I can't tell you all they do, but they are busy all day long, and some work in the night too. The wind fairies dry up the damp, and make the ground nice and hard; and the ice fairies, they get rid of those nasty grubs that spoil my plants; and the water fairies—oh! of course you know all the good they do: but perhaps you don't know how bright they all make this world, for you don't look as if you thought it very bright, Master Brough!'

'Perhaps I don't. It isn't always bright, is it, not even to you?'

'Yes, always; and I mean that it always shall be bright. I hate dull faces, dull colours, and dull speeches. Why should people be dull and sad, I wonder; even mother, who has had sorrow of her own, looks bright, and so will I.'

Amyot looked at the smiling face uplifted to his, and wondered in his heart whether if sorrow came to her, such as had visited him and Joan, she would still talk about the world being bright; and Tory looked thoughtful—perhaps he was thinking the same thing.

'Lance is a long while gone,' the child said at length, 'and I am growing tired ; we must soon go home.'

'We must wait here until he comes back, or we shall certainly miss each other,' Amyot replied, 'but I will shout.' So he did ; and from the rocks overhead there came back the mocking echo, 'Lance, Lance !'

'That is a wicked pixie answering you,' Primrose said ; 'a very rude fellow he is to mimic what you say. I wish somebody would pull his ears.'

But, nothing discouraged by the echo's bantering sound, Amyot raised his voice and tried again : 'Lance ! Jasper ! Percy !' but no Lance or Jasper or Percy replied.

An anxious look stole over Amyot's face, for the sun was going down, and to confess the truth, the Beacon Hill wood was not by any means such a familiar place to him as to his friends. 'If it gets dark before they come back, I shall find it hard to make my way out of this wood,' he said to himself, and Tory, guessing by force of sympathy his master's thoughts, began to whine gently.

But Primrose was still engaged quite happily with her own imaginings, and the grave faces of her two companions quite amused her. 'The lads have gone rushing after a wondrous butter-fly—I know their ways,' she said ; 'perhaps they have run a mile or two, but they will come back presently ; and we are very happy here, are we not ?'

'Very happy indeed,' Amyot declared, but in his heart he knew that this was not true. The strange tales he had often heard of all manner of wild and savage beasts who had once in-habited these parts, wild boars, wild cats, and the like, not to speak of pixies and hobgoblins, returned to his memory ; a night in such company would not be pleasant, and to his excited fancy the night seemed coming on with extraordinary swiftness. And Primrose—ought she to sit so long on the grass, which might, even now, be growing damp ? Amyot almost wrung his hands as these thoughts passed through his mind, and Tory again looked up in his face with a whine of anxiety.

'Perhaps it would be best for us to turn round and walk slowly home,' he at length suggested : 'surely they will overtake us.' But to this plan Primrose seemed loath to agree. Lance might be vexed—and mother always bade her stay with the lads.

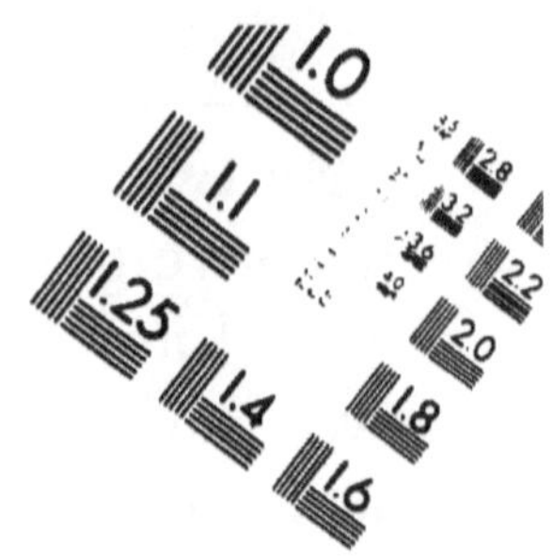

IMAGE EVALUATION
TEST TARGET (MT-3)

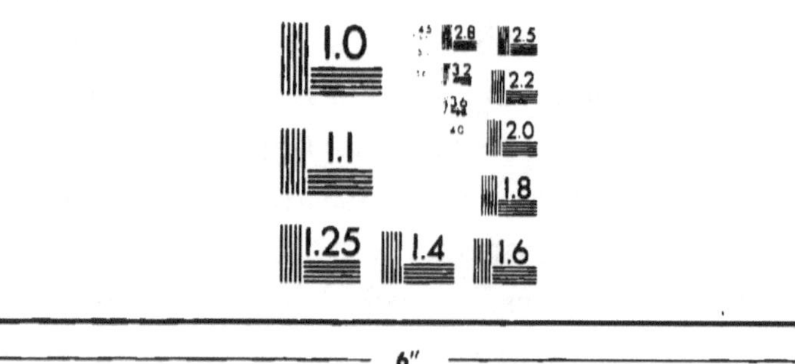

Photographic
Sciences
Corporation

23 WEST MAIN STREET
WEBSTER, N.Y. 14580
(716) 872-4503

Amyot reflected that the lads had not stayed with her, and grew each moment more indignant at their delay. Tory roamed about uneasily— looked down every path, and pricked up his ears at every sound : but alas ! no step could be heard—no movement but the twittering of birds among the branches, or the rustle of the leaves in the evening breeze.

The sweet contentment on the little one's face showed no variation ; it was very sweet in the wood at evening, she said, but it was getting a little cold—perhaps it would be well to run about. And so for a while they played a merry game of her own invention over some mounds of earth and some trunks of fallen trees.

The moon came out, and one or two stars peeped forth, and ' the light was so very pretty,' the little maiden said ; but she was getting sleepy, she would like to go to bed, if only Lance would come and carry her, for she was tired, and could not walk.

' Then I will carry you,' Amyot bravely said, ' and we won't wait any longer, for I am sure your mother must be looking for you, and Lance and the others must have missed their way.' And then he lifted her up and carried her what

he thought was a very long way ; but she was
much heavier than she looked, and before long
she slipped from his arms and said she would
walk, for he was not strong enough to carry a
person nearly as big as himself. Amyot did
not tell her, but a great fear had taken possession
of him that they had neither of them much
notion in which direction they ought to proceed,
and that it might be a very long time before
they reached home, even if she succeeded in
walking so far.

It was a piteous sight to see the child striving
bravely to drag herself along, though her legs
ached terribly, and her eyes positively refused
to keep open ; but she persevered for half-an-
hour, during which they seemed to make little
progress, so slowly did those tiny feet travel.
Then she stopped, and saying, ' I think it would
be rather nice to sleep out of doors such a warm
night,' she sat down at the foot of a tree, and
leaning her weary little head against the trunk,
was almost asleep in a moment. She roused
herself, however, to say, when Amyot, sitting
down beside her, drew her on his knees and
rested her head against his shoulder :

' Shall I tire you ? It is very cosy so, and
good Tory will bark and drive away all the

lions and tigers and bears, and you and I can have a nice sleep.'

'There's nothing else to be done that I can see. I can't make her walk,' Amyot reflected ruefully ; 'but I fear she'll catch her death of cold. Tory, come and sit close to her ; your coat will help to keep her warm.'

The dog obeyed, nothing loath, and licked his master's face in token of sympathy ; then the three sat still and silent. Primrose's soft breathing soon showed that she was fast asleep, but fear and anxiety kept the others wide awake.

CHAPTER V.

In which we take a Journey.

PENRITH town, as I have before observed, was between two and three miles from Brough-barrow—further than Deborah Jephson cared to walk ; for she was not so young as she had been, and stirring about the farm was all the exercise that she for the most part deemed necessary.

Therefore, when real necessity called her to the town, she was wont to make the journey in the farm waggon, seated by Mike's side ; and as the roads were for the greater part of the year very bad, the journey was not so short. as might have been expected.

It was a very real necessity and a very serious piece of business which took Deborah to Penrith on the special occasion we have in mind. She was expected there, and when the

waggon had made its slow way through the
town, and was pulled up by Michael at the door
of Blencathara House, it was no surprise to either
of the worthy couple to see Tory sitting on the
doorstep, watching for them.

'In coorse, he made sewer es I sud coom,'
the good woman observed, as she received his
somewhat subdued caress. 'Beest in t' do-
lorums aboot t' young maester, Tory?　Nae,
he's no' that sick sewerly.'

But hopeful as the good woman was wont to
be, she could not deny that it was a very white
face that lay on the pillow in one of the rooms
of Blencathara House, to which she was led by
Mistress Kirkbride, who, in much anxiety, had
sent to summon her to help in nursing her
young master. 'All that nursing and doctoring
could do she would gladly provide,' the good
lady said ; 'but it was natural the lad should
want his old nurse ;' and Deborah replied, with
a curtsy, ' Ay, ay—to be sewer.'

But for some days Amyot seemed to take
little note of who was about him ; sometimes he
slept a heavy sleep, sometimes he lay and tossed
about in feverish wakefulness, with wide open
eyes which seemed to gaze fixedly at nothing.
He moaned and rambled in his talk, so that

Jasper and Percy ran away frightened, and declared he had lost his wits. Then he grew quieter, and, to the relief of all, the surgeon said he would mend now ; all he wanted was to recover his strength.

'Bet that's nae sa easy dewn es ya 'mun think,' Deborah remarked to herself and to Mistress Kirkbride, when the days passed and the coveted strength still delayed its return ; 'bet it'll coom, niver feear. He's beean freeatan hissel' this mornin', an' sayin' es t' young mistress niver cooms nigh him, an' he's that weeary o' his loife, he canna put oop wi' it.'

Mistress Kirkbride said nothing in reply to this hint of Deborah, but soon after left the room, and before long the door was gently opened and Primrose's bright little face peeped in with the shy inquiry :

'Please may I come and see the poor sick boy ?'

'Like a sunbeam darting through a cloud on a rainy day,' Deborah thought to herself as she made the child heartily welcome ; and then, resuming her own seat by the window, and taking up the long grey stocking which was her constant companion, she listened with much interest to the children's talk.

' Mother says you saved my life—I mean you and Tory,' began the little maid. ' She says that if you had not kept me so warm, I should have taken a bad cold, as you did, and that she believes I should have died ; but I don't feel sure, because I am very strong and never do have colds.'

Amyot smiled faintly by way of response, and she went on :

' You must not talk, because you are ill, and talking will make you cough. I am going to talk to you and amuse you, and when you are well you shall tell me the things I want to know—about the long time you sat holding me while I slept, and about Mat and Joshua coming through the wood, and Tory running off to fetch them, and about them carrying us home, and about how silly the boys looked, and how mother sent them all to bed without any supper. It was so stupid of me to sleep all the time, and know nothing about it. But am I talking too fast ? Shall I be quiet a little while now ?'

Amyot made an effort to assure her that he wished for no greater pleasure than to listen to her voice, but she stopped him, laying her little hand on his mouth, repeating, ' Sick people ought not to talk ;' and then, replying to her own question, 'Yes, I am talking too fast. I think I'll talk to Tory, and then you need not listen unless you like.'

And Tory, well pleased at this arrangement, came and wagged his tail and seated himself at her feet.

'Yes, Tory, it was you that saved my life, so I'll love you for ever ; because it wouldn't have been nice to die like babes in the wood, would it ? But I never thought of dying—did you ? And, Tory, isn't it funny to see Lance so ashamed of himself ? Mother wished that his father would come to life again just to horse-whip him ; but I thought that would not have been worth while, because she might have asked somebody else's father to do it for her ; so Lance got off. But I tease him dreadfully—don't I, Tory ?—and tell him I won't be his wife now, because he would leave me to die in a wood ; and he can't say a word. But I don't mean it, Tory ; it's only fun, you know.'

Tory thought it was very good fun, and his tail thumped the ground approvingly.

'Oh, you dear dog, I do love you so ; now, shall we show your master how nicely you have learned to sing since he has been ill ; now, re-member all I have told you : sing softly, except when I lift my hand, and then sing loud, as loud as you can. Now, we'll begin,' and she began a simple ditty in as sweet a voice as a thrush's warble, while Tory obediently whined an accompaniment, keeping his eye on her hand, and promptly obeying the signal to sing loud or soft, as she dictated.

Amyot laughed almost like himself at this performance, and the little girl, greatly pleased to see him so well amused, continued to make Tory show off various feats which she had taught him during the quiet time of Amyot's illness.

'Count ten, Tory,' ten barks followed. 'How many brothers have I, Tory?' three barks replied, and so *ad infinitum.*

And thanks to the cheering influence of Primrose's visits, which after this became very frequent, Amyot began rapidly to mend. Deborah returned home, telling the boy that there was now no reason why he should encroach on the good lady's kindness, and that in a few days he had better come home as usual. This was by no means welcome news to Amyot, but he had enough right feeling to fear intruding, and his happy stay at Blencathara came to an end.

Broughbarrow looked more dull than he had ever thought it, as with Tory at his heels he approached his home one afternoon in September, right weary with his walk, and thinking that as there would be no one particular to talk to, he would go early to bed.

But a surprise was in store for him. Mike and Deborah greeted him warmly, and made him rest in his father's old arm-chair; but both seemed to have something on their minds, and before long out it came.

'Mappen ya've heeard es we've hed letters, ay, an' theear's yan fur ya, a reel girt an tew— likely it's from Mistress Joan,' Mike began.

This was good news; but something in Mike's tone implied that, to him, at least, the letters did not contain good news.

'Have *you* had letters, Mike—I didn't know you ever had letters ?'

'Bet why sudn't I hev' letters es weel es udther fooak ? Be this an is aboot yasell ; it cooms from that gran' gentleman, yer uncle, and it tells me es plain es can bea ta send ya reet aff t' him in Lon'on toon ; seems es he thinks we heven't moinded our dooty by ya, and sae t' Lon'on ya mun ga by t' furst coach es will tak' ya.'

Amyot listened breathless.

'It wasn't anybody's fault that I caught cold,' he said. 'Where's my letter ?—perhaps Joan will tell me more ;' and through his mind there rushed the thought, ' Home is very dull ; perhaps, after all, it will be better in London or at school.'

Joan's letter was speedily produced ; it was only the second that Amyot had received from his sister, for letter-writing was not an easy matter to the little girl, and Amyot rightly guessed, as he opened the sheet, that many hours had been spent in penning its contents, which ran as follows :

'Westerham, Kent,
'*Sept. 6th*, 1739.

MY SWEET BROTHER,—

'It is long since I wrote to you, and now I am almost beside myself to think that I shall not need to write to you on your birth-day, but all being well, I shall have you with me then. Uncle's letter will tell you all, except how glad I am. My grandmother has been so unhappy about you since we heard of your ill-ness, and she sent for Uncle Godfrey, and made him write that letter, and if only I felt sure that you would not be quite heart-sick to

leave Broughbarrow, I should go wild with joy.
But you will come, I know, because we owe
our grandmother all honour and obedience, and
you will love her dearly, as I do.

'And you will like this village, too, though
you will miss the Fells, and all the rushing
streams, and you will not understand the way
the people speak, it sounds so different from
the Cumberland folk.

'And now, dear Amyot, I have a certain
thing to tell you that makes me wondrous glad.
Grandmother, dear sweet lady, says that you
may bring my dear Tory with you—she will not
have him left behind on no wise. And tell
Tory, with my love, that I have found out that
he was born here; my grandmother says she
gave him, when a tiny pup, to our dear mother,
four years ago, just before she died. And
grandmother has still Tory's mother, but she is
a cross old thing, not like Tory at all. Grandmother says she has always had a dog of that
breed, ever since she came from France, forty
years ago. I wish poor Whig could come too,
but it would be a burden to you to bring both,
and he would scarce like to leave Deborah.
Dear Deborah! give her my love, and Mike
too. I would they could both come with you;

but, as grandmother says, it is best to wish only
for that which we are like to have. I have filled
my paper, and have writ a wondrous long letter,
so no more at present from

' Your fond sister,

' JOAN.'

The other letter to which Joan alluded was
from Mr. Pomfret, and was addressed to
Michael Jephson, giving full orders and direc-
tions about Amyot's journey, which was to be
by the next coach, lest the roads should become too bad for travelling. He had written
also to Captain Brough's lawyer, to make all
proper arrangements with the master of the
grammar school, who might naturally be disturbed at such a sudden departure. Thus all
was settled, and Amyot could not deny that
the prospect of a change was entirely welcome.

Home had looked so dreary after his late
sojourn at Blencathara House, that he would
have welcomed almost any change, and Joan's
loving letter had made his heart yearn towards
her.

True, there was a little heart-ache about the
friends he was leaving, a misgiving that when
far away he should find out that he missed his

boy friends and little Primrose sadly. But these
thoughts he tried to put away, and began to
look forward eagerly to the journey, and all the
wonders of London, and the new life at Westerham.

He had but three days for his farewells, and,
considering that he was scarcely strong enough
for the fatigues of the journey, it was perhaps
as well that he had not a lengthened period of
anticipation to undergo; for, as will easily be
imagined, excitement gave him little chance of
sleeping.

How strange it seemed to find himself once
more waiting on the high-road for the London
coach, as some months before he had waited,
with a lump in his throat to see Joan start.
Perhaps his throat was not quite free from such
inconveniences on this occasion, but it is pleasanter to be the traveller than the one left behind; pleasanter to have new circumstances to
anticipate than the dull monotony of the old life
without much that hitherto has made it happy.
It was sad to see Deborah and Mike and the
farm-men's regrets; sad to shake hands with
Lance, Jasper and Percy; sad to see the grave
expression on little Primrose's usually bright
face, for they had all come to see him start;

but it was pleasant to say good-bye to the many grey days of the past, and dash into something new.

The lumbering coach is toiling along towards them; the three horses pull up beside the little party in the road, and the door is opened.

'Plenty of room, young man,' says the fat driver—'Plenty of room,' echo six massive-looking persons inside—and Amyot shyly introduces his small person among their many packages, feeling much impressed with the idea that he is being buried alive. In consideration of his recent illness he had been specially provided with an inside seat; but Lance's whispered advice 'to go outside most part of the way' is a most welcome suggestion, and he determines to see if he cannot act upon it before many hours are over.

The small trunk containing his worldly all is stowed away, Tory has made his round of farewells, and ensconced himself between his master's knees; the long whip is solemnly whirled round the horses' heads, and Amyot feels that his childhood is over—the new stage in his life is reached, he is going to start in the world afresh.

The one link with the past is this little dumb

companion, who, with amazing forethought, has laid in a vast stock of patience and forbearance for this new chapter in his history. He is somewhat tearful and depressed, consoling himself, doubtless, with the reflection that this strange, lumbering machine cannot go on for ever—or, if it does, some deliverance from it will be granted to him, and that there is the sweet prospect before him of the meeting with his dear little mistress. His doggish heart will ever cherish fond remembrances of little Primrose, but Joan's image is still firmly enthroned in his memory, and all the sunny past, he tells himself, will return when these three labouring horses have plodded through their task of conveying him to her presence. Before long, he hopes, there will be some opportunity of cheering and encouraging these same horses, by jumping and barking in front of their noses ; but until that happy moment comes, nought behoves like patience, for truly they are very slow-going creatures, these coach-horses.

But hark, Tory! others are more charitable than thou.

'Wonderful changes since I was the size of him,' says one stout passenger to another, looking at Amyot. ' No coach like this un betwixt

Edinboro' and Lon'on in my young days.
We're growing a'most too comfort-seeking I
take it.'

'Well,' said his neighbour, a younger and less
contented mortal, ' I'd not find it amiss if they'd
make the road something better. 'Tis hard on
the nags—poor beasts.'

'But they're steady; keep a good steady
pace, slow but sure. A man has time to think,
still—though not so much as when I was
young ; but I fear me, come another hundred
years, folks will have no leisure to think out
one good thought in a lifetime. Didst ever
hear, sir, that some daft body has foretold that
in these parts coaches will run along the Fells
without so much as a horse to pull them—and
all to come to pass, so the old goody says, in
the space of the next hundred years.'

'Nay ! then the horses will have an easy time
on't. 'Twill be their millennium, I take it. But
the nags don't mislike their work, though maybe they would be well content to do it without
the help of the whip. But what's taking this
young man up to Lonnon? He's a young
traveller, that he is.'

Amyot, thus addressed, told his tale from the
time of his father's death to the illness which

had determined his relations to send for him to live near them.

The company in the coach listened kindly—thankful for anything to cheer the tedium of the way, and Tory came in for a share of notice. Then there came a very steep piece of hill, and the coachman's suggestion to his passengers that ' it was a fine thing to stretch a body's legs sometimes,' fell gratefully on the ears of both Amyot and the dog ; but two out of the six fat passengers declared that they preferred a level road for walking, and remained in the coach.

The day wore away very slowly ; probably both Amyot and his dog would have agreed, had they compared notes of their ideas, that it was the longest day in their life, and many more such days followed, until they both grew quite used to the coach and their companions, and it seemed ages since they had bidden farewell to Broughbarrow. Sometimes they sped along a smooth road between stone walls or hedges ; sometimes the coach toiled painfully up a long hill ; sometimes they passed through a town, causing much excitement to the inhabitants, and not a little to the passengers. The changing of horses was a welcome event to Amyot, and a great amusement to Tory, who seemed continually buoyed up with the hope that the new steeds would be faster, and scamper over the ground in the way he was wont to travel.

By the end of the week they had left hills and rocky country behind them, and were travelling through the flatter scenery of the Midland counties. Amyot had pretty well abandoned his inside place, and for the most part spent the days on the top of the coach, or by the driver's side, asking an infinite number of questions, and hearing tales of the wonderful adventures and hairbreadth escapes of the coachman and guard, and longing that some such good luck as a scuffle with highwaymen might yet fall to his share.

'But bless your heart,' said the coachman, 'they know better; these gentlemen don't interfere with me and Tom unless they've heard as I'm carrying quality with long purses and plenty of jewels, and such like; they know all about my cargo—the folks at the inns tell them all about the northern coach and her doings. And this time I've nothing so very particular in the way of passengers. No, I don't expect to be stopped on this journey; though, of course, Tom has his pistols ready.'

Amyot knew that already, having seen these

same pistols; but he was sorry to hear that there was little ground for hoping to see them fired. It was growing dark, and the inn where the coach was to put up for the night was still distant. The trees on each side of the road were high and thick; the air was still; strange shadows fell across the way; everything was weird and ghostly in the fast-fading light. Tory had squeezed close to him, a sure sign that he too felt something of the nameless fears that often haunt the twilight hour. It was just the time for a desperate deed, and Amyot held his breath and listened for stealthy steps until he could almost believe he heard them.

The coachman's remarks to his tired horses were growing discontented and impatient. 'Get along there, you, Nancy, get along; come up, Joe,' seemed to be losing all effect. The road was heavy, and the coach-wheels sank deeper and deeper in the mud, till at last, in the efforts to find a pleasanter footing, the weary beasts made a sudden swerve, and in a moment the coach had run off into a deep ditch, full of watery mud and slime, where it fell over on one side, to the unutterable dismay of some ducks who were half-asleep among the weeds and rushes, and the no small consternation of the stout passengers inside, who were also dozing away the twilight hours.

It was not precisely the kind of accident Amyot had been desiring, and the furious struggling of the poor, frightened horses as they kicked and plunged, and tried in vain to free themselves from their awkward encumbrance, was not a pleasant sight. He had fallen into a very soft bed of mud, and Tory had shared his fate; neither, therefore, had sustained any injury; but the coachman had been less fortunate, and when at length he was extricated from the ditch, where he was lying half-choked with watery mud, he groaned so piteously that it was plain he believed himself in a very bad way.

One by one the passengers scrambled out from the overturned coach, and then, with great difficulty, the plunging, restive horses were quieted and unharnessed.

'Like it or not,' said Tom the guard, 'all you gentlemen will have to walk on to the village— it ain't much above a mile—and send help to me and coachman. Send some stout lads and a horse or two, and lights—do you hear, gentlemen?—for it will be dark in no time now.'

There was no help for it; so, with much grumbling at the untoward accident, the mud,

the badness of the times, the depravity of things
in general and the weather in particular, the
passengers started in search of the nearest inn.

'You've only to go right straight forrard,'
was the guard's injunction; but 'right straight
forrard' meant through seas of mud and pools
of stagnant water, so deep and so black, that
before long Amyot was forced to carry Tory,
now no longer white, lest the brave dog should
be choked or drowned.

It was a very long mile that lay between the
scene of the upset and the wayside inn which
afforded the nearest lodging, and the darkness
had become profound before the luckless passengers reached it. Then there was much
exclaiming at their woeful plight—much wondering how such a mischance could have befallen
the London coach, before any stout lads could
be found who would go to the help of the
expectant guard and coachman.

'And you, my little man—why, you're little
but a mass of mud and dirt!' said the mistress
of the inn to Amyot, who was indeed in a
piteous plight. She looked kind and motherly,
and his tired face excited her pity; the gentlemen could be made comfortable by her husband,
she thought, but the poor child needed a

woman's tendance, and, without more ado, she led him, nothing loath, into her little kitchen, and making him sit down on a low bench beside the hearth, she set herself to pull off his boots and stockings, which were so soaked that they seemed glued to his feet.

'Hey! what's this?' was her exclamation, as Tory lifted his head from his master's arms and licked her face, 'you're both so much of a colour that I never saw the dog, poor beastie. Put him down, my dearie, and let him warm himself.'

But poor Tory was loath to soil her clean hearth by sitting down, and stood looking so miserable that a rough-haired lass, who was washing in an outhouse, brought a large tub of warm water, in which, after Amyot had soaked his numbed feet, Tory was immersed, greatly to his own satisfaction, and, it must be said, to his beautification. Then, a brimming porringer of bread and milk having entirely restored both boy and dog to cheerfulness, the kindly woman opened a folding-bed in a cupboard that led out of the kitchen, and Amyot was soon in a sound sleep, with Tory curled up on his feet. In that dreamless sleep neither of them heard anything of the commotion which greeted the arrival of the coach, some two hours after, and it was broad daylight when they were again ready for life and all that it might bring.

The coachman's injury was not so serious as it had at first appeared : ' A severe sprain, and perhaps a broken rib or so,' Tom, the guard, asserted ; a rest at the inn for a few days would set him up, and the landlord of the public-house was ready enough to take the reins in his place.

' The coach must not be delayed, or we should lose our character,' said Tom proudly, and accordingly, with fresh horses, they were soon again on the road.

And this slight catastrophe was the only adventure worthy of the name which Amyot met with on this his first journey ; as they drew near the capital they seemed to travel more quickly, the relays of horses were apparently more up to their work, and the amateur coachman seemed anxious to make sure of bringing his team in at the appointed time, and with as great a flourish as if he had been the fully-accredited driver.

Tom, the guard, too, blew his horn more frequently, and especially when the coach was passing through one of the little towns, which, as they neared London, lay at shorter intervals along the road; everything bespoke their speedy approach to the centre of life and industry.

Twenty times at least had Amyot asked, 'Is that London?' before the affirmative reply set his heart beating and his cheeks aflame. It was not all pleasurable excitement, for some misgivings mingled with the satisfaction he felt in knowing that his journey was almost at an end.

Joan was not in London; some days would probably elapse before he saw her, for he was to stay at his uncle's house in London until it should be convenient for him to be forwarded to Westerham; and of his uncle, Amyot had not the pleasantest remembrances. In her first letter to him, Joan had told him how strange everything had seemed to her in her uncle's house, how shy and awkward she had felt, and if his sister had seemed awkward, Amyot had a shrewd suspicion that he should feel doubly so. His coat and small-clothes were, he well knew, much more shabby than when he had started from Broughbarrow, and he had had so little to do with real gentlefolks, Mrs. Kirkbride excepted, that he feared he had never learned how properly to address them.

He hoped his aunt would be merciful to his delinquencies—she was, Joan had told him, a sweet fair lady; but of his uncle, and his quiet smile, Amyot stood much in dread; and then he recalled with sudden terror the outrageous conduct of Tory when Mr. Pomfret had parted from them in the spring.

'Oh, Tory,' he whispered, squeezing the dog close to him as they sat together on the top of the coach, 'that is London over there, where you see the smoke; and you and I will feel terrible strange among all the fine people there. I should like to run back all the way we have come, but we can't, so we must try to bear ourselves like other people; we must be careful to make our best bows, and we must not sit down without being bidden; and we must keep ourselves clean and smart. Do you understand, Tory?'

Understand! of course Tory understood, but there were difficulties in the way of this last-named duty; and as he licked Amyot's face, he whined plaintively as he shook himself and looked at his dirty coat.

Amyot understood the gesture, and replied:

'Yes, we *are* a pair of beggars, and no mistake, but when we have had a chance of washing ourselves we shall feel better; and one thing, Tory, you must remember not to tear nobody's coat—do you hear ?'

Tory hung down his head for a moment, but speedily recovering himself, looked at his master and blinked his eyes, his usual method of replying : 'I know, but it was not at all a bad joke, though perhaps it might not be safe to try it any more.' And then the pair were silent again, watching the streets of houses drawing nearer, and finding much to amuse them every few yards.

Perhaps, of the two, Tory was the most evidently excited when they were really travelling down the streets ; Amyot, looking at the crowded thoroughfares, wondered whether it was a fair-day that so many people were abroad, but the driver only laughed at this idea, and assured him there were not more than usual ; and after this the boy thought it best to be silent, lest he should make some other ridiculous mistake.

At length, after many turnings and windings, when numerous passengers seemed on the point of being run over, and only to escape by a miracle, the coach rattled up to an inn door and stood still ; and there, waiting beside a

hackney-coach from which he had just descended, Amyot at once spied his uncle on the
look-out for him.

It was pleasant to the fatherless boy to feel
that he once more belonged to somebody, and
Mr. Pomfret's greeting was sufficiently kind
and paternal to reassure him, and make him
forget his fears; in a few minutes more they
were seated in the hackney-coach, and starting
in the direction of Bloomsbury, where Mr.
Pomfret lived. Amyot wondered if this were
another town, but soon discovered that it was
part of London: one of the best parts, his
uncle told him; and Queen's Square, where
he lived, was almost like the country, being
open and fresh and breezy, looking over the
fields right away to the village of Hampstead.
Seeing he was interested, Mr. Pomfret went
on to tell him more about London, and pointed
out to him many objects of interest; the two
new churches of St. George's in the parish of
Bloomsbury, and St. George the Martyr at the
corner of Queen Square, also the fine new house
called Powis House, with its Corinthian columns
and splendid façade, built at the expense of the
French king, on the site of the old house of the
same name, burnt down in 1714.

Thus occupied and amused, the drive seemed a very short one, and the hackney coach stopped before a large house in Queen's Square, long before he had expected. It was such a handsome house, with such a wide entrance hall, and broad steps, that something of his shyness returned as he followed his uncle up the steps, and saw the tall footman who stood within the door. But on the staircase a lady was standing, tall and slight and most beautifully attired, at sight of whom Tory immediately executed a series of his best bows, thereby reminding Amyot of his duty, and eliciting great applause from Mr. Pomfret, who, up to that moment, had taken no notice of the dirty-looking poodle.

The lady came swiftly downstairs, and drew Amyot into her warm embrace, then, still holding his hand, she opened a door that led from the hall, and took him into a large parlour, the windows of which looked out into the square. His uncle followed them, and when Mrs. Pomfret seated herself in a large elbow-chair, he placed himself behind her, leaning on the high back of her chair.

The colour mounted to Amyot's forehead as he felt himself thus examined by two keen pairs of eyes. His aunt touched his forehead with her lips, and then looked at her husband, and smiling, said something in French; the boy blushed more intensely still, for he guessed that his own appearance and manners were the subject under remark.

'Poor fellow,' said his aunt, noticing his confusion, 'what a weary long journey he has had; he must be tired to death. Are you hungry, little nephew, or do you most of all desire to go to your chamber?—it is prepared and ready, and if you will, I will send you some refreshment upstairs.'

Of all things in the world, Amyot decided that to go to bed was the most desirable at that moment; there was a look in his aunt's cold grey eyes which made him shrink from her, though she still held his hand, and was stroking it with her soft fingers. So he lifted that beautiful hand to his lips, and bidding his uncle a respectful good-night, followed the servant to the sleeping-chamber prepared for him. Tory was sitting on the mat at the foot of the stairs; and, greatly pleased to recover possession of his master, he trotted upstairs behind him in a much more contented mood than the boy himself. For as he closed the door of the parlour he had heard, or fancied he heard, a soft rippling laugh from his aunt, and the exclamation, ' Such a prodigiously awkward lad, I never saw the like !'

How many flights of stairs they climbed ! He verily believed they must be ascending to the stars ; at Broughbarrow there was only one short flight of stairs to the bed-chambers. What folly to build houses so high ; why had Joan never told him of these ridiculous London houses, and why, oh ! why, had she never said how his aunt stared at people, and laughed at them as soon as their backs were turned ? Could Joan—his faithful Joan—have grown like Aunt Aimée ?

CHAPTER VI.

When Tory Finds his Little Mistress.

WAS he glad or was he sorry? This question Amyot vainly asked himself as he strolled round the Square garden about a week after his arrival in London, and the question had been suggested by the remark dropped by his uncle that day at dinner, that he was so vastly employed that he could not say when he should be able to find a day to take his nephew down to Westerham. His aunt had kindly pitied him, and assured Mr. Pomfret that he was pining for his sister; but though he scarcely allowed it to himself, even the prospect of meeting Joan had been almost forgotten in the strange delight and wonder of this new world of London.

The very bustle in the streets, the constant passing to and fro, the street cries in the early morning, the whirl of life and activity, had awoke

in him a passion to be doing something. He
had listened to the talk of busy politicians in his
uncle's house, had been admitted to the sight of
Dr. Meade's museum of curiosities and paintings
in Great Ormond Street, and had even caught
sight of many great men whose names were in
everyone's mouth. It seemed to him that years,
not days, must have separated him from the old
Cumberland life, and as he sauntered round the
Square garden watching Tory, whose happy
spirit found easy satisfaction in chasing the
brown leaves along the garden paths, he wondered whether even to be with Joan again would
be as enchanting as this wondrous fairy-land of
novelty and excitement, of new thoughts and
new aspirations. Tory he knew well would
rejoice to be again in the fields and country
lanes. Tory was feeling in no small measure
cheated, that he had not yet been able to discover his little mistress; but, always light of
heart, the good dog lived in hope. Well
washed and combed, he had recovered his self-
respect, and could find much to amuse him in
the town and its strange inhabitants. He was
contented to wait. Not so his young master;
when he listened to the discourse of those who
were doing great things in the world, he fretted

and fumed to think that for him years of school must intervene before he could command ships, fight battles, paint pictures, or write mighty books. His cousin Guy, a gay captain in the Grenadiers, hoping to see some service on the Continent, rattled on in merry guise of marches and victories, sieges and assaults, as if his wars were over and his laurels won.

Amyot listened, and resolved he would be a soldier and fight the French as his father and grandfather had done. Then of a sudden the dream was changed. Guy's half-brother Arnold had just returned from France, where he had been studying under the care of his stepmother's French relatives, returned, as his father bitterly complained, more French than English, more Papist than Protestant, but withal gentle, tender-hearted, full of lofty aspirations and fervent longings for the revival of faith in the land.

Amyot bowed at once to the fascination of his pure and lofty soul, and listened entranced to his tales of the saintly Archbishop of Cambray, who had dedicated himself in his youth to missionary work in North America, but had given up his heart's desire at his King's command, had then fallen under that King's dis-

pleasure, and in his banishment from Court and
Court favour had been sought out and visited
by the wise and good of all nations—'Your
grandfather among others,' Arnold added.
'Oh, that I had known him! but your grandmother will tell you more about him, for she
knew him, and has heard him preach too, as
well as the great Bishop of Meaux.'

And listening to these tales of holy lives,
Amyot forgot his warlike intentions, and felt
that Arnold was right when he said the war
with sin was the only war worth fighting.
True, his aunt laughed at her eldest son's
enthusiasm, and wished he would come down
from the clouds and dress and talk like other
people ; his uncle fumed and muttered some
bitter invectives against Popish plotters and
French traitors ; but, as Arnold's spirit was
never ruffled by jests or gibes, his young
cousin felt instinctively that he must have the
right on his side, and reverenced him accordingly.

It was a far greater pleasure to Amyot to
linger by Arnold's side in the Abbey of West-
minster, or in the great church of St. Paul's,
listening while his low musical voice related
wondrous histories of martyred saints and

heroic deeds achieved under the banner of the
Cross, or quivered with emotion as he spoke
of the mighty war yet to be waged, of the
world sunk in indifference or vice, than to drive
with his aunt in her chariot to Vauxhall
Gardens, where the gay world enjoyed itself
and forgot such dismal matters.

Mrs. Pomfret thought, and not perhaps
without reason, that a consciousness of his
awkwardness and rustic manners was the cause
of this dislike on the part of her nephew to the
society of the *beau monde;* indeed, it was no
small annoyance to her to be burdened with
the company of such a raw country lad. Her
step-son might be wanting in some of those
elegances of language which were generally
deemed essential to a high-bred gentleman, but
he was never *gauche*, and none had ever
received aught but courteous treatment at
his hands; she had never blushed for him,
though well aware that he was peculiar;
her second son was all that her fastidious
taste could desire; but this orphan boy
was a trial, and she much feared that he
would never grow into anything at all akin to
a gentleman.

To these lamentations her husband listened

with his smile of languid indifference, and replied :

‘ Do not distress yourself, my love ; if he turns out quite unpresentable, we must get him service in some foreign land where the chances of war or fever may save us the pain of being ashamed of him.   And, indeed, if my judgment does not much deceive me, his hot temper will endanger his neck long ere he be grown to years of discretion ; so make yourself easy— you will not be troubled with him long !’

‘ Nay ; I wish the child no harm : he is my sweet sister’s son, though he favours her but little.   My son Arnold tells me that he has parts and abilities, though he has no more manners than a dog—nay, not so much as his poodle !   But Arnold is vexed that you let him read what he will, and says he should be guided in his studies.’

‘ Then let Arnold guide him ; but no, the captain was loyal to King and Church, and his son should tread in his steps ; but I’ll not meddle with the lad—he must go to school ; that is, when he has paid his respects to his grandmother at Westerham.’

Probably this conversation determined the worthy but indolent gentleman to bring his

Westerham.

nephew's stay in his house to a speedy conclusion ; for the very next day he announced
that he had now sufficient leisure to ride with
the lad to Westerham, and that he had written
to announce their coming.

'Taking to the roads again,' thought Tory.
' Well, this time we can hardly fail to find the
little mistress !'

And the little mistress's heart went forth to
meet them, though duty and propriety kept her
from following the dictates of her inclination,
which would have led her far down the London
Road to meet the travellers when the long-
desired day at last dawned.

The little Kentish town was looking its
very best that autumn evening when Amyot
first saw it ; how often in after-years, when discontented with his lot, with himself or his sur-
roundings, or resting after a long day's march
in foreign lands, did he strive to recall that first
impression of the quiet little village street, the
green slopes of the park, the changing colours
of the tall trees, and the peaceful flow of the
little river which ran before his grandmother's
house. He might call Broughbarrow home,
but it was not long before Westerham was
more truly home to his heart than ever his

Cumberland birthplace had been, and Mrs. Darley's house was by all acknowledged to be most entirely and altogether home-like.

And there was no denying that it was very pleasant to be once more possessed of Joan, and Joan so grown and improved that Amyot could scarcely take his eyes off her. He wondered why she had never looked so neat and well arrayed at home, for his father, he knew, had always wished that she should be dressed as a gentle-woman, and had grudged no money spent on Joan's slips or hoods; but now she looked for all the world like a soft dove, and no wood-pigeon had ever cooed so sweetly as her voice sounded in his ear. And his grandmother, in her rich, but softly falling paduasoy, her snowy kerchief, and delicate lace cap—whence some braids of snow-white hair just escaped—was she not the loveliest old lady imaginable? Aunt Aimée's blue eyes were doubtless very beautiful —he had heard fine gentlemen tell her so a hundred times—but Amyot had shivered at their cold scrutinizing glance, while he gazed with undisguised admiration at the bright brown eyes that had such a loving warmth in them, even when they twinkled with amusement, as, indeed, they often did when they caught sight of him.

'I thought I should have been vastly afraid of my grandmother,' Amyot confessed to his sister, after a few days' residence at the red-brick house that faced the little river and the rich grounds of Squerries Court, where Mrs. Darley had lived ever since her widowhood. 'I thought she would have laughed at me as Aunt Aimée did, and I do hate to be laughed at. But, Joan, I cannot understand her, can you?'

'Who, dear grandmother, or Aunt Pomfret?'

'My grandmother. Sometimes she looks like a holy saint in a church window, when she lays her hand on your head, Joan, and says, "Que le bon Dieu te bénisse," or something of the sort, for I shall never be able to speak that silly French stuff, whatever she may say; and then sometimes all her face laughs, and she is as merry as my little Primrose—my fairy queen. Say, Joan, do you understand her?'

'Perhaps not quite,' Joan admitted: 'but I love her, oh! so dearly; and as for being like a saint in a church window, if they were half as sweet as she, I think it is quite right to put them in church windows, though Miss Johnstone says they make the church monstrous dark, and she believes it is wrong to have painted windows at all.'

'Miss Johnstone is vastly queer—why does she live here?' asked Amyot; 'she teaches you, I know, Joan, and she winds wool for grandmother, but she is not related to grandmother, so why does she live with her?'

'I never asked,' Joan replied; 'perhaps it is for the same reason as many other things that seem strange,' and she laughed her quiet laugh of deep amusement.

'What things?'

'Have you not noticed how many funny things and creatures there are in this house? —the cat with three legs; the parrot with the bald head; the ugly old butler with one eye; and the cook who is stone deaf; the dog who snarls when you stroke him; the pony that stands still every few yards, and—and——'

'The little girl who sees the worst side of everything and everybody,' said a low voice from behind her. The children started and turned round: the brilliant dark eyes of Mrs. Darley were fixed on Joan's blushing face, and she said, with something of reproach in her musical voice, 'What dost thou mean, petite?—is it such a chamber of horrors, thy poor grandmother's house, that thou fearest to dwell in it, and art begging thy brother to carry thee away?'

' Indeed, no, madam ; it is the dearest home in the world. We were only wondering why——' and she stopped.

'Wondering why! Ah! that is the way of the world now, always wondering why. Better not, chérie ; rest thy little brain, and be certain that there is a reason, and a good one, for all that seems strange. Yet, if thou must know this particular why, it is just simply this : here is an old woman good for nothing much, but able to give a home to many whom no one needs or loves or admires ; they are not ugly or strange or troublesome to her, and so she takes them in, and loves to have them—yes, curious little maid and all.'

'And clumsy country lad too, madam ?' inquired Amyot, with a deep flush on his face.

'Yes, yes! child, for sure. Yet, bethink thee, the cat makes the best of his three legs : thou hast a goodly pair of thine own, and a straight and comely figure—why, then, walk as if all the ground were newly ploughed, and thy body and legs had fallen foul of each other ?'

Amyot laughed. 'Joan had forgotten to name me,' he said ; ''twill go hard with me, madam, but I'll learn to walk as well as the cat !

My aunt was for ever ashamed of me, but I could not bear myself so as to please her ; and, to tell the truth, I'd no great liking for her fine beaux.'

'Tut, tut! be thyself, child. Imitate no one's airs, but be thine own *best* self, and let thy grandmother and sister be proud of thee.'

'I shall ever be that,' Joan replied, 'be Amyot what he will; I could not help it, madam.'

'Nay, nay, little simpleton—talk not such foolishness! Women, poor silly things, have a trick of loving even the drunken sot that would fell them with his fist ; but I speak not of love, but of pride : if Amyot grow not up a true loyal-hearted gentleman, such an one as men may esteem and women trust, then, Joan, thou mayest love him in a poor weak fashion, but thou will despise him in thine heart the while.'

'Nay, madam, nay ; I never could,' was Joan's response, as she lifted her steadfast blue eyes to Amyot's face, which none could deny looked honest and true and straightforward ; but the old lady repeated :

'Thou art wrong, pétite, I know thee better; thou wilt never reverence aught but worth ; look to it, Amyot, that thy sister may ever

hold thee as meet to be honoured as now she
doth.'

The old lady left them with the quiet step
and easy motion that had ever distinguished
her, and the children followed her with eyes
full of admiration, Amyot murmuring :

'She is the sweetest, loveliest old lady I
ever saw! I will be all she will have me ; but,
oh, Joan, tell me how! Think you I vex her,
as I did Aunt Aimée ?'

'Dear grandmother is never vexed except
by such things as you, Amyot, will never do, I
trust. She would have you bear yourself more
like a gentleman, and she looks for more dutiful
language towards herself; but when Miss
Johnstone lamented bitterly that you walked
into the parlour without so much as lifting your
hat, and that you neglected to open the door
for her, and said your voice was so rough it
made her feel quite nervous, grandmother said,
"He is a gentleman's son, and the sense of
what is fitting is there ; 'tis but the training he
lacks."'

'Any lad would make Miss Johnstone feel
nervous ; even you, Joan, forced her to seek
her scent-bottle to cure her fainting, when you
let the door shut suddenly this morning.'

'She suffers much from the vapours,' Joan replied. 'Amyot, we should not laugh at her.'

'No, indeed; the vapours must be dolorous things indeed, to judge by her countenance; but tell me, Joan, do you know the lad that would not terrify her?'

Squerries Court.

'Yes, indeed; there are brave young gentlemen living yonder at Squerries Court, who are wondrous favourites with her; and Master Edward Wolfe, of whom I have spoken many a time, and his brother James; they are ever mindful of her whims, as you call them, and treat her with true gentle courtesy. It was but yesterday she wished that you resembled Master Edward Wolfe.'

'And you, Joan, do you wish I resembled this paragon of a youth?'

'I would have you your own self, like none else; but yet I know that when you see him, you will like him well.'

'When I see him! is that likely? you have shown me the house where these lads live, but you said, Joan, that they had gone to school, and that their parents were about to leave Westerham.'

'Yes, so I did; but grandmother purposes to send you to the same school with them. She spoke to Uncle Pomfret about it when he was here, and they said that by the new year you would be well and strong and fit for school again.'

'I am well and strong now.'

'Nay, my grandmother said after the new year; and she said more that I do not mean to tell you.'

'I know,' said Amyot gloomily; 'that until I was a little less of a savage, I had best not mingle with these fine gentlemen, lest they should laugh me to scorn. Well, and if they

did, I have a pair of hard fists to defend myself,
and I know how to use them.'

' But we want you to keep your strength to
serve your country,' was Joan's soothing response.   ' Now tell me again about little Primrose, and Lance, and dear old Broughbarrow.
I wonder shall we ever see it again ?'

' To be sure;' and then, nothing loath, Amyot
suffered himself to be led into long, rambling
stories about his old friends and old life—
interesting enough to little Joan, but scarcely
worth relating.

Meanwhile, in her wainscoted parlour, the
windows of which looked out on the smooth
sunny river, Mrs. Darley was sitting in her
elbow-chair, lost in thought.   In spite of Joan's
flattering assurances, Amyot did not unfrequently contrive to vex the placid old lady ;
and when she had parted from the children,
after her brief conversation with them, it was to
be met by her ancient butler and still more
ancient cook, both full of complaints of the noisy,
unruly ways of her grandson.

She had heard them with her usual patience
and quiet dignity, and had quelled the angry
storm of their excited feelings by the earnest
appeal :

'The child is fatherless and motherless, and orphans are God's special care; not in haste will I meddle with His training. The world will deal him the rude blows which are the Almighty's rod. As for me, I will try to do the cosseting and comforting that the poor lamb as surely needs, though you, Hannah, and you, Doddridge, think nothing but stripes can benefit him, and would have him horsewhipped without mercy.'

'Nay, madam, but if you knew——'

'If I did, where would it profit me? I have resolved, and your complaints will not change me. We have been, perhaps, too quiet here; a little noise will make a change.'

And so she dismissed them, with the reflection that small trials are good for all, old servants not excepted.

And for herself too, no doubt. These small tumults were a trial, though, of course, only in a wholesome degree; they made her thoughtful, not sad. Sad! Who had ever seen Mrs. Darley sad? Possibly they suggested some regrets that she had not sooner insisted upon having the charge of her orphan grandson, and some uneasiness lest the six months during which he had been his own master should have made him too ungovernable for her quiet rule. Well, he must soon go to school ; and in the meantime she had little doubt that she could so arouse his chivalrous feelings that for her sake he would curb the haughty spirit that had so vexed the old domestics.

'If I can't manage a boy of ten, I'll take to my bed and order my coffin,' was the characteristic conclusion of the valiant old lady's reflections.

CHAPTER VII.

Finding his Level.

' A whimsical world this is, a restless ever-changing, never-resting kind of place; and the race of beings who proudly call it their own, grow every year more fidgety and given to rushing about.' Such was Tory's soliloquy, when, before *he* had well settled down in his new home, he found his young master carried off, and himself left behind with his little mistress. Well, it could not be denied that Amyot and the new home did not exactly suit one another, and Tory hoped that in his next experience his young master would find some comrades more congenial than Doddridge and Hannah.

Whether such was the case the good dog might have been puzzled to decide, had he been able to follow his master and judge for himself;

possibly, for his peace of mind, it was well that a sense of duty restrained him from gratifying his curiosity, and kept him in the quiet home at Westerham and the safe companionship of Queen Joan.

And where was Amyot? School had begun for him in sober earnest, and in the good town of Greenwich, among boys who for the most part were south-country lads, the northern boy was trying, and not very successfully, to hold his own.

See him one Sunday afternoon, early in the year, sitting lonely at one end of the large schoolroom; the others are talking merrily in groups, the room rings with their laughter, but no one talks to him; his face wears a scowl which is anything but inviting, his very worst look, as Joan would call it; and the peaceable boys have already learned to keep their distance when young Brough is in the sulks; and as good luck would have it, some time elapsed before the spirit of evil impels any of the war-like souls to interfere with him.

But it is not in boy nature to refrain from tormenting when such a ready victim is at hand. Some one passing inquires 'What ails Mr. Gruff?' and the smouldering fire bursts forth at once. Then follow many witticisms concerning the giant's castle in the mountains, the skulls and bones that are to be seen there, sure proofs of Giant Gruff's ferocity, and the room is soon in an uproar. The elder lads look on amused, till one, a slender boy with blue eyes, turning to his brother close beside him, whispers, ' Ned, there's a good fellow, get him away from them and take him for a walk. Mr. Swinden will give leave, I know. 'Tis like baiting a bear, and cowards' work at the best.'

The younger lad obeyed, and though it was no easy work to drag Amyot from the crowd of his tormentors, he succeeded in his attempt, and before many minutes were past, the pair were free from the schoolhouse and on their way to Greenwich Park.

More than once had Ned glanced at his companion before either of them spoke; the cloud was not yet entirely cleared from Amyot's brow, when the silence was broken at length by the very simple remark, ' I'm a fool to get so chafed by them. Don't you despise me, Ned ?'

' We had best forget them,' was the very prudent reply of his companion ; ' here's the church ; I love Westerham church better than this—what say you, Brough ?'

' I like going to this church very well,' Amyot

replied. 'Till I left Broughbarrow, I did not go much to church—my father did not take us often; but here I like the organ and the singing, and some other things also. What was that Mr. Swinden said this morning about a

Church of S. Alphege, Greenwich.

certain psalm tune, and a great man who made it up, whose body lies buried in the church—did you understand what he said?'

'Understand?—yes, right well; I have heard

the story many a time, and in former days
his tomb bore a quaint inscription—can I
remember it, I wonder ; let me see, it ran thus
—I have seen it written in an old book :

' "Enterred here doth ly a worthy wight
   Who for long time in music bore the bell ;
His name to shew was Thomas Tallys hyght,
   In honest vertuous life he did excell ;
He served long tyme in chappell with grete prayse—
   Fower sovereigns' reygnes (a thing not often seen) :
I mean Kyng Henry and Prynce Edward's dayes,
   Quene Mary and Elizabeth our Quene ;
He maryed was, though children he had none,
   And lyved in love full three and thirty yeres
Wyth loyal spouse, whos name yclept was Jone,
   Who here entombed him company now bears:
As he did lyve, so also did he dy,
   In myld and quiet sort (O, happy man !)
To God ful oft for mercy did he cry,
   Wherefore he lyves, let Death do what he can." '

' Tallys, yes, that was the name. I was
wondering whether his spirit stays in the church
sometimes to hear those tunes sung ; but I
suppose he has made hundreds more since then,
and perhaps he does not care much about his
old tunes now.'

' They're grand though, so people say who
understand, and I think, as James often says,
it would be a splendid thing to have done
something which will help people hundreds of
years after one's dead and buried.'

Amyot thought so too, but the church being left behind, his thoughts turned to less solemn matters; the green slopes of the park were before them, and the great domes of the Hospital, and beyond the smooth river with

Greenwich Hospital.

its many barges, their gay colours making the scene bright and pleasant.

Boy-like, they talked of ships and sailors, great commanders and naval victories, wondered whether it would be their lot to travel far from old England, and hoped they might have a chance of a brush with Spain. Amyot related to his companion many of the witty sayings and quaint expressions in a book which he had seen, when staying with his uncle in Queen Square, entitled 'The History of John Bull;' and the sentiments of John Bull and Nick Frog, with regard to the greed of Lewis Baboon, drew forth much applause from both the lads.

'Young Spitfire,' as he was familiarly called by his schoolfellows, had quite recovered his equanimity under the judicious treatment of Edward Wolfe before they returned to the schoolhouse, and submitted very tamely to a short lecture administered by that sage young man before they plunged again into the noisy crowd of boys.

'How many fights have you had since you've been at school, Brough?'

'Can't say; a dozen or so.'

'More than your share, Brough: you give no one else a chance. Try and stint yourself a bit. I've a score or two to wipe out; but one can't fight a fellow who has two black eyes to start with.'

Amyot laughed. 'They were all older than I,' he said. 'I don't fight the little ones.'

'Doubt if they were bigger—you're a young giant, Brough, and your fists were cut out of your own mountains; keep them to fight the Baboons.'

'Oh! they'll serve for Britons as well. But I don't want to quarrel, if they'd let me alone.'

'Why should they let you alone? You make fine sport for them, by being so ready with your sting. If I were you, Brough, I wouldn't condescend to notice all their gibes. It isn't a good thing to get the name of being such a hot-headed dog that no one can speak to you.'

To this advice Amyot made no reply, but, as young Wolfe told a friend afterwards, 'At any rate, he didn't bite;' which was as much as could be expected of him.

From this time forth school life grew brighter to our hero. He ceased to look upon his comrades as his determined foes, and before long his friendships were as many and violent as his enmities had once been. Moderation was a virtue he despised—everything was done

with vehemence which he deemed worth doing
at all; and consequently trifling quarrels,
insignificant breaches of rules, seldom had any
attraction for him, while outrageous acts of
insubordination, persistent fits of idleness, often
followed by desperate bursts of remorse were
the characteristic marks of Amyot Brough
during this period of his life.

'A most uneasy charge we have entrusted to
you, my good sir,' observed Mrs. Pomfret,
on one of the rare occasions when her chariot
had rolled to the door of the schoolhouse,
bringing her and her eldest son to see for themselves 'how her monstrous awkward nephew
was faring at his school.' She had little liking
for the expedition, but Arnold Pomfret had not
forgotten the eager attention with which his
young cousin had listened to his discourses,
fanatical as he knew they were not unfrequently
considered; and he had reminded his mother
so frequently of her duty to her orphan nephew,
that, to please him, and no doubt in some sort
to satisfy herself, she had made the great exer-
tion of driving to Greenwich.

Amyot had striven hard to show himself duly
grateful, and his dark eyes had sparkled with
real pleasure at the sight of his cousin; but his

aunt's presence always wrought in him a miserable consciousness of want of words, want of manners—in short, want of all that would have commended him to her. He would have opened out at once, had he been alone with his cousin. A walk with him by the river would have been felicity ; to have introduced him to his schoolfellows would have been truly too delightful ; but Arnold, always silent in his mother's presence, spoke little to the boy : though, whenever their eyes met, Amyot felt that the old kindly interest beamed forth in every glance, and that the gaze, which was at times peculiarly keen and searching, was yet the gaze of a friend who would hope the best. So unlike the cold stare of his aunt's grey eyes. Why did men admire her ? Why did Mr. Swinden treat her as if the ground on which she trod was hallowed by her foot ? Mr. Swinden was true as steel — that all his lads knew well. Could he not see how cold and hard his aunt was ?

Lucky was it for Amyot that his presence was soon dispensed with—Mrs. Pomfret wished to have some discourse with Mr. Swinden ; but the door had not entirely closed behind her nephew, when the above exclamation fell on his ear, ' An uneasy charge.' It might have been balm to the wound thus caused, had his master's kindly rejoinder also reached his ear.

'Nay, my dear madam ; without presuming to doubt your discernment, may I not suggest that if the task be somewhat difficult there is yet abundant cause for supposing that the labour needed will be well repaid. There is good stuff in the lad—a strong will, no doubt, but so much the better, say I ; a boy with no will of his own may be a pleasant companion, easy to guide and easy to live with, but he'll make no mark in the world, do no great things for himself or anyone.'

Mrs. Pomfret leaned back in her seat, and glancing at the mirror to see if the plumes in her hat were in good order, and if the patch on her fair cheek was becomingly placed, and being satisfied on these important points, turned with an air of languid interest towards the clergyman, and, yawning slightly behind her fan, said :

'It is too charitable of you, dear sir, to speak so benevolently of my poor little nephew. We know well that if anyone can make anything of him it is you, and you only. But our fears— yes, I own, our fears—are greater than our hopes. And yet, 'tis strange, his father was as pretty a man as ever I saw, and my dear sister was an angel. Whence he can have drawn this awkward, churlish temper and boorish ways, I know not.'

'Amyot is but a child, madam,' interposed her son; 'good-breeding and courtesy, if not natural, can yet be acquired—time, and the great advantages he finds in this house, will yet make him all you desire.'

'I doubt it,' the lady persisted. 'He is as sour-tempered as he is ungainly. You will find that I am right, sir.'

The clergyman smiled.

'Worse lads have made good men,' he replied. Then, as his guests rose to depart, he offered his hand to lead her to her chariot, adding, 'Trust me, madam, there is much good in the boy.'

It was never pleasant to Mrs. Pomfret to find her opinion disputed, and she took her leave with some hauteur and a stately curtsy. But not so her step-son; following his mother as the schoolmaster led her to the door, and having assisted her into her chariot, Arnold turned again, and, forgetting his usual reserve of manner, thanked him warmly for his kindness to the orphan boy, adding:

'From my heart I agree with you, and believe that you are right.'

'Did ever a man treat a poor woman so rudely?' complained Mrs. Pomfret, as her handsome chariot drove slowly from the door. 'Poor Amyot will learn small courtesy at his hands. Never was I so contradicted in my life. Are all schoolmasters thus unmannerly and overbearing, I wonder?'

'Few bear a better reputation than he, I believe, madam,' her son replied; 'and, in truth, I liked him for his honesty.'

'I thank you, son Arnold, for your courtesy. You liked the man because, forsooth, he contradicted your mother.'

'Nay, madam; it seems to me that you mistook his meaning. It is plain he likes my little cousin, and you would not have him deny that he has a kindly feeling towards him.'

'I would have the man know how to treat a lady; and you, Arnold, I would have you learn not to dispute with your mother.'

'Your pardon, mother; I had no such thought.'

He took her hand and raised it to his lips and the lady, appeased, turned the subject, and apparently had soon forgotten her annoyance.

Not entirely, however, for on meeting her husband that evening, she made him smile as she reproached him for having suffered her to go unprotected into the den of that monster of a schoolmaster, who had a profound contempt for womenkind, had contradicted her flatly, and put her entirely out of countenance, ' While my son, of course, took his part.'

' 'Tis a pity,' her husband replied, ' but Arnold must strive to defend you better this evening, for he must needs attend you to your card-drum at Lady Sarah's. I find myself prevented from accompanying you.'

' Arnold's grave face ill suits with the gay world,' his step-mother replied ; ' but, if truth must be spoken, he is wont to be more obliging in his attendance than my son Guy, who is ever on the wing after the last belle of the season, and is apt to think his mother can take care of herself.'

' And what report do you bring of the lad Brough ?' inquired Mr. Pomfret ; ' is school to his liking ?'

' He is well enough ; a prodigious tall boy for his ten years, but as awkward as ever, with never a smile or a bow to spare. I wonder is it pride or sheer carelessness ?'

'Both, may be! But the schoolmaster—what says he of the boy's understanding?'

'Oh, he speaks well of him—would hear nothing of his faults—so I fear there is but small chance of any amendment.'

'Well, well! Your mother, my love, thought the boy had his good parts, and if the schoolmaster says the same, we must be encouraged to hope that the diamond may be genuine, though but roughly cut. What say you, Arnold?'

'As I have ever said, sir—that Amyot has many faults, but withal he has a sense of honour, truth, and honesty, such as I greatly prize. My mother—may I say it without offence?—it seems to me that the lad grows more awkward and churlish whenever he is in your presence—and, if I dare say as much, it is but true that I once felt the same dread of your displeasure.'

'That time has long since passed away, I see full well,' the lady replied; ' 'tis I that must now stand in awe of you. A hundred years hence it will be the part of children to correct their parents—did I say a hundred years?—nay, who knows but you, Arnold, will stand cap in hand to your own children?'

'If I have any it is likely enough, madam,' the young man replied, with his grave smile ; whereupon Mrs. Pomfret retorted that she was sure of it, and should much rejoice at the sight.

CHAPTER VIII.

Admiral Hosier's Ghost Story.

'BROUGH, tell me, have you any notion what ails Ned Wolfe?'

'What ails him! Is he sick?—he looks well enough!'

'Not sick, that I know of; but has he got the vapours, or has he been flogged, think you, that he looks so downcast, and has not a word to say for himself?'

'How can I tell? Ask himself, if you must know.'

'Well, if you put it in that way, I can't say that I am specially set upon knowing, but being a compassionate kind of a being, I own I feel queerish when a fellow-creature puts on airs that make one think of churchyards and suicides and such doleful things, and so I made bold to ask your worship if you knew the cause of the poor youth's sad countenance; but I'll beg your pardon if I've done amiss, so you need not knock me down.'

Amyot laughed.

'You're such a droll chap, West; but how should I know?   Ned doesn't tell me his secrets.'

'Doesn't he?—you're often together; but what appeared to me so mighty strange is that James Wolfe is just as mad with joy as his brother is mad with grief, and for the most part, the two seem to have but one soul, and for ever think alike.'

'Truly you are right there, West; it is mighty strange, now I think on't.'

'And at the end of the half, too, holidays coming in less than no time, what can it import? Some quarrel between the loving brothers?— well, that would be marvellous, truly.'

'Small chance of that,' Amyot averred. 'James Wolfe is hasty, and doesn't always pick his words; but that they should quarrel— no, never; I won't believe it.'

'Then I'll give up guessing; but see, Brough, there they go: did you ever see big Wolfe so mighty well pleased, or the little one so sunk in woe?'

' James Wolfe is telling some piece of tidings;
look how the lads are staring at him ; let's
run and hear. What is it, what is it, Wolfe ?
Ned, tell us what your brother was saying but
now.'

' Nay, don't ask me,' half sobbed the lad ;
' if only I could go too ! but my father will have
but one, and I'm too young.'

' Your father, Colonel Wolfe? Why, is James
to go with him—a lad of thirteen to go to the
wars ? Well, who ever heard such luck !'

'Aye, but my mother thinks him too young,
and I always deemed that we should go together,' and Ned turned away to hide his grief.

His brother's bright eyes were dimmed for
a moment as he gazed after him, but murmuring to himself, ' We couldn't both leave my
mother,' he shook off the passing regret, and
plunged again into an animated discussion of
his future prospects. All envied him, as a few
months before all had longed that fate had
given them a share in Admiral Vernon's triumphs
at Portobello, and many were the mutterings
and lamentations that such good fortune should
befall only one.

' Such good luck, to have a colonel for your
father !' cried one.

' I'd give my ears to serve under Vernon !' cried another.

' To have to stay here moping over these senseless books !' added a third, little given to either moping or books.

' Well, you won't have to do that,' remarked Wolfe good humouredly ; ' the holidays are coming ; hurrah for home, sweet home !'

' And you're going never to return, Wolfe,' said a sentimental lad much addicted to writing verses ; ' never to return !'

' We'll have a real good supper on the last evening,' remarked a more matter-of-fact youth. ' A monstrous fine affair we'll have this half ; see to it, lads, that you get ready your best songs.'

And, like true Britons, they applauded this suggestion ; and the last night of the half-year, always rather a tumultuous occasion, was doubly noisy this midsummer, the masters being conveniently deaf, the feasting, shout-ing, and singing were kept up till late. Again and again the cry arose for one more song, one more toast ; but at length a silence fell on the noisy crew, and after much pressing the most noted singer rose to attempt the song of the evening, bowing low to the honourable

company, and asking their kind indulgence if
his voice (which, alas! was about to undergo
that change which the vulgar call 'breaking')
should prove unequal to the merits of the song.
He thus began :

HOSIER'S GHOST.

'As near Portobello lying,
   On the gently swelling flood,
At midnight, with streamers flying,
   Our triumphant navy rode ;
Where, while Vernon, late all glorious
   From the Spaniard's dire defeat,
And his crew with shouts victorious
   Drank success to England's fleet,

'On a sudden, shrilly sounding,
   Hideous yells and shrieks were heard ;
Then, each heart with fear confounding,
   A sad troop of ghosts appeared—
All in dreary hammocks shrouded,
   Which for winding-sheets they wore,
And with looks by sorrow clouded,
   Frowning on that hostile shore.

'On them gleamed the moon's wan lustre,
   When the shade of Hosier brave
His pale bands was seen to muster,
   Rising from their watery grave.
O'er the glimmering wave he hied him,
   Where the *Burford* reared her sail,
With three thousand ghosts beside him,
   And in groans did Vernon hail :

'" Heed, oh, heed my fatal story,
   I am Hosier's injured ghost ;
You, who now have purchased glory
   At this place where I am lost,

Though in Portobello's ruin
　　You now triumph, free from fears—
When you think of our undoing,
　　You will mix your joy with tears.

' " See these mournful spectres sweeping
　　Ghastly o'er this hated wave,
Whose wan cheeks are stained with weeping,
　　These were English captains brave.
Mark those numbers pale and horrid,
　　Who were once my sailors bold ;
Lo, each hangs his drooping forehead
　　While his dismal fate is told.

' " I, by twenty sail attended,
　　Did this Spanish town affright,
Nothing then its wealth defended
　　But my orders not to fight.
Oh, that in this rolling ocean
　　I had cast them with disdain,
And obeyed my heart's warm motion
　　To reduce the pride of Spain !

' " For resistance I could fear none,
　　But with twenty ships had done
What thou, brave and happy Vernon,
　　Hast achieved with six alone.
Then the Bastimento's never
　　Had our foul dishonour seen,
Nor the sea the sad receiver
　　Of this gallant train had been.

' " Thus like thee, proud Spain dismaying,
　　And her galleons leading home,
Though condemned for disobeying
　　I had met a traitor's doom.
To have fallen, my country crying,
　　' He has played an English part,'
Had been better far than dying
　　Of a grieved and broken heart.

'"Unrepining at thy glory
　　Thy successful arms we hail,
But remember the sad story,
　　And let Hosier's wrongs prevail.
After this proud foe subduing,
　　When your patriot friends you see,
Think on vengeance for my ruin,
　　And for England shamed in me."'

The bravos were loud and long; the singer bowed his acknowledgments to right and left, and then resumed his seat; the provisions had long before disappeared, the candles were dying down in their sockets, one or two of the younger lads had fallen asleep, in spite of the deafening din around them, and, as the cheers died away, a strange and most unusual silence fell on the group of lads.

'Speak, do—somebody!' whispered a pale-faced boy with large awe-struck eyes. 'I don't like to think of that night at sea, and the hosts of ghosts rising through the waters—three thousand of them, groaning and shivering in the moonlight! I say, it makes me feel all cold and shaky!'

'Does it? Would three thousand be worse than one?'

'I don't know. Have you ever seen one?'

'Oh, scores of times. Stray ghosts are as common as daisies in our parts; but I fancy it

isn't usual for them to go in troops, and I've a
notion that the man who made that song has
put things a little too strong. What say you,
West ?'

'Like things strong !' said West. 'Detest
your prim folks, who stick to the exact literal
truth ; 'tis a good stirring song, and never a
ghost too many in it.'

'Pity they stay there ; if I were old Hosier,
or his ghost, I'd take a trip to old England and
plague the life out of those who sent me on
such a fool's errand. What's the use of moping
and fretting about on the sea ?'

'Little good crying over spilt milk,' remarked
Amyot. 'It seems to me that Hosier had but
himself to thank for his troubles.'

'You're right there, Brough ;' it was James
Wolfe who spoke. ''Twould have been easy
enough to have dropped his orders into the
sea, or read them t'other way about !'

'Bravo ! that's it ! just so !' echoed the lads.
'Teach the land-lubbers to mind their own
business ; put the Ministers to bed, and bid
them hide their heads under the bed-clothes, if
the sound of a gun frightens them. Why is
Spain to keep all the good things in America
to herself, and go prying into our ships to see

what we have been at? England's got ships
enow, and brave men enow, to conquer the
world, if she might but serve herself of them!'

'Ay, ay! that she has.'

'And some day she will.'

'Some day she'll turn the tables on Spain,
and make the French mounseers quake in their
shoes.'

'Ay, ay; she will.'

> ' "And she shall flourish great and free,
>   The dread and envy of them all." '

'So she shall—so she shall!'

> ' "Still more majestic shall she rise,
>   More dreadful from each foreign stroke." '

'If she only gets a chance of one.'

'I tell ye, lads,' broke in James Wolfe, 'that
she shall!'

'Whist! whist! Some one's coming.'

'Gentlemen, having settled the affairs of the
nation, and had a merry evening, I now commend you to your beds. Dream of glory as
much as ye will, I'll never hinder ye!'

It was the head-master who spoke, a smile of
amusement and no displeasure on his face, and
the lads dispersed at once.

A few days after, Amyot found himself again

at Westerham—Joan mightily pleased to have him, but quietly content, as was her wont; Tory uproariously delighted, as also was his wont.

At first, while holiday-time was a novelty, and the change was pleasing, everyone—even the old servants—pronounced him wonderfully improved. He would sit for hours together, holding a fishing-rod, by the side of the little river, waiting with most marvellous patience for the rare excitement of a bite, till Doddridge said he was a changed boy, and he shouldn't wonder now if he turned quite a credit to the family—doubtless he had been well chastised at school; for Doddridge was a firm believer in the efficacy of pain, and could see no other method by which such a wild young colt could have been broken in.

Hannah, too, privately informed her mistress that she had never thought to like a boy so well: Master Amyot was nearly as manageable as Miss Joan, and very near as sensible as the dog Tory. But Mrs. Darley smiled, and being a far-sighted person, she was not greatly surprised when, after a week had passed away, some of the old complaints began to recur.

The fishing was wearied of, the fish being

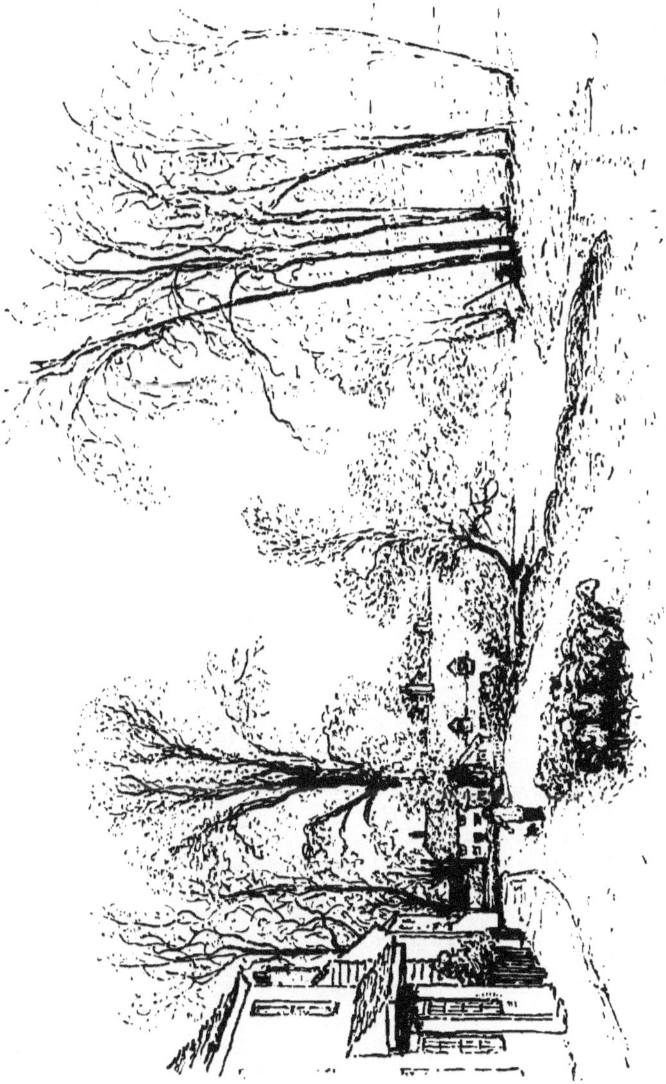

The River Darent.

stupid and perverse, and much given to an infatuated fondness for life; Joan and Miss Johnstone were so delicate that they could not walk if it was hot or wet; and Westerham was quite out of the world: there was nothing to do. Cock-fights were rare, and Mrs. Darley had a dislike to such amusements; so it came to pass one fine day that Amyot discovered that he was a most unfortunate individual, and the same conviction, by a strange coincidence, forced itself upon the minds of most of those with whom he came in contact.

Just at this period, and, to use Miss Johnstone's expression, as if he had been specially commissioned to avert some certainly impending calamity, there arrived at Mrs. Darley's house a most welcome visitor in the form of Arnold Pomfret.

'That dreadful boy entirely deprives me of my self-possession, dear madam,' the poor lady had observed. 'It is most providential that we should be protected by the presence of a gentleman just at this unhappy moment. I shall sleep in peace once more.'

''Tis well,' the old lady replied; 'sleep is a blessed thing, but my grandson shall never disturb my rest; and glad as I am to see my daughter Pomfret's step-son, for I like him, I need no protection from him—nor, I trust, from anyone. And, good Johnstone, I pray you, disturb not yourself for the humours of my grandson : 'tis a lad that lacks occupation ; we must find him work to do, and he will be well enough, and all this turmoil will cease.'

Prompted by this desire, the old lady was not long before she suggested to Arnold that, as he had a horse with him, and there was a sturdy old pony in her stable, he would be doing Amyot a kindness if he would take him out riding each day of his stay.

'The boy wants exercise,' she said ; adding, in a lower voice, 'and plenty of it ; provided thou dost not break any bones for him, I care not how long nor how hard thou makest him ride ; tire him out for us, good Arnold, and we poor women folk will thank thee ; and if thou carest not to ride thy horse to death, take him for a walk, and stride as if for a wager, till he is fain to beg for mercy.'

'Nay, madam ; what has the poor lad done to be so served.'

'Nought, nought, friend Arnold ; the lad is well enough, only I would fain save him from a fit of the gout, and my good Johnstone from a fit of another sort. But enough of that: thou wilt see for thyself how matters stand; and now to other points: how hast decided thine own affairs, for sure it is high time they should be decided?'

'But too true—it is high time; and, yet, dear madam, though I blush to say it, my mind is no more made up than when last I saw you. My father still presses me to study law, says he has much interest, and hopes he shall see me a judge one day; but though I am loath to go against his wishes, as I have often told you, the law has no charms for me.'

'And thine own wishes, Arnold Pomfret?'

The young man hesitated; then, looking full into the kindly face that was turned towards his, and the dark bright eyes that gazed through their long silver lashes at his troubled countenance, he said, with an effort:

'They have not changed, madam; but the questioning and the doubt remain.'

'The doubt how best to serve thy generation; whether to hide from thy sight all the evils that make thee miserable, and go and shut thyself up among those thou deemest pure and holy, and spend thy life in prayer; or whether to plunge into the sea of misery and wickedness and do what thou mayest to check the stream ?   Are these thy doubts, Arnold Pomfret ?'

'You have read me truly, dear madam, as indeed you ever do ; and now, what say you ?'

'Thou hast seen the monastery of La Trappe, thou enviest the good monks there ; thou hadst always a hankering after the Church of my ancestors, good Arnold, but yet thou callest thyself a Protestant ?'

Arnold hesitated.

'I scarce know what I am, save, I hope, something like a Christian.   I have thought little, too little, I fear, of dogma ; 'tis vice and cruelty and misery I want to combat—only tell me how.'

The old lady's eyes glistened.

'My son, I'll tell thee one thing : soldiers fight best when they see the foe, and I need scarce tell thee which of thy two plans is likest to thy Captain's.   Art astonished at me, Arnold ?   Didst think I would like to see thee a monk ?   Nay, nay, my son, I'm inclined to think I'm a pugnacious old woman, for I dearly love a hand-to-hand fight.'

Arnold smiled.

'It would be well if all had your cour-

age,' he said. 'To tell the truth, I believe
it is lack of courage that makes me long for La
Trappe. I'll put the thought away, and try to
face the other alternative.'

'And, Arnold, one more word.'

'The more the better, madam. I am happy
to be accepted as your scholar.'

'Nay, nay; my daughter Pomfret hath made
thee more civil than honest; who cares what
an old woman says? But, nevertheless, I will
speak my mind. Thou hast most surely the
weapon of zeal and good-will; and though
thou speakest of cowardice, I believe thee
brave to thy heart's core. Still, there are other
weapons: and ere thou enterest the combat, I
would have thee well equipped. See to it,
then, that all thine armour is forged in the
right armoury, and think not to fight till thou
hast well proved thy weapons.'

'I believe I take your meaning, madam; and
in this, as in all else, I am your loving pupil.'

'Nay, not mine, Arnold; take counsel with
thine own spirit, and with those fitted to instruct, not of an old woman who barely knows
enough to serve her own purpose, and maybe
instruct a child. But I must to my housekeeping cares; we will talk more another time,'

and the old lady bustled away, while her young companion took his hat, and calling Amyot to accompany him, started for a stroll by the river side.

Tory followed them; he liked Arnold, and was evidently relieved that his young master should be under some one's guardianship. He had done his best to keep him out of mischief, but this Kentish home was so different from Broughbarrow that the good dog's perplexities had much increased of late. In the north, few people had interfered with Amyot if he went bird's-nesting in other people's garden-hedges; the streams had seemed to be free to all; everybody had indulged and petted the brother and sister, especially after their father's death; but now times were changed—Amyot must behave like a gentleman, and a gentleman Tory was beginning to fear he never would be. But with this tall grave gentleman beside him the boy could scarcely get into scrapes, and Tory's heart was therefore light as in days of yore. He could hunt for frogs along the banks, he could bark at the stately swans in the little lake at Squerries Court, he could pay friendly visits at all the cottages where the doors stood open to invite him in, he could kiss the babies and have some fun with the cats.

Decidedly Arnold Pomfret's coming had been a happy event. Nor was it long before the young man discovered the meaning of Mrs. Darley's gay hints, and with the kindly feeling that ever distinguished him, he took upon himself to find occupation and amusement for the restless boy who was causing so much disturbance in the quiet household.

At first Amyot had stoutly resisted all proposals of pursuing his studies in holiday time, yet before long he found himself quietly submitting to be taught French, 'that hateful tongue, fit only for fine mincing dandies, traitors and cut-throats.'

'You will try to teach me manners next, cousin,' he one day remarked. But Arnold replied good-humouredly :

'I should be a poor teacher, having never learned. You must teach yourself, Amyot; good-breeding is the son or daughter of good feeling ; school your heart, and your head will bend.'

'And what about my legs ? My grandmother tells me they are much in fault. My sister can dance a minuet as prettily as any lady in the land ; but I—my legs are strong, but the hinges need oil, it seems to me.'

'You will find the way to make them supple in time,' was the reply. 'Can your sister take a good long walk, Amyot ? I think of taking her and you across the fields to-morrow, to the next village. It will be a pleasant walk, and I have a wish to hear a certain preacher, who I am told, is to preach there to-morrow.'

'Oh, Joan loves a walk. When we lived together at home we walked miles by ourselves, and she was never tired ; but now she walks only with Miss Johnstone, who is such——'

'Who cannot walk as far as you, which is but natural. Well, to-morrow we will see.'

To-morrow was hot and sultry, but not too hot for Joan if she put on her large hat, and not the silk hood which she usually wore to church. And the little girl was mightily pleased to be permitted to join her brother and their tall cousin in their walk. She was growing comelier than ever. Yet the quiet manner for which she had always been remarkable had rather increased than otherwise, so that Mrs. Darley was wont to call her 'her Quaker maiden.'

As they passed through the village they were

Quebec House, Westerham.

joined by Edward Wolfe, who, espying them from the windows of his home, ran out and begged leave to accompany them.

'I am so dull without my brother,' he said. And as Joan looked her sympathy, he added : 'I can't think how I am to live without him.'

Arnold Pomfret at once made him feel himself welcome to their party, and the two boys were soon quite happy, chattering over school doings, and school politics, while Joan, quite contented with her lot, walked demurely by her tall cousin's side, now listening to her brother and his friend, now answering timidly Arnold's grave remarks and questions.

Probably he was at that moment set on determining the question he had discussed with Mrs. Darley, for much of the road he seemed lost in thought, and Joan, who had conceived a vast opinion of his wisdom and saintliness, was sorry he should trouble to speak to her at all, since she felt quite sure that to do so, he must necessarily come down from some height of holiness or wisdom quite beyond her comprehension.

Returning home, he was much more inclined to talk, and Amyot and Edward Wolfe having exhausted the topics which had proved so interesting at first, were pleased to be drawn into conversation.

'The making of sermons,' Amyot remarked when they had proceeded a little way on the road towards home, 'must be a prodigious fatiguing business, a terrible hard way of earning a livelihood. What could induce a man to undertake it ?'

'Many different motives might lead a man to devote himself to such work,' Arnold replied, 'some worthy, some unworthy.'

'Some men love to hear their own voices,' little Wolfe remarked.

'Some say turning parson covers a multitude of sins,' Amyot observed, and Joan looked at him reproachfully. 'Yes, sister, parsons are huge villains, many of them.'

'This good gentleman must be right holy,' Joan asserted ; 'since he spoke so much of the comfort of a good conscience, he must needs know what it is.'

'Yes, he said that reflections upon a life well spent would help one to meet death comfortably,' Edward Wolfe replied. 'I wonder if one will be able to remember one's good deeds when one comes to die ; for the most

part I forget them, or perhaps I have never
performed any.'

'That you have,' Amyot broke in; ' I could
tell of many.'

Edward blushed.

'You make such a to-do about trifles,' he
said. 'I do truly believe I have never yet
done aught that I shall care to recall when I
come to die, but when I am a man perchance
I may.'

'There was a monstrous fine sentence near
the end of the discourse. I would I could
recall it, Ned. You have an extraordinary
good memory—tell me, I pray you, how the
parson proceeded after he had called upon
Innocence to come to his aid. Joan whispered
to me to ask to whom he was talking; she
verily thought he was addressing some one.'

'Did you truly, little cousin ?' Arnold Pomfret
inquired, much amused, and Joan, greatly
abashed, admitted that she had had some such
notion.

'I have no remembrance of the phrase,'
Ned Wolfe replied. 'I paid but little heed ;
my thoughts were on the sea with James.'

The address to Innocence which had thus
excited the children's wonderment had fixed

itself in Arnold's brain, and when he reached home he told Mrs. Darley of the little girl's mistake, repeating the words which had perplexed her :

'Oh, triumphant Innocence, oh, impregnable virtue, how art thou wanted in the day of distress, in the needful time of trouble ! How faint and languid is every earthly comfort without thee. Thou art the physician of the soul ; in all cases of extremity a very pleasant help, the only sure unerring guide. " Mark the perfect man, and behold the upright ; for the end of that man is peace." He, he only has courage to sustain the shock ; he has strength for the last encounter ; he has virtue to secure the victory. Happy man, enter into the joy of thy Lord, and dwell on the contemplation of thy virtues to all eternity.'

'And young Wolfe had a notion he should not remember his virtues !—a poor prospect for him,' Mrs. Darley remarked ; 'he will have no subject for contemplation throughout eternity. Verily, I trust the preacher is making good provision for himself.'

CHAPTER IX.

A Glance at London Life.

It was a balmy day in April, the month when
London looks its best ; the trees in Queen's
Square had a soft tinge of green ; the new
leaves had not yet had time to grow dusty, and
a faint smell of lilacs perfumed the air. Her
chariot, fresh-painted and fresh-lined, stood
before Mrs. Pomfret's door, and her gay son
Guy was in waiting to attend his mother on
her airing. Mrs. Pomfret had been ailing all
the winter months, and had scarcely crossed
the threshold since the cold weather had set
in : but the spring sights and sounds were
tempting her to lay aside invalid habits, and
show herself in the world again. But still
she lingered ; the horses shook their heads
and fidgeted, and Captain Guy paced the hall
impatiently, with many a muttered exclamation

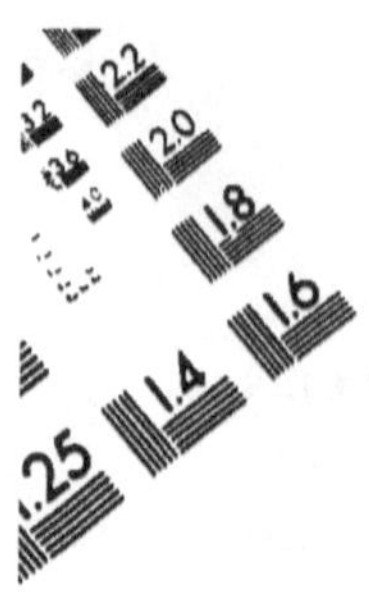

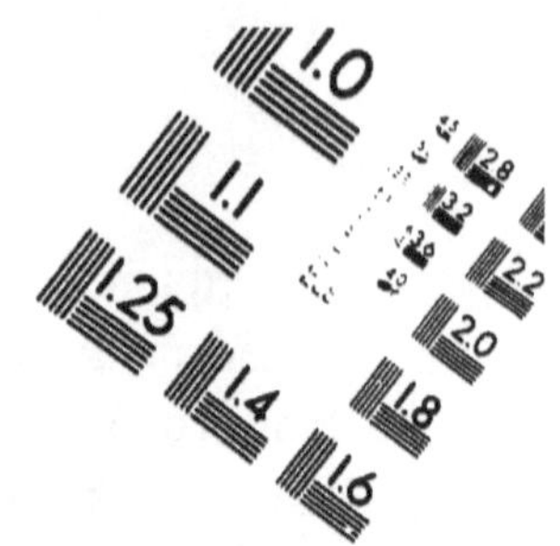

IMAGE EVALUATION
TEST TARGET (MT-3)

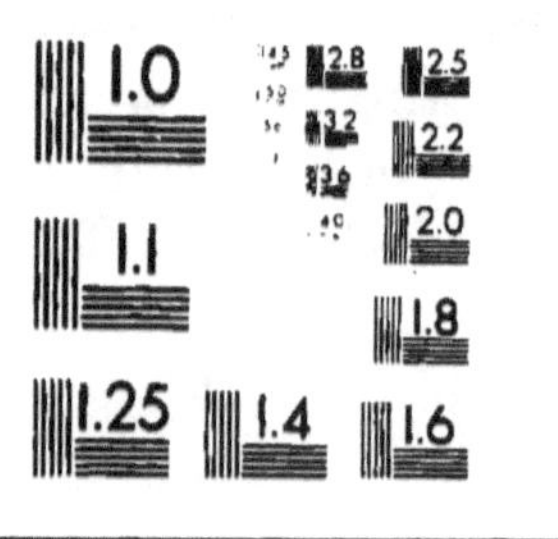

6"

Photographic
Sciences
Corporation

23 WEST MAIN STREET
WEBSTER, N.Y. 14580
(716) 872-4503

concerning ladies' whims and ladies' vanities;
till his father, opening the library door, inquired
whether there was aught amiss.   But as he
spoke a slight rustle announced the lady's
coming, and both advanced to meet her with the
gentle deference usually accorded to an invalid.

'You look pale, my love,' said her husband,
'but the drive will refresh you.'

'I look such a fright that I am almost determined merely to take an airing, and not go to
Ranelagh after all, much as I desire to see the
place.'

'Oh, for that matter, your paleness is becoming, my love, though 'tis a thousand pities that
your suit is so light a colour; a rich dark
tint would better have contrasted with the
delicacy of your complexion.'

'You are never pleased, Mr. Pomfret; this
suit has but just come from the milliner's, and
you had ever a fancy for primrose colour.'

'True, but now that you are pale——'

'Now that I am fit for my shroud 'tis a pity
I am not suited with it, you would say.   Well,
son Guy, have you no pretty compliment for
your mother, framed after your father's pattern?'

'Madam, the chariot is waiting; have I the
honour to hand you to your seat?'

Mrs. Pomfret deigned no reply, but permitted him to take her hand, and lead her to her coach, where she sank back, looking sad and weary, and scarcely spoke a word until they had arrived at their destination, the newly opened Ranelagh Gardens.

'Shall I secure a box for you, and bespeak some breakfast,' her son asked, as he assisted her to alight, 'or will you take a turn and see the rooms, and speak to your friends?'

'My friends will scarce know me,' she replied bitterly; 'when my hair was dressed this morning I scarce knew myself—such hollows in my cheeks, such lines around my eyes!'

'Nay, my mother, it seems to me you are fairer than ever; grieve not that my father thought you pale; it was but his care for you that made him mark how the fatigue of dressing had wearied you.'

'Well, enough of that. Find me a seat, and then let us have our breakfast. It is a marvellous fine place, and this is the room they call the Rotunda. I marvel that among all these crowds I see none of mine acquaintance. I thought it were likely I should meet with Lady Bel Finch, or Mr. Horace Walpole—they say he has been seen here many times of late. Ah!

there is my mother's old friend, Mrs. Wolfe. Go
to meet her, Guy, and ask her to take her dish
of tea in our company. And then, while I discourse with her, you can seek your own acquaintance. I would not tie you to my apron-string.'

Nothing loath, the lively captain went in pursuit of the good lady, and having delivered Mrs.
Pomfret's message, was successful in his suit,
and with great courtesy handed Mrs. Wolfe into
his mother's box ; and having seen them well
served with all that they required, bowed, and
went in quest of more lively company.

'A handsome young man,' Mrs. Wolfe
remarked. 'Going to the war, doubtless,
madam ?'

'To the war! Ah yes, and glad to go. But
he has seen some service already, and not been
altogether unnoticed. And your husband, my
d'ar madam, is he still abroad ? It is long since
it was my happiness to have any news of you.'

'The colonel has been long absent. He
went on that ill-fated expedition to Carthagena,
with Lord Cathcart ; and had not my son been
taken ill just before the fleet sailed, he had gone
with his father. It was sore against my will,
and right glad was I when sickness obliged the
lad to return home.'

'Ah, I have heard of that from my young nephew, Amyot Brough, your son's schoolmate, and right glad were the boys to have your son back at school again, though I warrant you Master James had hard work to bear the disappointment.'

'Well, he has his desire now, and in a few months he will be able to judge how a soldier's life will suit him. He goes to Germany in the summer with the King's troops, having got his ensigncy in the 12th of the line, Colonel Duroue's regiment. His brother will take it hard to part, but such is life.'

'"Such is life," you may well say, dear madam. But rumour had told me that your son's commission was in the Marines. My mother, visiting me a while ago, when I was sick, told me how your son had received his commission when staying with his friends at Squerries Court, and how he had waited on her most civilly to show her the document. I could have sworn it was in the Marines.'

'And so it was,' the old lady replied ; 'but James, poor lad, is but weakly, and a sea-life would soon make an end of him—at least, so he thinks, and so say those who have sailed with him ; and therefore he has contrived to exchange into his present regiment ; and mightily pleased is he, I can tell you.'

' I make no doubt of it,' replied Mrs. Pomfret ; 'the young men are all wild to be off to the Continent.　But, dear madam, what say you to taking a turn round the rooms ?　It is so long since I have been abroad, that I long to see something of my fellow-creatures, and there seems to be a gay company assembling.'

' Indeed, I have little doubt but all the world will be here ; 'tis the mode, and we must do as other folks do. Your gay son has found a party of friends, I see.　Will you join him, or shall we seek less lively acquaintances ?'

Mrs. Pomfret bit her lip and drew up her head, as her eye discovered Captain Guy walking at a little distance with a party of ladies whose loud voices and bold glances accorded but ill with his mother's ideas of good-breeding.

' They are no friends of mine,' she replied haughtily ; then, recovering herself with an effort, she added, ' Pardon my rudeness, dear madam ; my son has an unlucky passion—nay, I will not speak so seriously, 'tis nought but a fancy—for one of those monstrous ungenteel young ladies. It is well the war calls him hence, and for my own part I shall be glad when he departs ; for it annoys me that son of mine should be seen in such company. See but now——'

The ladies at that moment approached near enough for their eyes to meet, and one, a young lady in a robe of gaily flowered paduasoy and high hat with bright coloured plumes, turned her head and directed a prolonged stare at the discomfited Mrs. Pomfret.

Mrs. Wolfe smiled.

' An amiable daughter-in-law, my dear ! I agree with you, Captain Pomfret will do well to turn his thoughts to a fairer mistress— even his country. But be not distressed ; he is but diverting himself I make no doubt.'

' He shall not divert himself with a black-eyed doll who insults his mother,' Mrs. Pomfret indignantly asserted. ' Sir Claude,' to a gentleman who was approaching her with a low bow, ' you are truly a friend in need. I find myself tired to death with walking and standing about, and my son has disappeared at the very moment when I need his attendance. Might I crave so great a service from you, as that you will seek him out and bring him back ?'

' I am honoured by your commands. The truant shall be brought to your presence with

all possible speed—but, first, let me lead you to
a seat.'

This was soon done, and the gentleman had
soon discovered the gallant captain, and
brought him, with ill-concealed reluctance, to his
mother's side.

She was not slow to mark the signs of vexation, but, as long as Sir Claude lingered near,
contented herself with having gained her point ;
and it was not until half-an-hour had passed away
in lively talk with him and another gentleman
who had joined their party, that she vouchsafed
any reply to her son's inquiry whether she
wished to return home.   When at last, with low
reverences, they took their leave, the fatigue of
which she had complained again overpowered
her, and she replied sharply :

' Wish to go home ?—of course I do. Had you
not deserted me entirely, son Guy, I should have
been laid comfortably on my own couch by this
time, instead of being half-dead with fatigue and
stifled with the heat.   Seek the chariot at once,
and lead me to it, or you will have to carry me,
 warrant you.   Mrs. Wolfe, I pray you let me
have your company ; we can drive round by
Old Burlington Street, and part at your own
door.'

And to Guy's no small relief, for he by no means desired to be alone with his mother just then, the lady consented ; perhaps she anticipated the amusement of a further scene, but if so, she was disappointed. Mrs. Pomfret did but regret that her step-son Arnold, who was so much more dutiful and attentive, should have such a strange dislike to all scenes of gaiety that it was a real cruelty to force him into society.

'Not but what I do sometimes, for I count it my duty to do what in me lies to keep him from becoming altogether extraordinary,' she added, looking for sympathy to her companion.

'Mr. Arnold Pomfret extraordinary!—extraordinarily clever, you mean, my dear, or extraordinarily good ; nothing else, I am sure.'

'Ah, well, he is both clever and good ; but for all that he gives us much anxiety, his father and me ; for long he could not decide what profession he would follow. His father would have had him choose the law, and could have done much to advance him, but he would do no such thing, and after much deliberation he has taken holy orders, turned parson, which I can't say I at all approve, nor his father either.'

'Arnold will look a very pretty fellow in lawn sleeves : of course he'll be a bishop,' interposed Captain Guy ; 'he'll get a fat living in no time. For my part, I think it's not a bad idea.'

'I have known some creditable persons among the clergy : a few, at least,' Mrs. Wolfe replied ; ' but Mr. Arnold Pomfret will certainly bring lustre to the profession. A clergyman who has no taste for gaming, drinking, hunting, or the like, must seem something singular, yet the thought of it does one good ; and excuse me, madam, but I would be well content to see many more eccentric in such a fashion.'

'My mother speaks as you do,' replied Mrs. Pomfret, 'and had it not been for her persuasions, I doubt if we had ever given our consent ; but it is strange ; gentle and quiet as he ever is, and I must own, a most dutiful son to both his father and me, yet when he has made up his mind, Arnold is steadfast as a rock, and nought can move him.'

'So you did not try ?'

'Try to change him ? yes, indeed, and the more so, because it was plain he had no mind

to be such a parson as most : talked in a fashion
that he might almost have learned from that
strange woman, Lady Huntingdon, but that
he has never come nigh her ; and his father
wondered whether his brain was touched, so
earnest and piteous was his talk ; but there
again my mother reassured us, and as we could
make nothing of him, we let him take his own
way.'

'You interest me, dear madam. I shall
hope some day to hear the young man preach.
Right glad I am that he has not left the com-
munion of our own Church, as once it seemed
he might. But here is my home, and I must
wish you a good-day, with much sense of the
pleasure of your company, and grieving much
to have to part so soon.'

'A most tiresome old-fashioned creature,'
Mrs. Pomfret remarked, as she leaned back in
her seat. ' Guy, I am wearied to death of her
talk. It was most thoughtless of you to leave
me to her.'

' My dear madam, I truly thought you desired her company, else would I have found
you other society ; but I am a most luckless
fellow, and ever fail when most I desire to
please. But, tell me, sweet mother, will you

go with my father to the review at Blackheath next month. It will be a gay scene, and his Majesty and all the grandees will be there.'

'It will be pleasant on the river. Yes, if only I feel myself stronger I will go, and we can see the lad, Amyot Brough, at the same time. Your father is for ever telling me that I do not do my duty by the child. Let me see, he must be nigh upon twelve years old by this time. The little sister is eleven, I believe, and there is but a year between them.'

'He is a monstrous big fellow for twelve,' said the captain, 'and in boxing and wrestling he can beat all the school. I hear he has flattened one boy's nose, who could ill spare any beauty, and that all his comrades stand in awe of his amazing strength.'

'Well, if the day be warm we will go and visit the lad. I will have a basket of cakes and comfits prepared, that I may not be un-welcome.'

The weather favoured Mrs. Pomfret's intention, and the thought of change and variety lent something like a natural bloom to her cheek, which, when aided by the usual devices of art, might have enabled her to pass for her son's sister instead of his mother.

'Mr. Pomfret was right when he said pale colours became me not,' she remarked to her waiting-woman, as she surveyed her slight and graceful figure arrayed in rich crimson, and adjusted the soft lace which hung from her elbows. 'See that my hat is firmly pinned on.

Greenwich Park.

The wind is wont to be troublesome on the river. That primrose paduasoy may be laid by. I shall never wear it more. 'Tis a pity I have no daughter ; but now I think of it, when my niece Joan is old enough, if the fashion be not completely changed, it will suit her well; the child has such a pretty colour, and such a clear skin ; no garment will be too delicate for her to wear.

Give me my fan and gauze scarf, Félicité, I
hear your master call.'

The Thames was a gay scene that day,
crowded with boats and barges, bright with
their coloured awnings, and filled with richly
dressed visitors; flags hung from the house-
windows, the church-bells rang and cannon
thundered.   The greensward in Greenwich
Park was dotted here and there with more gay
groups; while on Blackheath the troops about
to depart to the war on the Continent were mus-
tered, to be reviewed and complimented by
King George, and much admired by all their
friends.

Not the least merry of the spectators were
Mr. Swinden's lads, proud to see their old comrade, now Ensign Wolfe,. among the officers,
full of exuberant loyalty, bloodthirsty hatred of
the French, and chivalrous pity for the wrongs
of Maria Theresa.   And of these lads, who
had all shouted themselves voiceless before the
day was done, none was more vehement in his
loyalty, more ardent in his military enthusiasm,
than our old friend, Amyot.   No longer now a
new boy or a stranger, he had thoroughly
adopted all the school traditions, had grown fond
of Greenwich, its park, its hospital, and desired

no better happiness than to stand for hours by the river, watching the ships and all the lively bustle of that constantly changing scene. One day he had quite resolved to enter the navy; the next, listening to the military enthusiasm of the two brothers Wolfe, he was equally determined to become a soldier; but soldier or sailor, one thing was certain, he would serve his country in foreign lands, and help to win back some of her old renown. Had not his grandfather fought under the great Marlborough at Oudenarde and Malplaquet, and should he sit down quietly on his farm in Cumberland, and think only of his own ease and comfort? No, not he! That dream had passed away. He would go to the wars and see the world, let Joan say what she would. And then he sighed to think of the years which must still pass by before his schooldays would be over, and the life he dreamed of could be realized.

CHAPTER X.

Wherein Amyot Brough betakes himself to the North.

SMALL apology, it seems to me, is needed for passing over with but brief notice the school career of Amyot Brough; rather, perhaps, should I apologize for bringing such an unworthy mortal before the world at all. My reasons for so doing, kind reader, may be hard to guess; yet I would pray your patience, and mayhap, if your long-suffering carry you through my tale, you may find somewhat to love, even in my rough and rugged hero.

We find him, then, once more in the little town of Westerham. It is again the summer holidays—the summer of 1745. Since that review on Blackheath, his military ardour has grown fiercer rather than diminished. The king, who won glory for England at Dettingen, made himself by that act worthy of all honour

in Amyot's eyes ; while the failure of the Duke
of Cumberland at Fontenoy was, he was sure,
no fault of the duke's or his troops, but all to
be laid at the door of the cowardly Dutch.

All the boy's talk was of sieges and battles.
War he must see. He would run away and
enlist if his uncle would not use his influence to
get him a commission. School? He had had
enough of school. Many lads were officers before they were as old as he ; fifteen was a fair
age, and none could say he was not tall for his
age and broad in proportion.

Such were his sentiments, and Joan, who was
the constant and patient recipient of all his
grievances, grew pale and anxious as she listened ; but there came a day when matters
arrived at a climax.

Mrs. Darley was away on a visit to her old
friend, Mrs. Wolfe, in London. It was a long-
promised visit, and should have been made
nearly a year before, when Mrs. Wolfe was
thrown into great grief by the loss of her
younger son, who had sickened and died while
away on the Continent. Mrs. Darley had longed
to go and console the bereaved mother, but her
own health had been delicate, and the visit had
been postponed. But at last she had gone.

Amyot had his sister to himself, for Miss Johnstone suffered much from 'the nerves' when he was at home, and seldom left her bed-chamber, and Joan was well content with his company. But it happened one morning, as she was sitting in Miss Johnstone's chamber reading to her, as was her daily custom, her ear, keenly alert for mysterious sounds, heard much opening of cupboards and shutting of box-lids in the chamber overhead—none other than her brother's.

'My poor head!' sighed Miss Johnstone. ' Joan, my love, do you think you have influence enough with your brother to prevail on him to forbear making that horrid noise in his chamber. Perchance if you could devise an errand to the village, he might be induced to undertake it. Do not tell him he troubles me, for that I well know is the very purpose of all this din.'

Joan rose quietly, and ran lightly upstairs. Tory, sitting at Amyot's door, greeted her appearance with a whine, which said plainly enough : ' Yes, there's something wrong going on ; see what you can do to prevent it,' and followed her into the room, where her brother, on his knees before a bureau, was pulling out and examining a quantity of clothing, while a travelling-bag, half packed, lay on the floor beside him.

'Amyot, brother!' Joan exclaimed.

Amyot, startled, sprang to his feet ; then, seeing her look of consternation, his face softened, he put his arms round her, and said fondly :

'Sister mine, be not vexed with me.   I thought it was a good moment, and that I would not lose the chance.'

'Lose what chance ?'

'Now you are growing pale, and putting on that miserable countenance which I hate to see.   Joan, sister, it must be so—I cannot be a boy any longer ; look at me—I must be a man, and do man's work.'

'A man should be patient and loyal-hearted, and bide his time ; but what will you do—where are you going ?'

'Listen, Joan, you have heard, as I, of the preparations making in France, and how men say the Pretender will shortly land in the North, and that there must the quarrel be fought out.   Is not our home on the borders, is it not my place to go and see to our property there ?—and who knows but I may find a chance of earning that commission which no

13—2

one will seek for me? I say it is a lucky
moment, and go I will ; my grandmother being
away makes it all the easier.'

'Oh, Amyot, wait but till she returns, and
ask her permission ; she will be at home, if all
be well, to-morrow.'

'Then will I be gone to-day !'

Joan wrung her small white hands.

'It will grieve her sorely,' she said.

Amyot uttered an impatient imprecation ;
then, checking himself, he said, taking Joan's
hands in his :

'Sister, I cannot help it, I must go ; my
heart is set upon it, and it is surely better to
go, my grandmother not knowing, than to
resist her will, when once it is spoken.'

'I know not that,' Joan replied ; 'and, moreover, I am not sure that grandmother would
forbid your wish.'

'Ay, but I am sure of it ; she will not believe but that I am still a child. Nay, Joan,
you must make the best of it ; win her to forgive me if you can—if not, you, at least, will not
cease to love me.'

'If I could, methinks I would,' Joan began
more passionately than Amyot thought was
possible with her ; then, choking back some

tears, she continued indignantly: 'Amyot, brother, you are a coward; Cousin Arnold would tell you so, I know.'

'Cousin Arnold and I do not always think alike,' Amyot replied, growing cooler as she grew warmer; 'but, yes, Joan, if you will have it, I am a coward. I like not to vex you, and I do fear to see my grandmother, lest she too should be grieved.'

'It is a poor spirit that will give pain, but cannot bear to see it,' Joan responded; 'but, Amyot, nought that I say changes your mind in the least; it is of no use then to talk and vex each other. When are you going, and how?'

'I shall walk to London, and take the mail —get some lifts on the way, perchance—but I have not too much brass, and must save it. Then we part in peace, Joan? I knew we two could never, never quarrel.'

'It would be of small avail,' she replied sadly. 'Amyot, I know you dread even to seem to be guided by me, yet this once—— there, your lips curl at the bare thought of it.'

'Nay, nay, Joan, you fancy; you have guided me oft, and shall do it oft again, but in this——'

'In this I may say nothing. Well,' she stopped, then added : 'if only grandmother would come home.'

The thought lent a fresh impetus to Amyot's activity, and when the old lady did alight at her own door, her grandson was already many miles away. Mrs. Darley was tired, and anxious to rest, and his absence was for some time unnoticed ; if she thought at all about it, she probably imagined he was out fishing, his favourite amusement. She had much to tell of her visit, of the news she had gathered during her absence, and it was not till she was in the middle of an account of the illness and death of her young favourite, Mrs. Wolfe's son Edward, that she noticed Joan's woe-begone face, and spied some tears ready to fall.

'What, love, didst thou so much care for thy playfellow ? But it *is* sad to think that the dear lad should have been far away from all he loved, when death came to him.'

It was not of Edward Wolfe that Joan was thinking, or rather, it was far less of him, than of one nearer and dearer; yet she was sufficiently interested in the old lady's tale to say :

'Was he then all alone, madam ? I thought

for certain his brother would have been with
him, so loving as they always were.'

'And I too, Joan, had always thought that
the poor lad must have died happy in his
brother's arms ; but, from what their mother
tells me, it seems that James knew not how ill
he was, and, moreover, his duty kept him at a
distance.   He grieved sore, his mother said,
and has wrote her a very feeling letter, in
which he tells her for her comfort—and it is
the best comfort a mother can have—how all
spoke well of poor Ned, and bore testimony
how he had ever done his duty ; and, indeed,
they were sons to be proud of, both of them,
so dutiful—— But, how is it, sweet one—what
ails the child ?'

' Nothing, grandmother ; I was but troubled
to think of Amyot.'

' Of Amyot! What of him, where is he—
out fishing, or rat-hunting, or gone to see those
fighting-cocks again ?'

' Dear grandmother, he grieved to seem un-
dutiful, but he has gone away.'

' Gone away! and whither ?—to see your
cousin, Arnold Pomfret ? It will do the boy no
harm ; nay, do not cry, Joan, it would have
been more civil had he stayed till my return,

and asked my leave, but as my daughter Pomfret says, he has never a very clear sense of
what is fitting.'

' But, madam, he has not gone to my cousin's ;
he has started for the North—for our home at
Broughbarrow.   I prayed him to wait and ask
your leave, but—— '

'To Broughbarrow!   The lad is mighty
strange ; what thinks he to do there ?'

' He is mad to go a-soldiering, madam, and
he thinks that if all we hear is true about the
coming of the Pretender, there may be some
fighting in Scotland, and he will make his way
thither.'

The old lady's pale face flushed with some
displeasure as she listened to Joan's tale ; but
seeing the young girl's distress, she smiled, and
patting her cheek fondly, said ' How is it, little
one, that thou hast such good sense and discretion, and thy brother none ?   Tell me, when
did this most valiant youth start on his journey,
and how did he mean to travel ?'

Joan told all she knew, and the old lady
paused to consider.   At last she spoke. ' Joan,
love, thy grandmother is getting old, and makes
many mistakes, and she scarce knows what to
do for the best ; but she thinks it may be well to

let the lad be. Thy uncle shall write to the lawyer who has control of the property, and from him we may learn what the boy is doing, and then I will write to the lad himself. And now to thy bed, child, and fret not too much about thy wayward brother; thy aunt would tell thee that crying makes bright eyes dim, and that for no brother in the world shouldst thou spoil thy beauty. I'm of another mind, and think that for no brother in the world shouldst thou mar thy peace, so long as thou hast one Elder Brother to bear thy burdens for thee.'

But though she spoke thus cheerily, and dismissed Joan to bed with a smile as serene as usual, and bade Tory not look so dismal, he would see his young master again, Mrs. Darley did not go to bed herself until she had written the letter which the next morning she despatched to London by a safe hand, to inform Mr. Pomfret what had happened.

'As the boy's guardian, I feel that you ought to know at once,' she wrote; adding, however, her own opinion that it might be well to let the boy have his will, and since he was bent on a military life, steps should be taken to obtain a commission for him.

This letter was brought to Mr. Pomfret as

he sat with his wife the next evening, telling
her some of the many astounding pieces of news
which he had heard during the day. 'The
French are certainly getting ready for an inva-
sion, nobody doubts that, my love; it is a well-
known fact. Marshal Belleisle says that if his
Government will give him but 5,000 men, he
will engage to conquer England in a week.'

'Mercy on us! what impudence!' ejaculated
his wife.

'And the King's abroad, and nearly all the
troops; true, the Ministers are coming to
London, but what can they do? There's a
rumour, but whether there's any truth in it I
really can't say, that the Pretender has already
landed in Scotland, and that he is publishing
manifestoes, and that sort of thing, setting a
price on his Majesty's head.'

'Better take care of his own,' observed Mrs.
Pomfret; 'but what was that letter they brought
you just now, Mr. Pomfret?'

'I have not read it; it is from your mother—
one of her pleasant little letters, no doubt, but
nothing of great importance, I imagine.' He
opened and read it, and uttered an exclamation
of annoyance, adding 'That boy is a plague.'

'What boy—our nephew! what is it, now?—

has he begun to make love to the milkmaids,
or got married at the Fleet?—he is so tall, I
begin to fear all manner of evil doings.'

Her husband read the letter, and folded it up
with the observation, 'Your mother is right, as
she always is ; it will be less trouble to humour
than to thwart him ; for your father's sake many
at head-quarters will be disposed to favour the
lad—a commission will not be hard to obtain ;
but for the present Amyot must take care of
himself.   I am not going into those bleak northern regions again in search of him, but I'll
write to the lawyer, as your mother suggests.'

'The boy will come to a bad end ; such self-
will and undutifulness cannot prosper,' Mrs.
Pomfret exclaimed. 'Well, I hope it will be
but a bullet on an honourable field of battle, but
my mind misgives me it is more likely to be a
gibbet by the road-side.   Poor little Joan !'

Unmindful of the high destiny thus predicted
for him, but yet not altogether easy in his mind,
Amyot reached his journey's end.

The coach deposited him before the well-
known sign of the Griffin in Penrith town,
where all looked much as it had done five years
before ; in fact, so familiar was every house and
shop-front, so unchanged were the faces which

gazed at him as he alighted, that he could
scarcely believe that he himself was so altered
as to be quite unrecognisable.

'Lile Amyot Brough, ta cap'n's lad ; nay,
thou'lt niver be he ?'

'What, Amyot Brough, o' Broughbarrow ?
Wull, I niver! Thoo's growed a ter'ble girt
fella. Hast cum to see ta land an' farm, an'
sich ? They'll bee verra pleased ta see ya ;
ga awa' heeam as fast as ya can—Mike he's to
heeam an' ta woife tew.'

And his heart warming at the sound of the
familiar brogue, Amyot quickened his steps out
of the town towards the old familiar road that
led to his home. On the top of the hill he
turned and looked back over the town : yes, it
was all just as he remembered it—the hill in the
distance with the beacon tower against the sky,
the church tower down below, and around it the
roofs of the town. He almost wished that he
had turned the opposite way, and paid his first
visit to Blencathara house. But then he remembered with shame how ill he had kept his pro-
mise of writing to his old friends there ; perhaps
they would have forgotten him, and not wish to
renew the acquaintance ; and for a moment the
thought flashed through his mind that he had

been rather reckless of his friends' feelings of late, and that there might come a day when they would prove equally indifferent to his.

But such unpleasant thoughts took to themselves wings as he stooped his head to pass in at the back-door of his own farm-house. (How strangely low that doorway had become since

Penrith.

last he passed beneath it!) Could such misgivings prevail amid the tumult of wonder and kindly rapture that greeted his appearance? It was long since he had felt so truly at home, and listening to the undisguised admiration which

his growth and general improvement excited,
receiving the rough but deferential service of
his childhood's friends, Amyot's spirits rose,
and he went to rest that night in the best bed-
chamber in the house, in a state of perfect
intoxication of self-sufficiency and self-satis-
faction.

CHAPTER XI.

Rebel or No ?

' AND my old schoolfellows—-Lance, Jasper and
Percy—all are gone ? Truly, I thought the
house was strangely quiet when I entered, but I
little dreamed of this.'

It was Amyot who spoke, standing in the
parlour at Blencathara House, the mistress of
which was busy with a bowl of water washing
some choice china, which never passed through
a maid-servant's hands. She had greeted her.
visitor with some ceremony, which recalled to
his mind the misgivings which had troubled it
the night before. He thought she was reproach-
ing him for forgetfulness and neglect ; and conscious that he was far from guiltless, he felt
abashed in her presence. For once, too, he
regretted that he had grown so tall, and wished
that Mrs. Kirkbride would treat him like a boy

once more. Her lack of friendliness made him
feel so awkward, while he could not but wish to
look his best to the laughing girl who, while
helping mother, was watching his every movement, and finding much sport in his awkwardness.

'Yes ; they are away on business, I may say,'
Mrs. Kirkbride replied, with some appearance
of mystery, and again devoted all her attention
to a delicate cup, which she handled with the
tips of her fingers.

'Away, not dead,' Primrose added. 'Master
Brough spoke in such a grievous tone, that he
appeared to think they were dead and gone.
They are well—at least they were a week
agone.'

'And you, Miss Primrose, are you well,
too ? You are marvellously grown, it seems
to me !'

'Nay ! From such a height as yours I
marvel you can see me. I must e'en mount
upon a chair if I am to pay you any compli-
ments !' And she laughed the silvery laugh
that Amyot remembered to have heard when
he was ill so many years before.

' Primrose ! your tongue runs over-fast, child.
Carry these cups to the press, and place them

carefully on the topmost shelf, and then go and help Maggie with her seam.'

The girl obeyed with no sign of annoyance at being thus summarily dismissed, and Amyot was left alone with the somewhat stern old lady, who, laying down the cloth she held, placed herself in a high-backed chair, and with some ceremony begged him also to be seated, remarking, ' I have a thing to say to you.'

He bowed—a bow that would have made Mrs. Pomfret shriek, but which he imagined was a triumph of elegance.

Mrs. Kirkbride was too much absorbed in her own thoughts to notice it, and, having turned to ascertain that the door was shut, began to speak in an undertone.

' You wish to know where my sons are at the present time ?'

' Nay, madam ; I would not be so curious.'

' Perhaps not. It is not your will to be curious, yet in this matter you are. I see it in your face, and I blame you not—youth is ever inquisitive. Now, as I do not wish that my matters should be talked about, and that Amyot Brough, or any other person, should go about the town saying " Mrs. Kirkbride's sons have suddenly left the place," I am minded to give

you my confidence ; believing that you, Amyot
Brough, have enough honesty to hold that
sacred which is told you in trust.'

' Indeed, madam, you may rely upon me.'

' It is well.   Then, Amyot, in brief, my sons
have gone to serve their King.'

' Joined the army, you mean, Mrs. Kirkbride.   I envy them their luck !   It is just what
I would be doing, but I cannot see my way.'

' You have but half read my meaning.   They
have gone to the North to seek the Prince and
offer him three loyal hearts, and any service he
may command of them.'

' The Prince, madam ! how, the Prince of
Wales is not in the North, and his Majesty
is abroad and not yet returned ;   at least, so
I believe.'

' The Prince landed in the Highlands on
the twenty-fifth of last month.   When you
left London it is possible the news may not
have been known.   Ha ! he will steal a march
upon them, and who knows but he will be
in London before that German Elector has
heard of his coming ?'

' Madam, you amaze me,' was all that Amyot
could say.

' Do I ?   Well, take time to breathe, my

poor boy ! If you want service, and the Elector
needs you not, Prince Charlie will find you
work and kindly smiles, and riches and honour,
if God prosper his cause, which I doubt not
He will, seeing it is the cause of truth and
right.'

But Amyot only gasped.

There was a long silence. At last Mrs.
Kirkbride spoke again, and this time on indifferent subjects : asked questions concerning
his journey, his sister and his school life, to
all of which Amyot answered as if in a dream.
Then, suddenly remembering some domestic
duty, his hostess hurried away, and a few
minutes afterwards the door was gently opened,
and Primrose came in.

' My mother hopes you will take your dinner
with us,' she said. Then, without waiting for
a reply, she continued hurriedly, ' I know what
she has said to you. Master Amyot Brough,
I pray you tell me what you have replied to
her. She says there will be fighting, and I
like not to think of you on the wrong side.
It is hard to think that you and your old
friends may cross swords, or, worse, may die
by each other's hands. It is foolish of me
to fancy that such things may happen ! But

I suppose they have in this quiet land ere now.'

'I scarce think there is like to be much fighting,' Amyot replied.

A few days before he had aspired to no greater happiness than to find himself on a battlefield; but the conversation of the last half-hour had changed his views, and his mind was such a turmoil of conflicting ideas that he scarcely knew what he was saying.

'And yet'—Primrose said doubtfully—'a great kingdom can scarce be won without much bloodshed; unless—oh, I pray that it may be so—the hearts of the people return to their rightful King.'

'I can never call him King whose father abandoned his crown without striking one good blow for it, and who showed himself near as fainthearted when he came over thirty years ago. Such men were never meant to be Kings of England, Miss Primrose. You cannot think they were.'

'Nay, if you look so fierce and speak so disdainfully I shall run away. I fear you, now you are grown so marvellous tall, and wear such a fine cut coat. But you will eat your dinner with us, and give me time to hear about

my dear friend Tory and all your travels. Nay,
do not hesitate—we will not poison you; at
least, not until we are quite sure that you may
not be won to the rightful cause.'

'Be quite sure of that, Miss Primrose. I
am King George's true man, and will serve
none else.'

'Nay, nay'—she stopped her ears—'I am
deaf. I will hear no treason. I go to tell
my mother that a fat duck and green peas
may make a loyal man of you yet. Contradict
me if you dare.'

And she danced away, singing 'The King
shall enjoy his own again,' leaving Amyot in
great dismay and perplexity.

It was rather a silent meal that followed,
and Amyot was glad when it was over, and
he could escape to think over what he had
heard. The Pretender had really landed.
Rumours of such an event had reached him
on his journey, but this was the first certain
information he had had. He wondered much
whether any considerable number of men had
joined his standard, and especially whether
others beside the Kirkbrides had gone from
Penrith.

He determined to step into the Griffin and

other inns of the town on his way back, and
pick up all the information that he could, and
judge for himself whether the feeling of the
townspeople inclined in any degree to the
Jacobite cause. This he did, and found that
if he wanted news he could have enough and
to spare, but as abundance is often more
embarrassing than scarcity, so he was soon
forced to admit to himself that he should go
home little wiser than when he set out, except
in the one important fact which he had learned
from Mrs. Kirkbride.

'Ya wants ta knaa what's gaan on; what's
dewan awa to Noarth,' said the landlord of the
Griffin. 'Wull I beant sewer whedther theears
any feytin theear as yet; bet I've heeard tell
as theears no gitten aboot in t' sea, it's that
full o' ships a bringin' forran sodgers frae t'
Continent.'

'Neea doot,' added a bystander, 'thae idle
fellars hoop ta git sumat ta dew, or leastways
ta git paid fur dewing nowt.'

'I heeard tell,' said another, 'as ta rebels
wur coomin reet doon ower ta Fells a-burnin'
ivverything an' a-murderin' all that coom in ta
roaad. Thousan's an' thousan's on 'em.'

'Na, na; thae'll be reet awa in Scotland yet.

Mappen it'll be a gae bit afoor thae cross ta
boorder. Penrith toon will be true ta King
Geoarge, I rakkan.'

' I's none sae sewer aboot that—wha knaa's
bet theear rebels amoong us ?'

The speaker looked round suspiciously, and
valiantly challenged anyone who was not
satisfied with King George to come out and
fight out the question in the backyard ; but no
one stirred.

' Theear be a bodderin' kind o' chap as
thae call Mounseer Saxe, a chap o' mickle
prate, wha ses as he's coomin' ta dew mighty
girt things, he an' ten thousan' meddlin'
forraneers. Has ta heeard whedther he's loike
ta be coomin' this roaad ?'

' Na, na ; I rakkan thae forraneers wull na
fash theersells aboot us ; hawiver, thae be alus
fratchin' amoong theersells. M'appen thae've na
quite fergitten ta aald Dook o' Marlboro', an'
ta lesson he giv' 'em.'

' Ay, ay, pity he's deed an' gaan.'

And thus they discoursed up and down the
town, till Amyot, tired of listening, went home
to talk to Mike and Deborah, and to sit in his
father's old elbow-chair, and wonder what he
had best do.

And this wondering continued for many days, until he could not help admitting to himself that he wished himself back again under guardianship and tutelage, since to live an idle life at Broughbarrow had been no part of his dream when he left Westerham ; yet how to find work to do, or whether now to wish for service, he could scarce decide.

The northern towns, lying among their mountains, and hidden away, as it were, from the world's bustle and notice, were not very bustling places in those days, whatever people may think of them now. The people who lived in Penrith and its neighbourhood were addicted to much consideration before they took any important step, and Amyot had soon fallen into their ways again ; and so the days drifted on, and no decision was made. His dream of fighting the rebels side by side with his old friends and schoolfellows had been rudely disturbed, and it was not easy to reconcile himself to the idea of fighting against them.

Mike and Deborah could not tolerate the notion of his going soldiering ; what call had he to go and get killed for any man, be he called George or James ? It made little difference, in their opinion, which was King, and certainly their young master had nought to do with any man's quarrels. They entirely approved of his coming home, and had no doubt at all that he must have found 'them southern folk' most feckless and ill to do with ; but now that he had come home, what better could he do than bide there ? To go further northwards would be a senseless move, since everyone knew that across the border lived a set of people little better than savages, with bare legs and a most uncommon kind of dress, not to mention a barbarous style of language, and a mighty fine opinion of themselves. Michael had seen one of these savages come riding into Penrith on the top of the coach, and could never forget his huge stature and horrid dress.

So it was of little use to consult him, and the days slipped by, one after another, wiled by continual quest of news, and discussion as to the turn that events were likely to take. August had passed away, September was far advanced, and still Amyot was living idly at Broughbarrow, when, sauntering down the hill, by the ruins of Penrith Castle, one early morning, he noticed an unusual stir in the quiet little town. Old people who had not left their doors for many years were making what

speed they could to follow their more active
neighbours to the market-place, bare-legged
children were running and shouting, men
looked eager and excited, women awe-struck
and alarmed.

'What is it?' Amyot eagerly inquired, his
heart ready to hail any news with delight, so
tired was he of waiting for the something to
happen which was to decide his fate.

'A great victory, nay, I mean a great
defeat,' was the reply of a young man, who
had just dismounted from a worn and jaded
steed. 'Your pardon, friends, but my horse
and I have come many a weary mile, and I
scarce know what I say, while he, poor beast,
scarce knows how to stand; but yonder fellow,
who rode with me, can tell you more, for he
was in the fight, which good luck, I grieve to
say, was not mine.'

He extricated himself from the mob, which
was fast collecting round, and repeating: 'Ask
yonder fellow in the red coat,' he turned his
horse's head down a by street, and, walking by
the poor stumbling beast, sought a less frequented part of the town, followed by none but
Amyot, who, with some indistinct notion of
recognition, some floating idea of having seen

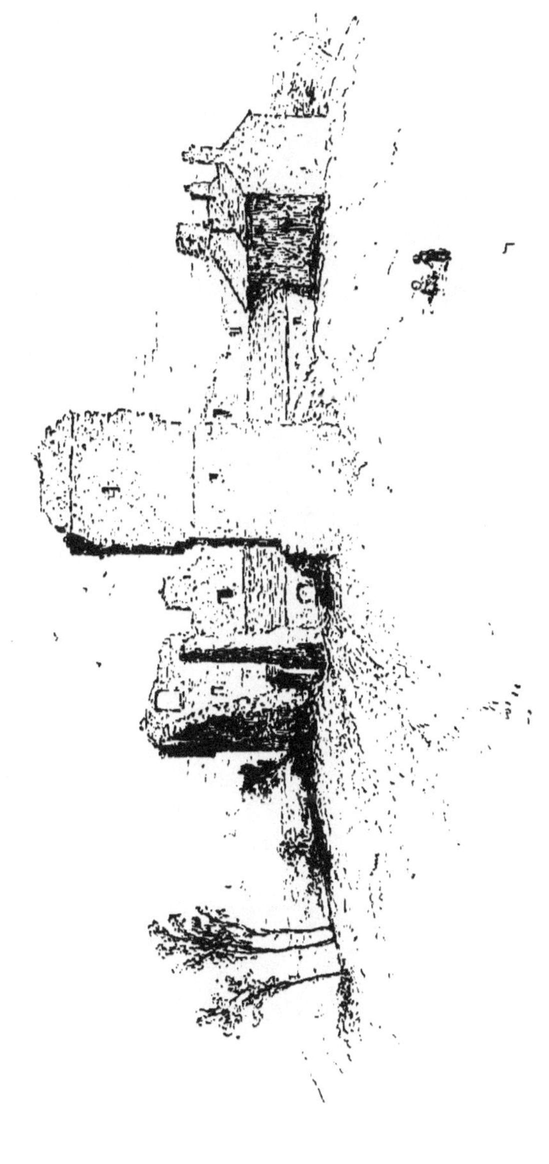

Penrith Castle.

the man before, resolved to keep him in sight
and see whither he was going.

So slowly did the weary horse proceed, that
it was not easy to loiter in the rear, and before
long, the man seemed to have an uneasy consciousness that he was being watched, and
after glancing furtively over his shoulder at
his pursuer, turned sharply round and said :

' I pray you, young man, have you any
business with me, that you thus dog my foot-
steps ?—if you have, speak out, and pass on !'

He looked full at Amyot as he spoke.
Amyot returned the stare, but, at the same
moment, recognised the weary traveller as
none other than his old schoolfellow, Lance
Kirkbride. The recognition was mutual.

' Amyot Brough !' ' Lance Kirkbride !' passed
their lips at the same moment ; and then the
two young men stood still and looked hard into
each other's faces.

' You here, Brough ?' said Lance, after a
few minutes' silence ; ' who would have thought
of this? What brought you to the North again ?'

' Never mind me—what's the news ? Is it a
victory or a defeat ?'

' Both,' and Lance smiled triumphantly.

' You don't mean to say,' Amyot exclaimed

in amazement, ' that the Pretender has fought
and won the day ?'

' I said nothing of the sort ; but so it is—the
Elector's troops fled without striking a blow.
Old Cope, who commanded them, is off, I know
not and I care not whither.   What, Brough, art
going to swoon ?—is it joy or fear ?'

' Where was the fight ?'

' Not very far from Edinburgh, at Prestonpans ; the Prince took General Cope entirely
by surprise, and the world too, I fancy.   Did
you expect such news ?—not if your face tells me
truth !'

' I never was more surprised in my life,'
Amyot confessed ; ' but you, Lance—have you
left the rebels, that you are here just when
fighting is in fashion ?'

' Have me hanged for a rebel if I have !'
Lance replied ; ' but have a care how you talk,
Brough ; keep a civil tongue in your head, or I
may be minded to rid his Highness of one dis-
loyal subject, though he were a friend of my
own in days gone by.'

' Perhaps it were well to part ere we come to
blows,' Amyot replied, ' for neither of us will
brook the name of rebel—no ! not even if spoken
in jest.

'Then we'll agree to drop it from our conversation; neither of us being on duty here, we may bear each other company and do no harm. Come with me to see my mother—it is with her I have business, a matter of a certain sum of money, and then I do but stay to rest my poor beast, and be gone. Come with me, and drink one glass to bonnie Prince Charlie; none will be the wiser, and none the worse.'

'I'll have none of your Prince Charlie,' Amyot replied doggedly; but he walked by his old friend's side notwithstanding, and even let him talk of the victory without giving vent to the rage and disappointment that were choking him.

'I had better not go any further,' he said, as they reached Blencathara House; 'their exultation will put me beside myself.'

'Nonsense, don't be a fool—are we not old friends; why should a change of Kings divide us? Ah! there's Primrose—my bonnie bride that's to be—and the old lady peeping between the curtains to see who's coming. It's a robber, mother mine, to steal thy hoarded gold, but well I know thou'lt give it with a glad heart for thy King.'

It was with much reluctance, and a most downcast mien, that Amyot suffered himself to be drawn into the rejoicing group, where he stood scowling and muttering : ' Fool that I was to come—fool that I am to stay !—why don't I go ?' and yet he lingered. In fact, he was unwilling to miss the chance of hearing any part of Lance's tale, though each sentence made him more savage than the last. Confident assurance that all would go well, that victory would follow victory, that clan after clan would come to tender homage, that the nobles would flock to the victorious Prince, that a post or two would bring the news of King George's flight, so that when Christmas came the toasts would all be for the restored King James—this was the strain poured forth by the jubilant household, while the bringer of good tidings was feasted and made much of, as if the victory had been won by his unaided arm.

Primrose's bright eyes danced with glee as she listened to Lance's tale, then, glancing to the dejected and sullen face of their guest, as he stood leaning, with half-averted face, against the window frame, listening in gloomy silence to the never-ceasing flow of question and answer, but taking no part in the talk, she observed roguishly :

' Master Brough has grown as grave as

he is tall; they have overloaded him with
learning at his Greenwich school; it terrifies
me much to be in his company. Brother
Lance, I pray you contrive some grave and
thoughtful speech, or he will despise us one
and all.'

'Amyot Brough is a good fellow—you shall
not make sport of him. Remember, Primrose,
how you once said he saved your life.'

'Aye, and so did you, brother Lance; but
Master Brough, I beg you, forget your woes—
who knows but we shall be vanquished to-
morrow? Let's dance and sing while we may.'

'With all my heart, only ask me not to join
you.'

'Aye, but I do; think you that your King,
worthy man as he may be for aught we know,
bears such a woe-begone face as you? Pluck
up your courage, Master Brough, for after all,
'tis the good cause that has conquered, and you
can't deny it!'

'Hush! hush, Primrose!—deny it he can and
will, and I promised we would not forget we
were old friends. Mother, I have feasted like
a king; now for some discourse. What!
Amyot, wilt begone? Well, maybe 'tis best—
we'll meet again in less troublous times.'

They shook hands, and Amyot left the house
and walked quickly away. Going home, he
heard many variations of his friend's tale, but
the substance was always the same. The Pretender had made a sudden attack on General
Cope's army, his dragoons had fled almost
without striking a blow, the victory had been
complete. The Pretender was quartered in
Edinburgh, and growing every day more
popular there.

'He'll be in England in a few days,' he said
to himself; 'in London in about a fortnight.
What will the end of it all be? My uncle,
aunt, Joan, my grandmother—what will they
all do?'

CHAPTER XII.

Concerning the Affair of Clifton Bridge.

'Nay, Mike, why should you come?   Deborah, keep him at home; these cold days make his rheumatics worse, and if I can't rest at home that is no reason why he should not bide in his elbow-chair after the day's work is over.'

'If ya wud bide ya'sell, mappen es hed dew ta sëam,' was all Deborah's reply.

But the old man shook his head. and with much lamenting concerning these bothersome rebels, he persisted in dragging his stiff limbs along the road and over the fields, wherever it pleased his young master to roam.

'I would really be easier if you would go home, Mike,' Amyot urged more than once. But the faithful old fellow was obstinate, and only replied :

'I wud loike ta see es weel es ya ; bet, hawiver, thae wars meeak a terble girt bodderation, an' fooak meeak mickle prate aboot things es thae knaa nowt aboot. What dusta think it matters whedther ta King be caed George or Jëames—'tis a' ta seeam ta me.'

This, a question which had already been discussed until Amyot was quite weary of it, failed to excite him to any reply, and, with his ear strained to catch every distant sound, he continued to trudge along in silence, until Yanwath Hall was close at hand; and there he stood still to listen and allow Mike, who walked very feebly, to overtake him.

'The roads are awful and the sun is setting. Ask leave to rest in the kitchen until I come back, Mike; I will but go as far as Clifton Bridge, and then return.'

'Nay, nay; I's gaan wi' ya. Bet tell ma, what dusta think es ta'll see?'

'Who can tell?—most likely nothing. Nevertheless, as all say the Pretender is retreating and the Duke is close behind, and neither army can be far from here, there's no doubt but I may see or hear something.'

'Weel, ga an; I canna keep pace wi' ya, bet I'll folla an' keep an eye an ya.'

Glad to be in some degree free, Amyot

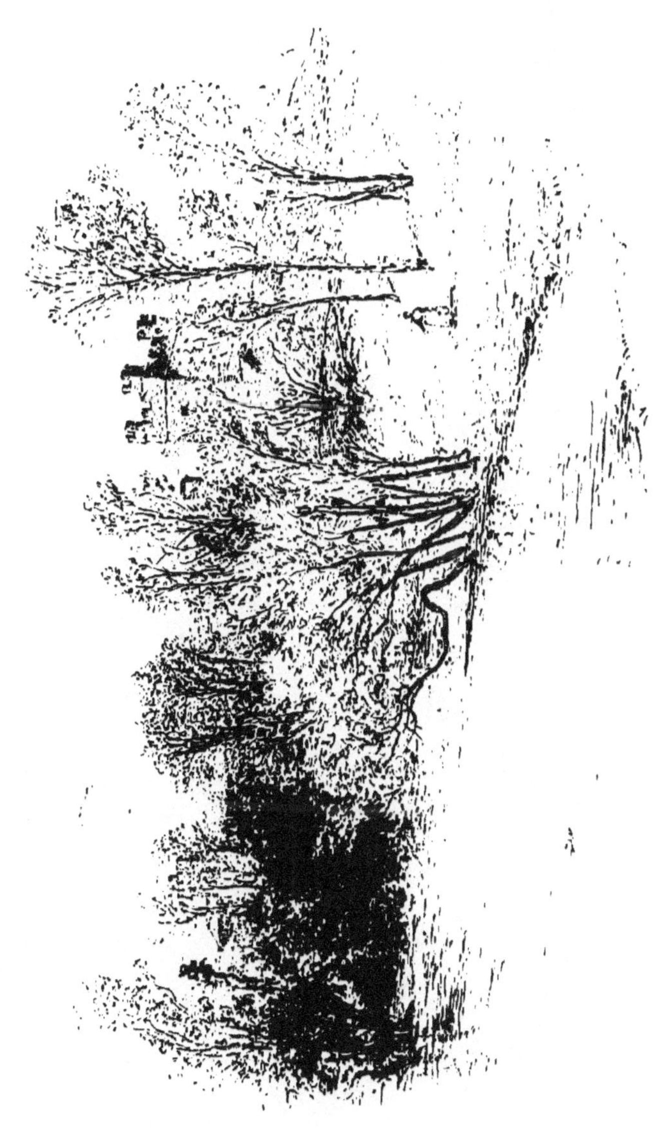

Yanwath Hall.

quickened his pace ; but he had not gone very
far when he stopped suddenly, and, stooping
down, laid his ear close to the ground to
listen. What was it ? Only the moaning of
the winter wind in the leafless trees, or maybe
the complaining of some forlorn ghost, wandering over the moor, or the water rushing over
the rocks in the river below ? All these sug-
gestions occurred to him, but his imagination—
keenly awake to explain the sounds as his
boyish love of adventure desired—ascribed
it to far different causes. It was, he felt convinced, the tramp of feet, the movement of a
vast body of men—and that near at hand.
Was it the rebel army, or that of the royal
Duke ?

Looking back, Amyot saw that the sounds
which he had heard had also reached the com-
paratively dull ear of old Mike, who, while earnestly signalling to him to go no farther, was
making great efforts to overtake him.

It would have been too cruel to disappoint
him, so, rather reluctantly, the lad turned back,
and in a few minutes the two stood together
consulting what they had best do.

' Ya'll be fer feightin' wi' oor fists, I rakkan,'
Mike said ; ' but mine are good fer nowt, an soa

I perpose es we lig a lile bit amang these yer bits o' brushwood an' listen ta 'em es they ga alang. If it sud be that Pertender chap, I'm no fer sayin' bet ya might heave a bit o' a steean at his heead. I's varra sartan we'd dew jist es weel widout un.'

Amyot laughed, and preferring to stay with his old friend, made no objection to concealing himself among the low bushes by the river-side, and there they remained for more than half-an-hour before any of the advancing host made their appearance. Travel-worn, bespattered with mud, weary and dejected, appeared most of the men, and the officers looked even more dispirited. It needed no great discernment to discover that hope and many of these brave fellows had parted company, while on many a brow hung the cloud of bitter resentment and savage despair.

The main part of the army were on foot, and as troop after troop passed, struggling through the mud, keeping but poor order, cursing the cold, the wet, and their leaders, Mike whispered to his young master :

'They bea a daft lot a chaps. What fer cuddent they bide at heeäm ? Rakkan they'll ha' had theear fill o' travellin', an sarve 'em

reet. Better 've beean mindin' theear pleughs.
Hoo many think ya ther beä ?'

But Amyot had no idea, and the old man
rambled on :

'When I teeaks to feightin' I'll bea an officier
an' ride ma nag, not ga trampin' throo ta mood.
Bet look ya, Master Amyot ! I rakkan that 'un
bea ta chap es had thowt to meeak his fooartan,
that yalla-haired yoongster wi' ta heead a hang-
in' doon a'most es if he wer gaan ta be
hanget.'

Amyot looked, and wondered if Mike was
right ; but the Pretender, if this were he, was
already past, and still the stream of men continued their weary, toilsome march towards
Penrith.

At length there was a pause. Amyot had
heard a soldier say, as he passed, that the artillery was still far behind, and that the Prince
would halt in Penrith until such time as Lord
George Murray, in command of it, should overtake him. In Penrith, therefore, they would
lodge, and perhaps in the neighbourhood ; and
full of this thought, and fearing that in their
absence Deborah might be alarmed by a party
claiming shelter at Broughbarrow, Amyot and
Mike lost no time in scrambling forth from

their hiding-place, and making their way by short cuts homewards.

All was, however, peaceful at Broughbarrow; and to the question asked by Deborah and the maids—what should they do if the soldiers came?—Amyot and Mike replied:

'We'll all go right off to bed, and if anyone knocks we'll take no notice—no, not unless they set the house on fire.'

'Which mappen they wull,' Deborah replied.

But, as she had no better suggestion to offer, she was compelled to adopt that already made, and in spite of her misgivings the household were left in peace until the morning.

There was much sighing and lamenting on the part of the worthy couple, Mike and Deborah, over the restlessness of their young master: off to the town he must be as soon as he had got his porridge, though sure it must be a most unsafe place, with all those soldiers about, whose guns might go off any minute; not to speak of their wicked ways, which every one knew were too awful to be named by honest folk. But he was not to be controlled: he would see and know everything, and the morning was passed by him loitering about the market-place and Dockwray Hall, watching the rebel

Dockray Hall, Penrith.

officers as they paced the town and went in and out, for Amyot hoped to have another sight of the Prince, whose adventures had made it quite allowable even for those who cared nothing for him to stare at him.

Amyot half-expected and half-feared lest he should meet Primrose Kirkbride. She could not now triumph over him, or speak with sure confidence of the good cause which must succeed; the retreat from Derby would have taught her not to be too confident, and, remembering this, Amyot thought it might be more possible to feel at ease with her than when last they had met; but, notwithstanding all that had passed, Amyot knew well that she would hope on to the very end, and that her disappointment would be very painful to witness.

But he did not meet her; and as the day wore on, he bethought him that in all probability other regiments would be coming in, convoying the artillery, and once more he betook himself to the highroad and the adjacent fields, for the paraphernalia of war was growing more and more attractive to him, and the quiet of home more and more distasteful.

As he sauntered along and drew near Clifton Moor, he found that a body of the rebel troops,

under the command of a French officer, was
waiting there the arrival of Lord George
Murray, in order to be in readiness to render
aid if necessary.

The sun was setting when the first lines of
the looked-for regiments appeared on the dark
edge of the moor : the red glow in the sky lit
up the scene, but a thick cloud of dust sur-
rounded them, and to the inexperienced eye of
Amyot all seemed in confusion.

Suddenly, from another quarter of the moor
appeared another host, and these were plainly
cavalry in rapid motion, dashing at full speed
towards the bridge, with evident intent to take
possession of it ; while the Highland regiment,
which had been awaiting the coming of their
artillery, advanced to meet Lord George's force
—and thus united, the rebel army came on to
dispute the passage of the bridge.

There was a brisk discharge of musketry,
then a hand-to-hand encounter with swords and
bayonets, and Amyot, from his post of observation among some furze-bushes, rejoiced to think
that by good luck he had chanced to be spec-
tator of a real battle.

That the dust and smoke greatly hindered
his view he cared but little : he could see the

tumult, could hear the din and battle-cries, the English kettle-drums and trumpets, the pibroch's shrill screech, could feel his heart thump against his ribs as now the Highlanders, and then the Royalists, and now again the Highlanders, seemed to prevail.

But the night was fast closing in, the darkness coming on apace, and with the shades of night came disorder and confusion ; the English dragoons turned and took to flight across the open moor : their opponents held the bridge.

Suddenly the moon shone out, and the discomfited dragoons perceived how small was the number of their assailants, rallied, and being reinforced by two fresh squadrons, tried to recover their lost ground, but again the light failed them ; the tide of battle slackened, and though for some time longer Amyot could hear the sound of strife, the rush of flying horses, the cries of the wounded, the words of command, the leaders cheering on their men, before long the tumult lessened, the darkness settled down on the moor, and Amyot discovered that it was bitterly cold, and that he had best seek his home.

As far as he could guess the Highlanders had returned to Penrith, the Royal troops had retreated to the edge of the moor, falling back on their main body; but as he crept along under the hedges, he was again and again passed by rushing horsemen, or forced to hold himself still and quiet, while troops of straggling foot - soldiers marched by. Once he stumbled over a motionless body, lying with white face upturned to the skies; a moonbeam lit it up, and Amyot shuddered as he gazed. The soul had parted in agony, and the pale countenance was still convulsed, the hands were clenched. Then he heard a horse struggling and writhing in pain, snorting and kicking, and turning aside, lest the animal's feet should strike him, he heard another sound, this time a human voice, which was giving vent to a cry of pain.

'One of those Highlanders,' he thought. ' Englishmen don't cry like women; but I've heard that those savages cannot bear pain: well, I suppose they'll send somebody to look after their wounded—at least, I can do nothing.'

And as, in truth, the wounded horse's struggles and the wounded soldier's moan were causing his heart to swell unpleasantly, he was hastening to get away from the place, when a voice cried :

'Here, for the love of heaven, stop a moment!'

Glancing fearfully at the dead soldier's face Amyot did stop, hoping that the wounded man, wherever he might be, would not, at least, look like him. Then he groped about in the dark, over mounds of earth and stunted bushes, until he fancied he could discern something like an arm which beckoned to him. Picking his way carefully, he was soon beside the wounded man, who, conscious of his approach, said :

'Stranger, will you give me a hand to recover my footing ? I am sore hurt ; yet, maybe, if once on my feet, I might be able to find my way to some inn ; for to lie here in the cold will certainly make an end of me before morning.'

'Where are you hurt ?' Amyot inquired, stooping down, and trying to pass his arm under him to help him to rise.

'I scarce know. A sword cut here, a bullet there, and my arm broken in falling from my horse, yet my legs, I think, are sound, if once I could struggle to my feet ; nay, not so,' as Amyot used some force. 'I cannot bear that ; it must be slowly. I feel strangely numb and stiff.' He groaned heavily, and his voice was choked and thick as he said : ' Maybe 'tis of no use—I am worse than I thought.'

' I am very strong,' Amyot replied ; ' let me try to raise you slowly and gradually ; place your uninjured arm around my neck.'

The sufferer obeyed, murmuring to himself :

' I've done it before now ;' but to this remark Amyot paid no heed, being wholly engrossed with the effort he was making.

It succeeded ; the wounded man recovered his feet, but leaned heavily on Amyot, who said kindly :

' I fear you can never walk as far as the inn, and I could not quite carry you ; if you could make shift to walk a short distance, I could leave you sitting under the hedge, and run to my house, and fetch some strong lads to carry you there.'

' No, no,' said the other hurriedly ; ' that must never be—rather would I die here !'

' But why ?' Amyot inquired wonderingly. ' Count my house an inn, if so you will ; I did but name it because it is nearer by a mile than the nearest inn where you could be tended as you need.'

' But you are rash,' the poor fellow replied,

while he moaned with pain. ' I am one of the Prince's men, and to cut the matter short, you, Amyot Brough, will never house a rebel.'

Amyot started back, and had almost let the wounded man fall in his astonishment ; then, remembering himself, he said :

' If that rebel is Lance Kirkbride, I cannot leave him here unaided ; and indeed, Lance, for one night there can be little risk. Come, say no more : try to walk, and let it be as I have said.'

' It were better to leave me here,' Lance replied ; but he did not resist further. With many a heavy groan and exclamation of pain he struggled on, stumbling in the darkness, tripping over roots of trees, clinging to Amyot in desperation, until the latter was fain almost to carry him, so slow was their progress.

There was much shaking of heads in the kitchen of the farm that night, and some subdued grumbling. The young master's doings were enough to break the hearts of all quiet folk, who liked to have things go on in their ordinary course, and hated being mixed up with battles, wounded men, and such-like. Was this all the good he had done by running up and down the country all day, to go for to pick up a dirty, muddy, quarrelsome fellow of a soldier, and bring him home and put him into the best bed in the house? Folks should reap as they sowed ; doubtless this fellow had done his best to break other folks' arms—it was but right he should be served the same : so Mike said, and so Deborah thought. But, happily for poor Lance, before an hour had passed, her woman's heart had softened towards him, and she had helped Obed, the old shepherd, to set his broken arm with as tender and motherly a touch, as if he had been Amyot himself, and even condescended to say that he had behaved under the operation almost like a Christian, and very nearly as well as a dog.

It was not until the morning that she discovered that the injured man was one of Mistress Kirkbride's sons, who had turned rebel, and then her consternation was extreme.

' Master Amyot, what wasta thinkin' of, ta ga an' fetch yan girt rebel heeam ? Whaariver sall we put un if any o' ta King's fooak come nigh ta place ? He's ower big ta hide, an' if they light on un, they'll be fer larnin' un ta mind hes aan wark, an' let other fooak's aleean.'

' Perhaps the King's folk won't come nigh the place,' Amyot replied ; but though he put a bold face on it, the same difficulty was pressing sore upon him, and he could see no way out of it.

Lance, too, had thought of it, and was urgent to be allowed to get up and depart; but, much as she dreaded the consequences of his presence in the house, old Deborah could not but see that he was even less fit to move than the night before: his cheeks were burning with fever, his wounds were painful in the extreme.

'Nay, nay, bide quiet,' she replied to all his entreaties; 't'hoose is weel oot o' ta road, an' if summun cooms peerin' about we'll meeak oop some tale ta tell un; bide quiet, an' dunna fret ta sell;' and quieting him, she grew quiet herself.

Not so Amyot: he roamed about like an uneasy ghost; and it was not till the afternoon that he began to feel secure against unpleasant intrusion, and able to laugh at Lance's fears.

Then, as all seemed quiet, and no travellers could be seen on the highroad, he ventured to leave the house, and walk into Penrith to give Mrs. Kirkbride news of her son. Deborah bade him not be absent long, and enjoined him to tell the good lady that she need not come to Broughbarrow, since one rebel was as many as she could do with—

more would perchance bring the roof about their ears. This errand Amyot performed with all the speed he might, but darkness had set in before he reached home again. It seemed to him, as he approached the farm on his return, that Mike and Deborah must be making more merry than was their wont. Through the kitchen window he caught sight of a roaring fire blazing in the hearth, and as he drew near he heard a hoarse voice trolling forth an ale-house song. 'Lance in delirium, or Mike got drunk,' was his first thought—his second, one of much more real alarm, which made him hasten his steps, and brought him to the door with rapid strides. He lifted the latch hastily, and found his fears most fully realized ; a lively scene was before him : half a dozen soldiers of the Royal army were seated round the fire, their arms and caps on the floor, while Deborah with her frying-pan, and Mike with a side of bacon, were busily engaged preparing their supper. The parlour-door stood ajar, but that it was also occupied, Amyot saw at a glance. Three tall officers were lounging around the fire which they had caused to be lighted, while one of the lasses was busy spreading the table for their repast.

' Ta yoong maister,' Mike observed, as Amyot entered and stood silent with amazement, gazing at the scene before him ; the soldiers looked at him carelessly, but one of the officers, perceiving him from the inner room, came forward, and said courteously enough :

' We have taken leave in your absence, young gentleman, to seek lodging here, for one night only ; you are, I hear, a loyal subject of his Majesty's, and will, we hope, esteem it an honour to lodge his soldiers.'

Amyot bowed : ' Sir, my house is at your service, but I fear the lodging is scarce sufficient.'

' Oh, for that matter, the men are well enough where they are : your housekeeper has found us excellent quarters ; we shall be lodged far better than most of our comrades.'

Amyot bowed again, feeling too uneasy to enter into much conversation, and was sitting down wearily, when Deborah, contriving to pass near him, whispered :

' Hoot, then, all's rect aboot yan chap, we've sided un oop ;' adding aloud, ' Ta bacon an' eggs is jest ready ; ga in an' tak yer meeal wi' t' gentlemen in t' parlour, an' let un see es ya maister an' nowt else.'

It was not easy for Amyot to stifle his anxiety

and curiosity sufficiently to do the honours of his house with perfect ease and equanimity; nevertheless, as there was some passable wine still remaining in the house, laid up there in the captain's time, his guests expressed themselves entirely satisfied with their entertainment, and gave their host much information as to the progress of the rebellion, their rapid march in pursuit of the Pretender's army, and their expectations of seeing a speedy end to the whole affair. All would go well now the Duke had taken the command—the men would fight for him; there would be no more blundering, no more Prestonpans muddles; the Scotch would be taught loyalty at the sword's point. Carlisle, too, must learn a lesson—and much more to the same effect.

Amyot would have been in high spirits had not anxiety for Lance been the most pressing subject on his mind, and when he found that Mike was actually leading the officers to the very room where, in the afternoon, he had left his friend in bed, his wonderment could scarcely be concealed. On pretence of seeing to the welfare of an ailing horse, he called Mike to come with him to the stable, and when fairly out of all possibility of being overheard, he eagerly inquired what they had done with Lance.

'Na, then, Deborah, she telt ma niver ta let ya knaa. Them es knaas nowt can tell nowt, ses she, an' I'm ta sceam way o' thinkin' masell.'

'But, Mike, you must tell me. I cannot rest without knowing; besides, I want to see him. I told his mother he should be well cared for; therefore I must see that he's well and comfortable.'

'Deborah 'll see ta un her aan sell; he's all reet, I tell ya, bet ya'll no see un till we're clear of them cattle,' pointing with his thumb to the kitchen, where the soldiers were already sound asleep. 'Please God, thear Dook wull sune want 'em, fer it's what we dussent. They've amost itten oop a side o' beacon an' eggs an' butter an' sich, an' what fer?—jest ta meeak theirsells meear crabbt an' cankert, an' boddersome than ivver. Sich mak' o' fooak dunna soot ma noways.'

And as Amyot could wring nothing more from him, he was forced to go to bed in utter ignorance of his friend's whereabouts, though pretty well convinced that his hiding-place was not far distant.

CHAPTER XIII.

Of Events after Culloden.

THE dark cold days of that cold winter were coming to an end; the grass was growing greener, the daffodils were again brightening the earth, and the primroses beginning to peep forth, and with returning spring young hearts must perforce wake to new life and happiness. It had been a very long dark winter at Blencathara House. Primrose could never remember any winter when everything had seemed so gloomy, and many was the day when she had accused herself of having been cross and troublesome, since, had this not been the case, mother would surely not have spoken so sharply to her. Primrose did not know how often suspense and anxiety makes the voice peevish, and the brow contract into a frown, or she would have comprehended why she found mother so hard to

please when week after week passed and no
news came to her from the north. True, there
had been some bright days in January, after
word had come of Prince Charlie's victory over
General Hawley at Falkirk; but that had been
the last gleam of sunshine, and each day the
widowed mother grew graver and more silent.
She would sit watching the fast-falling snow
with eyes that told of a vast anxiety, and Primrose had a strong suspicion that many a night
she never took her clothes off, but paced the
room through the long hours of darkness, finding
it more possible thus to bear her load of misery.

But spring was at hand : the birds knew it,
the young lambs in the fields knew it, the
flowers felt it, and Primrose's heart rebelled
that she too might not bound and skip and sing
with joy. Why should such terrible news come
just when all nature bade her be glad, and when
she had every 'mind to obey the call ? It was
hard, it was cruel, she said, as she stood beneath
her favourite old yew-tree in the garden, and
looked with loving eyes at the snowdrops that
grew around its roots.

' They are so sweet, so pure, so heavenly ; but
no one notices them now Lance is not here, the
boys are away, and the mother's heart is break-

ing; and I am selfish—I do not fret as she does; I have such a way of thinking things will come right, I can never be as sorry as I ought,' and even as if to verify her words, the girl's lips parted in a merry smile as she saw that her solitude was invaded by her tall boy-friend Amyot, who had passed through the house and sought her in the garden, directed thither by the maid who had admitted him.

'Your mother is too sad at heart to see me,' he said, 'but you, Miss Primrose, can still smile, I am glad to see.'

'It is my way to smile when I would fain weep,' she said; 'laughing is but a foolish trick with me—it means nothing—at least, if I know myself; but, Master Amyot, have you come to laugh at our woes? If so, I think you would have done well to stay away.'

'Indeed, I am in no laughing mood, though glad to think the war must end now. I came to know if by chance you had any tidings of my old friends. Nay, no news! then must we hope the best.'

'Yes, so say I; but mother can do nought but sit silent in her elbow-chair and listen, and if you, Master Amyot, had but knocked at the parlour-door, she would have started as if she had been shot; so great have been her fears for all these terrible months, that her brain seems on fire, and her eyes have a look as if they had not closed for years.'

'It is sad,' Amyot said; 'then must you too rejoice that the war is over, and her rest has come.'

'Ah, but we know nothing. And rejoice, say you!—how can I rejoice that our bonnie Prince is a fugitive, gone we know not whither—a price set on his head, and that barbarous Duke hungering for his life?'

'The Duke is not all his enemies paint him; his soldiers adore him, and your bonnie Prince, maybe, has his failings too; but do not let us talk of them and quarrel, as we always do; rather, tell me more about your brothers—when did you hear last from them?'

'From Lance, a month ago, soon after he had rejoined the army; he was nearly himself again, thanks to Mistress Deborah. Mother will love her for ever for her care of him, and I most of all for hiding him in the hayrick, for it has given me many a merry laugh since the day when Lance told me about it; and oh! it does one good to laugh in these sad times.'

'But your mother would ill bear the lecture

old Deborah gave her about training up her sons to be rebels, and making them quarrelsome and the like; I tried hard to stop her, but she said she had it on her mind, and it must out.'

'Mother would bear anything from her for her care of Lance; and I think she was more diverted than offended at Mistress Deborah's urgency.   She laughed when she told me: poor mother, I have not heard her laugh since.'

'Ay, well; when they are home again safe and sound, and the Pretender has got his deserts, and peace is restored to old England again, we will all laugh and be merry as in the good old times.   But, how now, Miss Primrose, why so solemn?'

'Can the old times ever be again?   Mother said there would be executions and confiscations, and what not; and it is well known how all her savings have gone to help the Prince.'

'The mean villain!' Amyot exclaimed; but Primrose added, 'And willingly; she has given all willingly, and with little thought of recompense, though Lance did say it was putting the money out at good interest.'

'Not a penny will she ever see!' Amyot exclaimed.

'But herself, will she be safe? The Penrith people are so wondrous loyal to King George, that those few who have come boldly forward to support the right will scarce be forgotten by them, I fear.'

'Does your mother fear ill-usage from them? Then surely it were best that she should leave the town for a while.'

'But that she will not do, since here only will she hear tidings of her sons. But I trust none will molest her in this house; she will not stir abroad, and none of our friends come near us; it is but through the maids that we hear any news. You are our only visitor, Master Amyot; how long will it be ere you grow tired of our company, or fear to be acquainted with such desperate rebels, I wonder?'

'Long, I trust,' was Amyot's fervent response.

And then Primrose changed the subject, and would hear all he had to tell of his sister and grandmother, and the contents of the last letters he had receive dfrom Westerham.

'It sounds so pleasant and peaceful,' she said. 'Why did you come away from them all into this turbulent North?'

'I hoped tc take service in the army, and it

seemed to me that I had best go where work
was to be done, but I doubt whether I had not
better have stayed : my uncle, it seems, is
making interest for a commission for me, and
Joan tells me that he has good hopes he will
succeed — Joan tells me it is more than I
deserve.'

' Then do you think of returning to them ?'

Primrose's face grew a shade more anxious.

' My uncle bids me stay where I am, since, if
he succeeds in my behalf, I may be ordered to
join one of the regiments now in Scotland, so
I wait, you see.'

' I am glad ; and when you come again, if no
bad news comes, I will ask mother to see you ;
but not to-day—she is too cast down, and I
must not stay idling here ; I must go to her :
it is bad for her to be quite alone.'

' Then I will go ; but should any news come,
will you send me word ? When Sammy brings
you the milk, you could send me word if you
have heard aught, or if I could be of any use.
Do not laugh, Miss Primrose ; who knows ?—I
might be of use, if only to journey with your
mother from this place, should she choose to
move.'

' If so, I will let you know,' Primrose pro-

mised as they parted, 'but I have no thought
that we shall need your help.'

Amyot secretly hoped that she might, but he
had no suspicion how soon his aid would be
requested. Only two days had passed when
the cow-boy, returning in the evening from his
visit to the town, sought his young master, and
delivered to him a small note, which ran as
follows :

' Am I wrong, dear friend, to take you at your
word ? My mother says, " Torment no one
with our woes," and if they were only mine, I
would say so too ; am I writing nonsense ? I
fear I am ; well, then, if this falls into any
hands but yours, I hope it will not be comprehended. But if your lad says truth, and he
will be able to give you this, none perceiving it,
I would make bold to ask whether you are
likely to have business in the neighbourhood of Appleby to-morrow, and could give a
lift to two poor beggar-women who are constrained to journey thither, and who will be on
the road by the time the sun is up. One is but
feeble, and I would be glad to think her feet
need not bear her all the way. The travellers
we looked for have passed through the town,

but made no long stay. It seems to me an idle waste of time to put my name to this, as it concerneth none but you, who know it well.'

'Oop ta soom mischief agean,' was Mike's comment when his young master drove off in the small waggon well loaded with hay and straw the next morning. ' He waan't tell ma wheear he's gaen wi' all that stoof—arter soom o' these bodderin' rebels agean. Waal, they they mud sow theer wild oats, fooak say.'

Meanwhile, Amyot, weil pleased with his errand, was jolting along the rough roads at a very leisurely rate, for the double reason that the nature of the road permitted no better pace, and that he was well convinced that he had started earlier than was necessary. It was a sweet-smelling morning ; the hedges were still only just touched here and there with green, and a slight frost had left its bright spangles on the twigs : but the birds were twittering their new loves, and the world was waking to new life and hope.

'She said two beggar-women : could she have meant herself and Mrs. Kirkbride, or one of the servant-maids with the old lady ?—surely Primrose would never call herself a woman ; she is nothing but a child—not so old as Joan ;

and grandmother does not call her a woman yet. And where they can be going, I can't imagine, that they should start by this road; but it's all one to me. I am glad Primrose asked me to help them. And this road is wondrous quiet at this hour; even Primrose will see nought but fays and pixies.'

Half an hour passed in these musings, while the stout farm-horses moved slowly along, only occasionally quickening their pace when they came to a slope in the road, or a few yards of tolerably smooth ground. One or two work-men had passed on their way to their daily labour with a 'Good day ta yer,' and a grin which Amyot shrewdly divined to mean, 'That young fellow don't know much about his busi-ness.' But as long as they asked no questions, he told no lies, and prudently refrained from entering into conversation with anyone.

Many a glance had he cast behind him, many a fixed gaze into wood and meadow as he jogged along, but still no female figure could his eyes discover.

'Primrose loves a joke; and sometimes it seems to me she dearly likes to make a fool of *me.* Could she have sent me on such a fool's errand as this seems like to be? No—never!'

Amyot said, the hot blood mounting to his cheek at the thought. ' But they may have been hindered ; Mrs. Kirkbride may have fallen sick, as Primrose feared she would.   But what may that be—is it a trunk of a tree or a brown cloak—by the roadside ? Gee-up, Fanny, and let's see.'

The brown object remained very still and motionless as the cart drew nearer; and Amyot, keeping his eyes intently fixed on it, had almost decided that it was nothing but a stump of a tree, when another brown object emerged from the shelter of the hedge, and approached the cart, while a plaintive voice said :

' For the love of heaven, master, give a poor body a lift to the town.   My baby is a sore burden, and my old mother is sick and feeble, and I am broken-hearted.'

A sob seemed to end the speech ; but the bright eyes that peeped shyly at Amyot's face from under the faded brown hood were full of laughter ; and the baby, so tenderly pressed and fondly regarded, was no stranger to Amyot, since years before he had seen it in Primrose's arms, and very roughly handled by Lance and his brothers.

Poor Mrs. Kirkbride was sitting a few yards

off, so weary, so heart-sick, so indifferent to all
that concerned her, that she could not summon
even the ghost of a smile as she let herself be
hoisted into the waggon, and laid in as easy a
posture as possible among the bundles of hay ;
yet she tried to thank Amyot, who could
scarcely bear to look at her, so sorely had the
sorrows and anxieties of the past few months
aged and wasted her.

But Primrose's spirits rose again instantly.

'Never mother hated child as I hate you,'
she said, addressing her old doll. 'Oh! the
weary weight you have made yourself this
dreary morn! Master Amyot, will you think
me a brute if I leave the creature to end her
days in a ditch, for I am much inclined to fling
her from me. With those bundles to carry, I
have no need of dolls. Why did I bring her,
say you? Oh, to touch your heart, to be sure.
It was a last thought ; for I have not handled
her for many a long day, not since the boys
went to the wars : but taking a last look at the
old toys I spied her, and I thought—what did I
think ?—oh, never mind—of course I thought
you could not refuse to take pity on a child; but
give me leave, and I will fling her into the ditch.'

'I can do without her, Miss Primrose.'

'Are you sure ? I doubt you. What, dear mother, art comfortable ? does the waggon jolt too much ?'

'Nay, I am well enough, but tell him—tell Amyot about the boys.'

'Yes, dear mother,' and the girl grew sad and sober while telling Amyot that two days before Lance had suddenly appeared among their little household; he had relieved their worst fears by bringing the news that without any harm except a few wounds of a trifling nature all three brothers had escaped from the battle near Inverness, and would live to fight another day. 'But oh! Lance was in a terrible state,' Primrose said, 'he made me tremble all over by his rage, and the fearful things he said. I wish I could forget it, but I can't, and poor mother, she was glad to see him safe, but his words made her grow white as ashes—wars are dreadful things.'

'Was he so angry that the battle had gone against the Prince ? I thought they had almost lost hope before then.'

'Lance never had, and he said that had they made but a fair fight, it would not have seemed so shameful ; but Lance *is* brave, and so are the other boys, let people say what they will.'

'And where are they now?'

'Ah, how do I know?—fleeing for their lives! for Lance said they had vowed they would not become prisoners, as many were—hundreds, I believe. They mean to go abroad, if they can find a passage on some French vessel; but how can we tell?—it will be long before we hear of them, and mother says we must not expect to see them again for years: she feels as if she had lost them entirely.'

'And why are you and she leaving Penrith, and why are you going to Appleby?'

'Lance thought we had better go away for a time at least, because you know the Penrith people are so very loyal, and besides, we are nearly beggars: Lance thinks Blencathara House will be confiscated, and he said we had better go right away and hide ourselves somewhere. Mother has an old cousin at Appleby, and we thought it would be best to go there for awhile, until things are quieter, and then perchance we shall go to London, and find some quiet hole to hide our heads. Don't look so dismal, Master Brough. I am gloomy now, but I shall soon be happy again; I can't be dismal long. I've tried, and I don't succeed.'

Amyot looked at the bright eyes which shone

even through the girl's tears, and wondered
much ; and then he looked at the haggard face
that lay back on the hay in the cart, noticing
the deep lines and wrinkles, and the tightly
compressed lips which told of bitter suffering
long borne in silence, and then he wondered
more ; but he said nothing for some time.

At last he spoke. 'Shall you like to be at
Appleby ?'

'Oh yes! I am glad to have mother right
away from Penrith, though I fear she nearly
broke her heart to go ; but it seems to me she
will best bear all she has got to bear if she is in
a new place. How far shall you be able to
take us, Master Amyot ?'

'As far as you wish to go.'

'Nay, my mother said I was not to be
troublesome ; you shall take us just as far as
you will, and then the two beggar-women will
go on the tramp again.'

'Mrs. Kirkbride cannot walk.'

'Yes, she can ; she walked stoutly enough
when we started, though I own she was getting
tired when you overtook us. You little thought
to have found us so far on the road, I reckon,
Master Amyot.'

'That I did not, indeed. I was beginning to

think you had sent me on a fool's errand, Miss Primrose.'

'You thought so ill of me as that?' the girl replied, colouring. 'Nay, I marvel not, for I am sadly silly, I know full well.'

And while they talked thus, the good horses plodded on their way, not unseldom finding their burden stuck fast in a rut, which required all their efforts and all Amyot's energy to master.

Once or twice, towards the middle of the day, Amyot let them rest for a while, while they took their food ; but Mrs. Kirkbride looked uneasy at these delays, and at last, when towards evening Amyot said he thought they were not far from the town, no persuasions would induce her to remain in the waggon ; she wished to walk— she was determined ; and Primrose, seeing her mother resolute, became again the timid child, and agreed without objection. The old lady thanked Amyot with agitated vehemence, and lading herself with her bundle, set forward at a feeble but rapid pace towards the town. Primrose lingered but to say farewell, adding, 'We will never forget your kindness—some day, perhaps, we may meet ; but who can say where ? I shall know you again, Master Amyot, and if you meet my brothers, be kind to them.'

'Stay,' Amyot said; 'I must rest the night in the town.   I shall wait awhile here to breathe the horses, and then come slowly on; if your mother is weary, urge her to wait for me.'

'Ah, you do not know her!—but good-bye,' and Primrose darted away.

CHAPTER XIV.

Wherein Two Letters are Received.

MRS. DARLEY sat by the window of her parlour, which window was open to let in the pleasant scent of flowers, and that she might exchange a word or two if she wished it with Joan and Miss Johnstone, who sat sewing in the garden outside. The old lady was sitting at rest, her hands lying idly in her lap—even her knitting had been laid aside ; but two letters lay on a little table before her, which she had just laid down, and her spectacles lay by the side of them.

She had read these letters several times, and each time laid them down with a half smile on her face, which had made Joan long much to know their contents, but no hint had as yet been dropped by the old lady.

The door opened, and Mrs. Pomfret, then

on a visit to her mother, entered the room, and
sank into a lounging chair with the languid
grace which, well or ill, she never lacked.   She
carried a tiny dog in her arms, at sight of which
Tory, who was crouched at Mrs. Darley's feet
in an attitude of adoration, uttered a low groan
of disapprobation.   Tory had his own opinion
about dogs that lived in lady's laps, and that
opinion was not a favourable one.

' How sweet and balmy the air is,' Mrs. Pomfret murmured ; ' if this house, madam, were but
larger, and more suited to your rank, I should
say I held you much to be envied.'

' 'Tis well it is but small, then,' Mrs. Darley
replied, with her quick repartee ; ' I never desired
to excite anyone's envy, least of all my children's.'

' Dear mother, you entirely mistake me ; I
do but venture to think you might keep a little
more state.'

The old lady laughed good-humouredly.
' Have a care, Aimée, or we shall fall out.   I
have lived so long alone that I cannot bear dictation ; no, not a word.'

' Madam, dear mother—dictation !—and from
me !'

' Well, well, never mind ; tell me in what the
house is lacking.'

'Truly, it lacks nothing that would make for comfort; it is but style, and, your pardon, madam, but the serving might be more attended to. Doddridge is scarce fit to be seen, and your own woman might pass for Noah's wife straight from the ark.'

'Good; does she look so venerable?'

'Indeed she does; and your own attire, madam, is, to say the least, not as becoming as it might be.'

'Va, va, ma fille, c'est assez, n'en parlons plus. What, must I not speak French?—is it high treason? Well, in plain English, then, and English sounds very ugly sometimes — we will each go our own way: you love rich colours, et moi, j'aime le gris; and for the house, be content to breathe the fresh air, and put up with the old barn. Art thou not glad to be away from London, and all the fearful doings there?'

'Yes, indeed; my husband wrote me word of the gaping crowds staring at the heads on Temple Bar, and people letting out spy-glasses at a halfpenny a look; and he tells me that he is thought wondrous queer that he went not to see the beheading the other day. Truly, I hope he will not be reckoned a Jacobite, but he had an old kindness for Lord Balmerino, and could

not bring himself to face the sight, though it
seems to me it was a pity.   Such things do not
happen every day, and it is well to be able to
say one was there.'

'Then it was a pity you quitted town, my
daughter.'

'I! Oh! I could never have stood the sight;
besides, for me it would have been unseemly,
but Mr. Pomfret goes everywhere.   I marvel he
stayed away; but of course he will hear all particulars, and I doubt not will give me full details
when we meet.'

'I have a letter from your husband here,
daughter Aimée.'

'From Mr. Pomfret, madam? You terrify
me! Is aught amiss?   Oh! where is my per-
fume?—my poor nerves, they are all on the
flutter!'

'Aimée,' said the old lady, putting on her
spectacles, and looking sternly over them at her
daughter.   'Thou lovest English, so I will tell
thee my mind in that very uncivil tongue—thou
art a goose.'

'Ah, you never suffered from nerves, and
know nothing of the misery they cause; but
tell me, why has my husband written to you
and not to me?'

' Because, maybe, he had no stomach to write
about scaffolds and falling heads, and knew that
I could content myself without such details,
while thou, Aimée, wouldst feel thyself de-
frauded, if he told thee not the ghastly tale.
Mais enfin, he wrote to me on business, being,
as I am, much concerned in my grandson
Amyot, though the lad concerns himself but
little about me.'

' Ungrateful young viper !'

' Nay, it is but a wilful slip. Your good
husband writes to tell me that he has at last
gained a commission for the boy, and has wrote
to bid him come to town forthwith, for that it is
likely his regiment will shortly go abroad.'

' Well, I am glad, and I hope he will fall
into the hands of severe officers, who will teach
him his place ; for if ever lad needed discipline,
it is Amyot Brough. And what does Joan
say ?'

' I have not yet told her ; the child comes to
me at mid-day to read me the lessons, and then
we have some discourse ; I will tell her the news
then. I believe she will be glad, for Joan has
sense beyond her years, and knows what will
be for her brother's good. I have another
letter too, and that is from thy step-son, Arnold

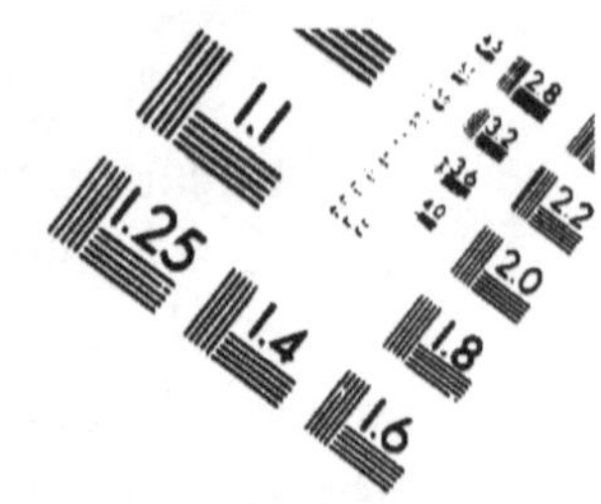

IMAGE EVALUATION
TEST TARGET (MT-3)

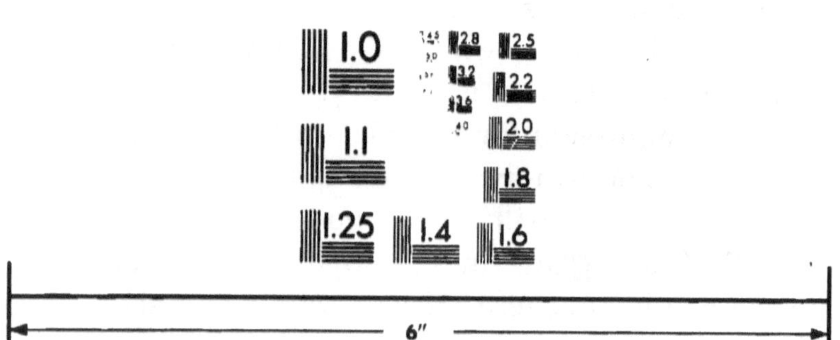

6"

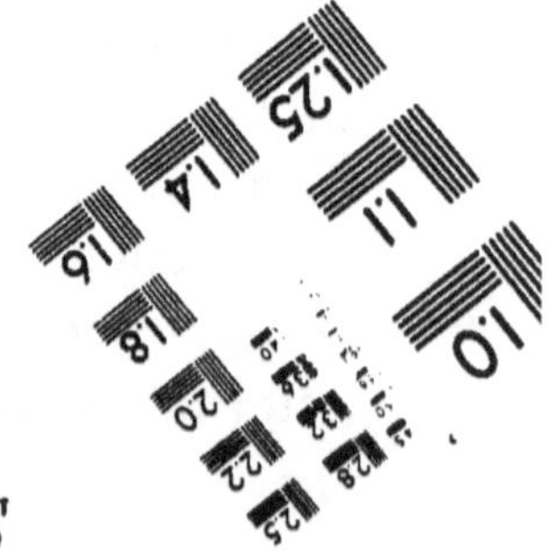

**Photographic
Sciences
Corporation**

23 WEST MAIN STREET
WEBSTER, N.Y. 14580
(716) 872-4503

Pomfret ; but that I guess thou wilt scarce care to see.'

'Arnold's letters are ever the same—prodigious wise and saintly ; he is fast losing his wits. I often wonder whether his mother was quite in her right mind when she died, but I like not to ask Mr. Pomfret—he has never named her to me.'

Mrs. Darley smiled, the same tender half-sad smile which had passed over her face as she read the letter ; but she did not offer to show it, and merely said :

'Arnold is right enough about the brains ; it is but an old head on young shoulders, and a mind full of sympathy with the troubles in the world, but hard perplexed to find a cure.'

'Then why not let it alone ?' said Mrs. Pomfret impatiently.

The old lady's smile had gone by this time, but she gazed with a sweet tender expression at her beautiful but fretful daughter, and replied in a slow and musical voice :

'La charité de Christ nous presse, étant persuadés, que si un est mort pour tous, tous donc sont morts.'

' Oh yes, the love of Christ !—fanatics always talk of that ; but my belief is, God meant us

to be comfortable, and Arnold makes himself
vastly uncomfortable and dolorous; his parish
must be a prodigious doleful place; he has
asked his father and me to go and visit him, but
Mr. Pomfret seemed not over-desirous, and I
feel certain it would be the death of me, with
my poor spirits and palpitations.'

'Worse than the spectacle of the beheading,'
Mrs. Darley suggested ; but Mrs. Pomfret made
no reply, and the subject of her step-son's
eccentricities was dropped for the time being,
Mrs. Pomfret soon after leaving the room.

It was a very pretty girlish figure which Joan
presented when she came as wont to read to
her grandmother at noon. Mrs. Darley liked
soft colours, and dressed the girl almost like a
Quaker, but as she had a clear skin, and a bright
colour, no depth of hue was needed, and the
pale blue slip, and white muslin apron and bib,
with the little muslin cap restraining her fair
hair, made her as elegant a maiden as even
Mrs. Pomfret could desire. To her grandmother's eyes she was all that a modest girl
should be, and Mrs. Darley was not a fond,
easy-to-please grandmother. Joan had learnt
to be careful that her curtsey should express all
due reverence, to be mindful to be free with

neither words nor looks in her elders' presence,
not to forget that her person being comely was
a choice gift to be guarded, and her clothes,
being costly, must be carefully handled and dis-
creetly put on. A careless curtsey, an awkward carriage, an apron awry, a thoughtless
stare, a hesitating or too forward answer, were
offences which Mrs. Darley never passed
unnoticed, and Joan, though not by nature
awkward or rebellious, had learned her lesson
at the cost of some tears, and many hours of
painful reflection in her own little chamber.

'I love not to be for ever saying the same
thing; it is weary work to me, and to all who
hear me,' Mrs. Darley had been wont to say;
'therefore, Joan, thou must learn to remember;
and to strengthen thy memory, I will have
thee spend this forenoon in thine own chamber,
and commune with thine own spirit awhile,
asking thyself is it fitting that a young girl
come into her grandmother's presence with a
rent in her slip, and ink on her fingers, and
with a reverence that testifieth neither honour
nor affection. What sayest thou ? it was Tory
that tore thy slip ? Nay, then, I asked not
who tore it ; it needed not that thou shouldest
cast blame on thy dog, poor beast ; thou hast

other slips, so that excuse will ill suit thy purpose. And since I must e'en set thee matter for thy meditation, I will add one other question for thy self-examination. Is it meet that a young girl answer when she is reproved ? And now go, and I pray thee give me rest from fault-finding for a season : it takes away my appetite, and sets my voice in the minor key, ay, and no doubt adds a dozen wrinkles to my withered old face.'

Such had been Mrs. Darley's system, and whatever may be thought of it, in Joan's case it had answered well. The thoughtful child of Broughbarrow Farm had grown up a marvellously sweet and unselfish maiden. While her grandmother's eye rested on her as she stood before her with the sacred book in her hands, prepared to read the lessons for the day, she said to herself, ' It is not strange that others too should be attracted by her winsomeness.'

The reading over, Joan heard the contents of her uncle's letter with unfeigned delight, and prettily expressed gratitude.

' Then Amyot will soon be in London,' she said, ' and you, madam, will you permit him to come hither after the ungracious manner in which he left you last year ?'

'If he has time, and is not at once despatched to join his regiment ; but he will have to beg my pardon, tall man and commissioned officer as he is. It is long since you heard from him, Joan ?'

'Two months and more,' Joan replied. 'It was some weeks after the battle, and his friends, the Kirkbrides, had left Penrith, and he was feeling very lonesome. Oh, Amyot will be glad to hear these news, and to have his matters settled.'

'Thy uncle Pomfret is coming this afternoon to conduct his wife home : he may have more to tell us. I trust Amyot's is not the same regiment in which his cousin Guy is captain. Guy would be but a bad guide to Amyot, and yet the lad might perchance be taken by his merry tongue.'

'Amyot likes Mr. Arnold Pomfret best,' Joan replied, whereupon the old lady turned round quickly, saying :

'Ah ! does he ? and thou, petite, dost thou like his reverence Arnold Pomfret, whom some think half mad ?'

'Oh yes ; we both like him ; he is so—— grandmother, I cannot think of the word I need —so real, so honest. I never can think of him as a clergyman, because they are not what they seem to be, are they ?'

'Fie, for shame, child, what heresy!' the old lady stopped her ears, but her dark bright eyes laughed, as she said to herself, '*We* both like him, that will do for the present. Now, child, you may go.'

Mr. Pomfret arrived in time for dinner, and brought Joan the enchanting news that her brother had come to London, and was staying at his house in Queen's Square; he had received orders to join his regiment almost immediately, but he hoped to be able to pay his respects to his grandmother before doing so. The regiment would probably be ordered abroad before long, but how soon was quite uncertain.

'Now that the Pretender is disposed of, we shall be able to teach our neighbours a lesson,' Mr. Pomfret said. 'The French think the world was made for them. I see no reason why we should not think it was made for us. We taught them to respect us at Blenheim and Ramillies; they agreed to give us what we claimed in America. Nova Scotia and Newfoundland are ours, but they can't get over it; they are jealous. They would shut us up in this little island, and bid us be content with it. Why should we? We have better fleets than Holland or France, our trade must grow; why should not England assert herself, and take the place that is plainly hers.'

' I am sure I hope she will, if it will make things cheaper,' said his wife ; 'tea is such a frightful price.'

' I have a great respect for England, my adopted country, and the English, my dear husband's nation,' said Mrs. Darley ; 'but I have ever thought they were quite too fond of asserting themselves ; and though my colonel fought at Blenheim, I should have liked him quite as well if he had been defeated instead of victorious, and I think that, angel though he was, a little less of victory would have improved his character.'

' But you are entirely English now, my dear madam,' Mr. Pomfret replied gallantly. ' You will rejoice to see the power of our great nation felt, and her dominion grow and increase, so that when the population of our great cities becomes too dense, there may be homes for them elsewhere, in lands where they may still feel themselves Englishmen and Englishwomen.'

'Yes, yes, if we are in danger of being crowded, it is well that new lands should be found for those who may need them. I detest a crowd —not that we ladies can be squeezed to death, so long as our hoops continue the mode, but

fashions change every day, and you poor gentlemen have no such defence. Tory, my good
dog, I pray you sit not so close to my feet.
You or I must go to America.'

Mr. Pomfret laughed.

'You cannot, I see, my dear madam, believe
in either the numbers or the wealth of our
nation. Your French blood makes you despise
us, whether you will or no.'

'Despise you, mais non, but I feel for my
poor people, whom you have robbed of Acadie,
and whom you mean to spoil of much more of
their possessions. There is only one thing I
do not grudge you, which you got by your
peace of Utrecht—it is a thing I never desired,
and you English may have it and welcome.'

'That is an old subject of dispute, dear
madam, but I hold that, be it pleasing to our
ideas or not, still, if others trade in negroes, it
is but fair that we should have our share, and
being great in commerce, it is but natural that
we should make good profit by that trade as by
others.'

'Money, money, nought but money,' sighed
the old lady.

'Well, mother, we can't live without money,
though I own that down in this quiet place you

seem to have but little need of it ; but come to
live in London, and you will find your purse
soon grow light.'

'And take to gambling, as my grandson Guy
doth when he likes not to trouble his father ;
how much has he lost in the last month, I
wonder ?'

There was an awkward silence after this
remark. Mrs. Pomfret rustled her fan, Mr.
Pomfret took snuff repeatedly ; at last he resumed :

'But we are not to be allowed to extend our
commerce unmolested ; both French and Dutch
are crying out that we are claiming a despotism
of the sea, and mean to destroy the trade of
other nations ; we must be crushed, say they,
our Ministers must be cured of their "délire
ambitieux," as if they have not as great a right
to be ambitious as other Ministers.'

'Well, well, Mr. Pomfret, do not weary us
with politics ; have you nothing more enter-
taining to relate ? Everyone has left town now,
I suspect ? Truly, I cannot stay there long if
this heat continues.'

'Nothing much has been spoken of, save the
executions and the flight of the Pretender ; no
one doubts now that he has got safe to France,

and we hope he has learned his lesson and will not return.'

'Poor young man!' sighed the old lady; 'I am glad he has got safe away, though, indeed, he has cost his country much sorrow, and many lives. Did Amyot tell you aught of his rebel friends in the North?—here is Joan dying to hear.'

'He said there had been some hanging and confiscating in Penrith and Carlisle, and that his friends were like to be beggars, their house being confiscated, as indeed was to be expected; they themselves, I think he said, had all escaped further mischief. The lad seems to have a kindly heart, and spoke with real pity of the troubles he had witnessed.'

Joan blushed and dimpled at hearing this praise of her brother—it was long since she had heard aught but blame of him; *she* had always believed in him, but it was delightful to hear that others did not think him hopelessly bad, and her heart sang within her.

Before she retired to rest that night, Mrs. Darley wrote a letter, on which she bestowed some anxious, and not a few merry thoughts. Having no secrets from our reader, we give it entire:

'It being plainly evident to me, my dear young friend, that you are in marvellous great haste for a reply to your letter, I proceed to put my thoughts on paper without loss of time, albeit I know not when an opportunity will present itself of despatching the epistle to that far-off wilderness wherein you pitch your tent. Well, if so, you must summon patience to your aid, as methinks you will need to do in a weightier matter than the mere answering of your letter.

'And this leads me to the subject-matter that you suggested for my meditations, with regard to which I would strongly commend to you the need of being in no haste. And this the more, because when last we communed of the life to which you have devoted yourself, you were entirely determined that the service of the Church would permit no earthly affections; and if I did not wholly mistake your meaning, you were then minded to forswear for Christ's sake all tender ties and earthly loves. You will remember that I smiled, and thought but lightly of your stern decision; nevertheless, I honoured you for the thought, and I had little notion that even then the love which you now confess, had taken root in your breast. How now, my son ?—did you so ill understand your own heart, that your words could so belie your thoughts ? You will say, " Chide me not, since I own that I *had* thought never to be married, save to my flock, and do now confess my weakness." Yes, but I do chide thee : he that changes once may change again, and fickleness is my abhorrence. So I say to you, " Wait ; give yourself to your work, and try yourself— whether it be not a passing whim, such as oft besets your brother Guy, who, butterfly-like, is ever caught by the last bright flower that he chances to light upon, and had even once thought to have honoured your fair one with his hand, and what he calls his heart, had I not warned him off with a voice like a screech-owl : I am ever diverted when I think of that day."

' But for you I have not such a fixed aversion, as you know perhaps too well. I could like you passably, were I but sure of you, and that will I be, ere you have my child. May you come to visit her, you ask. Nay, that you may not ; but if your cure of souls permit it, you may come to visit *me*, and I will put you through as strict a catechism as ever did spiritual director : so, if you are minded to come hither, see that your confession be well prepared and honest, for I will have no evading of my questions; you know me of old, I think, and will testify that I am wont to have my will.

'And now that you have heard my mind, and are doubtless much chafed and vexed with me, let me tell you that it affords me great diversion to think that you have so soon descended to the level of ordinary weak mortals, and are even half persuaded that you cannot live if the good thing you desire be not granted. My good young gentleman, you are too impetuous; bethink you, ere you thus set your mind on earthly happiness. Not live without her! fie, for shame! you are indeed fallen from the pinnacle of lofty imaginings on which I last beheld you, and I must indulge myself a space with gazing at your humiliation.

'Yet it is unseemly and unchristian to laugh at others' woes, and well do I perceive that the fall hath grievously damaged you in your own esteem; for that I am not disturbed. You will seek for new steeps to climb again ere long, ay, and I like to see you climb—the falls are no matter, they grieve me not. But my sermon hath been marvellous long and tedious, wrote, like too many a discourse, when the eyes are heavy with sleep, ay, and it might all have been wrote in four letters—"wait ;" and to stimulate you to this mighty effort, I would remind you that the child is but a child, and will be naught else for some while to come ; therefore say I again, there is no call to haste. And now, lest the cocks should crow ere I be laid on my pillow, I will bid you farewell, commending you to much deep study of your own heart, and to some gentle discipline of your unruly will.

'I am, most truly,

'Your sincere though severe friend,

'PAULINE DARLEY.'

CHAPTER XV.

Concerning a Christmas Rout.

'AND where did you say the Christmastide is to be passed, with your mother at Westerham, or with Arnold in his tumbledown rectory, or in our own home, my dear Aimée?'

'My mother has promised to come to visit us, and she will bring Miss Johnstone, my niece Joan, and her own women; Arnold, I trust, will also bear us company. So we shall be a merry household; my nephew Amyot must enjoy himself as much as in him lies, seeing that in January he will go to the wars, and learn what hardships really are.'

'Nay, they have a pretty time of it, many of these young officers,' Mr. Pomfret replied; 'good rations, plenty of cards—and the Dutch and German maidens are not uncomely. Guy leads a merry life, by all accounts.'

'Poor Guy, would that he could be at home,' sighed his mother; but she glanced at her husband, whose brow had contracted with a frown, and said no more. Deep play had brought Captain Guy into difficulties, and his father spoke his name with unusual bitterness. An easy-going father, allowing his sons much license, and seldom interfering with their tastes and pleasures, and that partly from indolence, partly from indifference, Mr. Pomfret had at last been roused to something like stern language towards his youngest son; he had paid his debts many times, but he vowed he had now done it for the last time, and Mrs. Pomfret had written and told her son that she much feared his father meant what he said.

Merry Captain Guy said it was 'very hard, too desperate hard,' and then he joined a lively band of brother officers, who were wiling away a long evening at cards, and the stakes being inconveniently high, he lost another £500 before going to bed, and not being quite tipsy enough to be unconscious of his awkward predicament, had serious thoughts of shooting himself for one half-hour; but on second thoughts remembered that he had an elder brother who had more than once befriended him in his schoolboy scrapes, and might do so again. Therefore the shooting was delayed for the present, Captain Guy having a faint notion that such a performance was rather a cowardly way of getting out of the difficulty, and determined to write without loss of time to Arnold, who was one of those lucky fellows possessed of independent means, having inherited property from his mother.

It was the receipt of this letter which had determined the Rev. Arnold to obey his father's request, that he would pay them a visit at Christmastide. An old penniless tutor of his would gladly supply his place at Swynford, and set him at liberty to see his mother, and talk over with her the state of Guy's affairs.

Arnold was a little ashamed of the pleasure he felt in the prospect of this visit to London, after more than a year's absence from civilized society. It was impossible to conceal from himself that his mother's conversation, which, with all his high respect for her, he had been apt to find wearisome, would now be most pleasantly refined and elegant ; his father he had always honoured as a man of cultivated taste and extensive reading, but now, as compared with the boorish country-folk among

whom he had been passing his days, Mr. Pomfret appeared to his son a being belonging to
another world, to associate with whom would
be a kind of intellectual Paradise—and as he
thought over the names of old friends to be
visited during this short stay in London,
Arnold instinctively began to count the days
till Christmas, as when he had been a schoolboy going home for the holidays.

Mr. Pomfret had spoken of his son's home
as a tumbledown rectory; but at that time
he had never seen it, and only thought of it
as Arnold had described it, an old rambling
house in desperate need of repair. Had he
seen it, his fastidious taste would have pronounced it utterly uninhabitable, since, in many
of the chambers, the flooring had entirely de-
cayed, and nearly half the roof had been blown
away in a storm.

But the Rev. Arnold Pomfret, having a
strong desire to fit himself to understand the
sufferings and hardships of his flock by per-
sonal experience, had felt a great sense of
exultation when he first examined his vicarage,
and noted its many weak points and manifest
sources of discomfort. Nor was it until a pig
had pushed a frail door off its hinges, climbed

up the stair, and taken up its. abode close
beside him during the night, and geese and
ducks, and many other kinds of flying fowl had
roosted in all the various chambers where the
window-frames were glassless, and owls and
jackdaws had built in every chimney, that he
had reluctantly confessed to himself that a
house in ruins did not necessarily incline the
soul to soar above the world of time. and
sense.

An easy bed might doubtless lead to too
much folding of the hands to sleep, but a
night disturbed by the scampering of rats and
hooting of owls had also its disadvantages.
and revealed to Arnold the painful and humiliating fact that if a man cannot sleep at night,
he will perchance doze by day ; while a roof
full of holes, implying much dripping of rain
on the floors in wet weather, and doors that
have so shrunk that no bolts will hold them
shut, and other such small inconveniences, instead of affording the soul room to soar
heavenward, as might be expected, seem but
to keep it more earthbound than ever.

How differently had Arnold Pomfret fondly
dreamed ; but, alas for his theories ! to become
skilled in the art of sympathy, he soon found that

he needed initiation into the pains of rheumatism, sore throats, and ague fits—good things in their way, but not quite the kind of suffering he had prescribed for himself, and entailing the awkward consequence, that while he was lying in his comfortless bed, watching the smoke wreaths that filled the room, counting the rats that gambolled over his pillows, and setting himself diligently to learn this grand lesson of sympathy, the hungry flock found themselves unfed, untended, unshepherded.

It was humiliating, but not the less comforting, to acquiesce in the old parish clerk's dictum :

' You bees too delicate a gentleman to live in thiz way ; we'll fetch along sum bits of glass and mend them winders, and we'll patch up the roof and make he watertight, and the rats— well, I know a dog as will make an end of they, and next time you come across the bishop you should tell him as yer house is coming down about yer ears, and bid him see to her.'

But the bishop did not often come to Swynford, and Arnold had contented himself with these slight improvements, and with planning others in the future, when he went to spend his Christmas in London.   How luxurious did the

Queen's Square house look on the night of his arrival! 'Surely it was wrong to live in such comfort,' was his first thought, instantly checked, however, as the remembrance of his hardly learned lesson came back to him; and he shuddered at the thought of the house he had left, and wondered if he had done right to leave his old half-paralyzed tutor in such a place.

It was Christmas Eve, and the late four o'clock dinner was going forward when he arrived. Mrs. Pomfret, elegantly attired, at the head of the table; Mrs. Darley, in her soft grey brocade and plain white muslin kerchief and cap, beside his father; the elderly spinster, Miss Johnstone, on his left-hand; Amyot and a young brother-officer to the right and left of his mother; and opposite the vacant place which had been left for himself sat Joan, in the seat she loved best, between her grandmother and her brother. How homelike it seemed! The heart of a traveller from the arctic regions could not have bounded more joyously at his home-coming, than did Arnold's as he responded to the merry greetings which welcomed him.

'Half-frozen and entirely starved,' said Mrs.

Pomfret; 'sit there, son Arnold, and eat and warm yourself: between the Christmas log and your cousin's bright eyes you must needs thaw presently.'

And amid this merry buzz of voices the country priest was soon conscious that not only was his outward man thawing, but the cold, cheerless wall of restraint and endurance which had been growing round his heart was giving way, and social enjoyment was warming his whole being. Was he ashamed to own it to himself? Blame him not, reader; he had looked so much and so often on the dark places of this earth, and the sad lives of those less fortunate than himself, that he could scarce tell whether he had any right to forget them for a moment and be happy.

'Give us some traveller's tales, cousin,' said Amyot; 'the last from a journey has ever some adventure to relate—did you meet with no mishaps as you came hither?'

'Nothing worse than a terrible snow-storm, through which the horses struggled knee-deep, and we were near blinded by the snow which beat in our faces—but that is a mischance scarce worth naming.'

'I love much a veritable tempest of snow and

hail,' said Amyot's friend, Lieutenant John James Pownal, a young man of Canadian origin, lately arrived in England; 'but in your England the tempests are a bagatelle — I mock at them.'

'Why say in *your* England?—you are English too, lieutenant,' said Mrs. Pomfret. 'You told us that your father is English, though your mother is French, and that though your English is not quite perfect, you wished to be considered an Englishman and nothing else.'

'Ah, it is true ; but see you, madam, my England is across the sea, and your climate here—but it is abominable ; there is nothing one can see of worse—how you can suffer it ?—that astonishes me ; but you are a wonderful people —more I see, more I admire.'

'But you have not seen much, Jack,' Amyot broke in ; 'the parks, Vauxhall, Ranelagh, Bagnigge Wells, Marybone, that's about all, isn't it ? You scarce know London ; and as for the country, why, you've not set foot in it since you arrived.'

'I am a soldier—I am to my king ; I go where he will, be it to the end of the world, be it nowheres. I am all to him, my dear Brough.'

'Well, King George has a mind to send us

to Flanders, I hear; how will that suit you?' asked Amyot. 'Cousin Arnold, do you not envy us our luck?—real war at last!'

Arnold Pomfret smiled. 'I had never a taste for bloodshed,' he replied. Then, turning to his father, 'Have you had late news from my brother, sir?'

'Late enough,' was the answer; and the family having by this time quitted the parlour and retired to the drawing-room, Mr. Pomfret drew his son aside, and related at full his vexation concerning Captain Guy.

When they rejoined the ladies the card-table had been set out, and the two ladies, together with Amyot and Lieutenant John Pownal, were occupied with cards, while Joan, on a low stool by Mrs. Darley's side, was disentangling a skein of fine wool for her grandmother's knitting, and watching her brother with eyes which seemed full of pensive anxiety.

Mr. Pomfret quitted the room, and Arnold drew near to Joan, saying:

'We have scarce greeted each other, cousin, and I have had it in my mind ever since I arrived to congratulate you on your brother's good fortune. He seems wondrous content and merry.'

'It is what he has long coveted,' Joan replied, 'and I am glad for him ; but for myself—yet that matters nothing.'

'For yourself there is much anxiety in store,' Arnold responded ; and as she met his glance of sympathy, the young girl's eyes filled, and she cast them upon her work.

'Hey now, what's this ?' said her grandmother, turning round suddenly ; 'my sport is spoiled.   I'll play no more, daughter Pomfret ; here's a parson come among us, bringing the vapours and the dismals, and I know not what mischief beside.   I thought gentlemen of your robe were called ministers of consolation, sir. Perchance you make it your practice to bruise that you may have somewhat to bind up ; if so, I take it you are a quack, and nothing better.'

'Nay, madam,' said Joan, dashing away the tears.   'My cousin said naught amiss—he did but wish me joy of Amyot's success.'

The old lady shook her fist at Arnold.

'He has but a melancholy mien,' she said. I mistrust him wholly.   Joan is a soldier's grand-daughter, a sailor's daughter, and a soldier's sister ; she shall send her hero to the wars with songs, not tears.   Fie upon thee,

Arnold, I know thou wert at the bottom of the mischief; I tell thee I see it in thy face.'

'Sister,' whispered Amyot, as Joan, confounded at having attracted so much notice, shrank away into the shelter of the deep window, and stood half concealed among the rich hangings, 'you do not truly grieve that I have attained my heart's wish! you were ever so unselfish, Joan, and so brave withal.'

'And so am I now, at least, for the most part; it was but the thought that came to me, how happy we all are to-night, and perhaps we may never all be thus merry together again; yet I am not truly sad—it is but for a moment.'

'We shall all be together again many a time in the next fifteen days, I hope; and on Friday, Joan, my aunt tells me she means to take you to the great rout given at her old friend's, whose name I ever forget, in Great Ormond Street. Jack and I, too, will be there, so we shall see you dance, which is what I love, and hear you praised, which, too, I love amazingly.'

'You are so silly, Amyot,' Joan said, blushing. 'You do not truly believe all the fooleries men talk?'

'Do I not! When they talk of you, sweet sister, I believe all they say; and if you will but wear your pale blue dress, which you think so fine, I shall win my bet with Jack for certain.'

'Amyot! that a man should bet about his sister's dress. You are so monstrous silly.'

'Nay, it is not your dress which our bet concerns—it is your fair face, sweet sister.'

'Then I trust you will lose your bet, and gain more wisdom,' Joan said, with her old dignity, as she withdrew herself from his embrace, and quietly returned to her seat by Mrs. Darley, who, scanning her tenderly, said:

'It is all well with thee now, little one. I marvel not that long stern face gave thee a fright—like a death's-head on a tombstone. We must teach him to smile again; he has quite forgot the secret, in that terrible land of ghosts and hobgoblins where he dwells.'

The rout referred to by Amyot was destined to be long remembered by more than one of the family from Queen's Square, and by Amyot and his sister, perhaps, most of all.

It was the first assembly of the kind at which Joan had appeared, both Mrs. Darley and Mrs. Pomfret having up to that time con-

In Great Ormond Street.

sidered her too young for any but small enter-
tainments ; but now that she might be called
a woman, the case was different. ' It was time
she should be seen,' Mrs. Pomfret said, and
Mrs. Darley added: 'Time, too, that she should
see for herself what the world was like.'

The world put on a very dazzling appearance to the young girl that night, for the rout
was given partly to honour the officers of a
certain regiment about to depart for Flanders,
and the ballroom was filled with gay uni-
forms, and the lights and decorations were
splendid.

Joan's wish had been to see, and not be
seen ; but this was not to be. One after another of Amyot's friends begged to be favoured
with the honour of her hand for one dance, and
Mrs. Pomfret was so well pleased at her niece's
popularity, and so well contented to be free
from the charge of her, and able to betake
herself to the card-table, that Joan soon lost
sight of her altogether.

At length, growing somewhat tired, she was
about to beg her partner, Lieutenant Pownal,
to discover where her aunt was, and to lead her
to her, when her ear was caught by the sound
of her brother's voice in hot dispute from a

small room close by.　Lieutenant Pownal saw her cheek grow pale, and guessed the cause.

'It is nothing,' he said reassuringly ; 'your good brother, madam, he is a little excitable, he cannot suffer that one contradict him, and all the world cannot comprehend his character —there is all.　I pray you be not disturbed for so little.'

'It can scarcely be a little thing to move Amyot so to forget himself,' Joan said ; 'can you speak to him, sir, and tell him that his sister needs his company ?'

'Without doubt I might do your commands,' said the young man, with some hesitation ; 'but shall I not rather have the felicity to lead you to your aunt ?　I can scarce leave you standing here, while I plunge into that crowd and seek out your brother.'

'Yet I might put an end to such an unseemly dispute,' Joan said timidly, 'if so be you could persuade Amyot to come to me.'

'It will be an uneasy matter, madam, but your commands do me great honour—behold a seat ; I fly to execute your orders.'

He disappeared, and to Joan's anxious heart ne seemed to have been absent nearly half an 1our, when the loud altercation gradually subsided, and she saw her brother making his way towards her, his brow contracted, a flush on his face, and his whole bearing sullen and angry.

'What is it, sister; where is my aunt? Could not Jack have taken you to her, instead of tormenting me with his importunities that my sister needed me, my sister was ill, in distress —a thousand other follies?'

'Take me to her; I know nothing of the ways of this house, and cannot walk through all these rooms by myself,' Joan replied evasively; then, as he drew back, saying, 'Jack will take care of you,' she persisted : 'Nay : nay, brother, I need you ; come with me but a few yards,' and as he unwillingly complied, she went on hurriedly, 'What has befallen, Amyot? why such brawling and angry words in a gay company such as this, and in another person's house too?—surely you have forgot yourself—do not go back to that room.'

'Not go back!—forget myself!—Joan, you are a child ; there are things no man may endure, and the man you heard me talking with is an ill-bred rascal as ever breathed.'

'Then have naught to do with him,' Joan was saying, when her brother broke forth again as his eyes followed a figure which passed them hastily, and went down the stairs. ' Ha, has he got away, thinks he ; not so fast, you old rogue, I'll keep an eye on you, and pay you yet. Now, Joan, to the whist-tables to find my aunt.'

He hurried her along, paying no heed to her entreaties that he would stay with her and forget his wrath at least for one night. ' I pray you, brother, spoil not all my pleasure thus,' fell on deaf ears, and he had no sooner discovered where his aunt was seated, than having found Joan a seat beside her, he mingled with the gay crowd around and disappeared.

Joan tried hard to stifle her uneasiness : her brother in this mood of stormy passion had ever been terrible to her, and as she pressed her hand to her head, and felt the throbbing of her temples, she wondered whether he had any just cause for his resentment, or whether his griev-ance was now, as it had often been before, purely imaginary. Mrs. Pomfret was too much engrossed with her game to notice her disturb-ance. She had asked her if she was over-fatigued, but being reassured on that point, had said no more, and Joan, engrossed with her own thoughts, watched the motions of those around her as if in a dream.

Suddenly she was awakened. Her uncle had brought his wife and niece to the rout, had left them after awhile, promising to return and escort them home : Joan now saw him making his way through the company, guided by the lady of the house to the table where his wife sat ; she had been wondering how soon he would come, and a glad thrill passed through her as she spied him, for the gay scene had become intolerable to her since Amyot had so abruptly departed, leaving her in doubt and fear, and she fervently longed to be at home. But her gladness was but momentary—what was that strange look on her uncle's face? Joan never remembered to have seen it before ; had he been gambling and lost all that he possessed ? His niece knew that such things had happened before now to richer men than he ; but then she had heard her aunt say Mr. Pomfret did not lose money at cards. Had he been drinking? That, too, she believed, was not his habit, though many gentlemen of fashion went drunk to bed every night, and if others, why not he ?'

'Dear aunt,' she said timidly, 'here is my uncle.'

'Well, child, what then? are you in haste to

go ; why, mercy on us, Mr. Pomfret, what ails
you ?—have the French landed ?'

'Mr. Pomfret, madam, is the bearer of ill
news,' said her friend, the mistress of the house,
'but I grieve to say it is private sorrow, which,
though we may all share it, falls chiefly on himself and you.'

'On us ! for pity's sake speak, Mr. Pomfret !
Is it my mother?—tell me—I shall swoon away !'
and she grew so pale that Joan sprang forward
to support her.

'Nay, do not be alarmed, all may yet be well,'
said Mr. Pomfret soothingly ; 'it is briefly this :
Arnold has met with an accident, being knocked
down by some drunken fellow in the street,
close outside this house, whither he had come
to hand you into your chair and walk beside
you home as he promised. The chairmen tell
me that he had been standing there some
minutes talking cheerfully to them, when some
drunken young officers rushed out of the house,
and one of them snatched a torch from a link-
boy, and struck him a violent blow on the head,
felling him to the ground, and the other seized
his friend by the arm and dragged him away,
so that we have no clue to the perpetrator of
this vile outrage.'

' And our son Arnold, what of him ?'

' He was lifted into a chair and carried home, and there he lies, still unconscious ; but the surgeon says he thinks he may recover.'

' He may recover ?—when they talk in that fashion, they know there is no hope. Ah me, that I had never come abroad this night !'

' My love, do not reproach yourself for this mischance ; rather, let me take you to the chair, which is in waiting, that we may the sooner be with our poor son. Our kind friend here will permit your sudden departure, and excuse the discourtesy.'

' Indeed, sir, I grieve at the cause most truly ; but I would not detain you an instant. Most glad am I that you have but a short distance to traverse. Your charming niece will accompany you, doubtless. I must come and see you both well cloaked and hooded, that you may take no chill in leaving this hot room.'

A few minutes after, the anxious parents were at their own door, and Joan, burdened with a new fear, which she dared not to name, could scarce bear to look at her uncle, so sad an expression did his usually cheerful face now wear.

'I must rest awhile ere I see him,' Mrs. Pomfret said, sitting down on a couch in the parlour, where two wax candles, giving but a faint light in the spacious apartment, yet served to make her pale face look even paler than it really was. 'Go to him if you will, Mr. Pomfret, I will follow shortly. Joan, love, do you fear to look upon wounds and suffering ?—if you knew how I dread it !'

'Can I do aught for you, madam ? Fetch you a glass of water, or my grandmother's bottle of strong essences ?—you look ready to faint.'

'I can scarce keep myself from sinking, Joan, yet your uncle, I know, desires my presence in his son's chamber ; but oh, if he should be dying ! Did you ever see death, child ?'

'Once —long ago '—Joan's thoughts had ravelled back to the dark evening, seven years before, when her father's lifeless body had been brought to his home ; 'it was not fearful, madam.'

'You speak truly ? Joan, you are a blessed child ; give me your arm to mount the stairs.'

'Nay, stay a minute.' It was Mrs. Darley's voice, and the old lady entered brisk and lively

as in her merriest mood. 'We want no sighing and moping upstairs, and you are such a
poor creature, Aimée, that I have told your
husband I shall send you to bed, and nurse
your son myself.'

'You, mother?—an old lady of your age turning sick nurse? Nay, that may never be.'

'That may be, and that shall be. Joan, do
thy grandmother's bidding; take thine aunt
to her room, and leave her not till she is laid
comfortably to sleep; then take thy pale cheeks
to bed. It hath been an ill rout for us to-
night.'

'But, mother, tell me, how is my son?'

'Thy son hath been in ugly company, as I
shall tell him, if ever he finds his wits again;
but I have hopes he will live to mend his
ways. The surgeon has bled him, and that
was a sight thou likest not, so it were well
thou didst not come straight to his room.'

Mrs. Pomfret uttered a little shriek, whereupon the old lady stamped her foot impatiently,
and said:

'Come, come, thou wouldst make a poor
nurse. Go to rest now, and to-morrow, if God
wills, you shall have a sight of your son in
better case than he is at present. But I must

return ; there is none with him but his father, and that silly old housekeeper, who is sure he will die, and who knows but she may smother him, to make her words true, if I do not keep watch ;' and she trotted away.

It was not an easy task to prevail on Mrs. Pomfret to go to rest. She would lie down on the couch, and so be ready if needed. She must see poor dear Arnold ; she loved him as well—nay, better than her own son. Again, she dared not see him—he might be dying, and she could not look on death. Joan was ready to sink with fatigue ere she had succeeded in inducing her aunt to go to her chamber, and allow her woman to undress her ; and when at last that was done, and, true to her custom of exact obedience, she also had followed Mrs. Darley's direction, and sought her own room, and had crept cold and miserable into bed, sleep seemed further from her eyes than ever in her life before.

Would her cousin Arnold live ? Joan wondered whether her grandmother had really the hope she seemed to have, or whether the old housekeeper, who had known Arnold all his life, would prove the truer prophet. Could he be even now dying ? Could that strange power, called Death, be even now entering the silent house, and claiming a victim, while none perceived his approach ?   Joan held her breath and listened. The wind sighed in the chimney—a hollow moaning sound—the stairs creaked, a door swung to with a heavy thud ; no other sound reached her ears, except the call of the watchman from hour to hour, and the voices of some link-boys, as they ran by the side of the chairmen, or lighted foot-passengers on their way. Soon all revellers had gone home, the quiet and silence grew more intense, and Joan wondered why she did not sleep.

'If I only knew, if I only felt sure it was not Amyot, I *could* sleep,' she moaned ; 'for death is not a terrible thing, and Cousin Arnold, I am sure, fears it not. But then his poor father—and if it was Amyot, I could never bear it, I could never look at them again. Oh, brother, if you only knew how miserable you have made me !'

Thus she murmured to herself, tossing on her bed, till, no answer coming to her anxious questionings, she fell into a fitful slumber, starting and waking, and sleeping again ; and thus the long hours of the night passed away, and the late winter morning came at last.

CHAPTER XVI.

Humiliation.

Whither away so fast, Jack?'

'To church. Will it astonish you so much
o hear that I have the habitude of assisting at
ne service every Sunday?— but truly I know not
where to go.   One has told me there is a handsome new church called St. Giles-in-the-Fields,
ut I doubt if I can find the road there. Where
lo you go, good Amyot?'

'Well, I had half thought of going to the
hurch near my uncle's house—St. George the
Martyr, they call it—because there, perchance,
 may meet my sister. Give me your company,
ack.'

'Willingly. A sight of your fair sister will
uch augment the fervour of my devotions;
nd truly, the parsons do little to aid us to—
hat do you call it in English?—raise our

souls to God ? Is that well said—*comme il faut ?*'

'It is most entirely "*comme il faut*"—your English is most elegant, Jack ; but you are starting in the wrong direction. Let me guide you.'

The service had begun when the two young men entered. The church was new, and the congregation most fashionable—far too fashionable to concern itself much with the prayers, doubtless considering that the parson was paid to repeat them, and could of course perform his task unaided.

Amyot and his friend were led to a pew not far from the reading-desk. Many plumed hats turned as they passed up the aisle, and more than one pair of glasses was raised to inspect them ; but neither of the young men could distinguish among the elegant ladies, the face and form of which they were in search.

'Queer that none of the family should be in church !' whispered Amyot to his companion. 'They must have overslept themselves.'

But his friend shook his head, firmly convinced that such an explanation was inadmissible.

It was not till near the close of a very eloquent discourse upon the necessity of laying up such a fund of good works as must secure popularity in this world, and also make an entrance into heaven certain, that Jack Pownal twitched his friend's sleeve and whispered :

' My eyes are better than yours : beside the pillar near the door I see an angel form. Let us lose no time, when he shuts his book, in making our way to the door.'

And Amyot, looking eagerly towards the spot indicated, discovered his sister, attended by her aunt's woman, and half hidden behind the pillar.

The sermon ended just at that moment, and they were soon outside, waiting for Joan. She had a preoccupied air as she came towards them, and started violently as her brother approached, saying :

' Sweet sister, have you no eyes for me, and are you walking for a wager ?'

' Amyot—Lieutenant Pownal—I beg your pardon—I did not perceive you. But oh! brother, I am glad we have met: now you can clear up my doubts. Come with me a few steps from all this crowd, so that we may speak freely.'

' Speak freely ?—aye, to be sure. What's amiss, Joan ?—you look wondrous grim.'

'Then you know nothing ? Oh, I am so relieved—-so thankful !'

' Know nothing of what ?'

'Of my cousin Arnold's accident : how he was thrown down on Friday night, as he was standing waiting for my aunt to come from the card-party, and struck on the head and grievously hurt, so that we know not whether he will recover. My aunt is ill with grief, and my uncle is sad beyond description.'

' But how did it happen ?' Amyot inquired, a look of some uneasiness passing over his face ; while Lieutenant Pownal seemed inclined to speak, but checked himself.

' It happened only a few minutes after you parted from me so hastily. The chairmen who saw the mischance said some drunken officers, leaving the ballroom, attacked him savagely, with no provocation, and then, having done the deed, fled like cowards as they were !'

Joan's eyes flashed as she fixed them on her brother, and then waited breathless for his reply.

The colour rushed to his brow ; he uttered a half exclamation as he met her indignant gaze ; then his eyes fell, he dropped her hand, and, turning towards his friend, he said :

'Then you were right, Jack ; and it *was* all a horrid, villainous mistake !'

'I fear so, indeed,' Jack Pownal said. 'I told you you had missed your man.'

There was a dead silence.

Joan looked from one to the other in despair.

'Tell me,' she said, at length. 'I cannot understand what you mean, brother. Was it you that struck that coward blow, and all unprovoked ?'

But Amyot did not speak ; his brow was bent, his eyes fixed on the ground, his lips compressed ; the red flush had passed away, and an ashy paleness had succeeded. Thus he stood, silent and motionless, until anguish drew from Joan the passionate exclamation :

'You did it, you did it, in a fit of vile passion ! Oh, I am glad, so glad that father and mother are dead, and no one left but me.'

Then he lifted his head, and with white lips said :

'Tell her all, Jack, for God knows it was a mistake, and, what is more, that I never meant to take anyone's life.'

'Miss Brough,' said the kindly lieutenant, 'might we not make a tour round the Square garden, and then I will recount to you the affair as it arrived ; your brother is not altogether the veritable rascal you believe him, and God is good, so be not too miserable. This is how the thing has arrived. There is a certain parson, a quite other man from monsieur your cousin, a beggar, a sot, a veritable demon, and he is for ever and always on the heels of your brother— he gives him no peace. Now, Amyot is not prudent—I speak it to his face—he has played with this demon, and the demon has cheated him, and he wants his money, and Amyot, you see, will not pay. He says he will fight, but no, the little parson fears to be killed—he is in no hurry to go to see his friends in the other world, although I do believe they must love him right well; but no, he will not fight, and he will have his money, and I say to Amyot, " Pay him, and deliver yourself from him ;" but no, Amyot will not, and they quarrel, quarrel, as you, madam, did hear the other night. But you are unquiet, and I relate the affair in a manner so tiresome. Enfin, this is what did arrive. The parson ran out ; your brother conducted you to your aunt, and ran after him. I followed to see the mischief, and I saw Amyot seize a torch from a boy and strike a parson on the head ; truly, he meant but to frizzle up his perruque for him, and scorch him a trifle. But the parson was so exceedingly astonished that he started back and stumbled, and fell on the stone steps, and lay there as if dead; I was affrighted: I seize Amyot's arm and drag him away, but I did say to him that very night that the parson was not the man at all, but larger—taller, I mean, by the head, at least. This is all my history, and I grieve exceedingly at the calamity; truly, I am in desolation for you, madam, and for my friend.'

'You are very good,' Joan said sadly. 'I thank you much, sir, for your explanation. It is something better than I feared, yet it is plain that my brother's passion is the cause of all our sorrow, nor can it be denied that he meditated harm to some one, though not to my cousin.'

'In verity, it cannot be denied,' Jack replied; 'when in a passion, the good Amyot should be sent to Bethlehem.'

At last Amyot spoke:

'And now, sister, that you know all, what would you have me do? It is an evil mischance, but I see no way to mend it. Is my cousin truly so much hurt?' For Joan was weeping, and tears were so seldom her resource, that Amyot's worst fears were aroused by the sight.

'I scarce know; my grandmother is hopeful, but my uncle's face is woful to behold. Amyot, I know not what to counsel you.'

'Oh, for that matter, the counsel I need is soon spoken. I am not going to hide this deed of mine—my uncle shall know all about it, sooner or later; all I need to know is, whether to go to him now and tell him, or wait till his grief be something lessened, and it may not cause him so much vexation to hear that I am such a ruffian. Tell me which will be best for him, Joan; trouble not yourself for me. My aunt said once she feared she should live to see me hanged in chains, and if I go on at this rate she is like to see her words come true. Nay, Joan, don't sob in that fashion; truly, I meant to take no one's life.'

'It is so miserable,' Joan said; 'not that I fear that uncle will not credit your story, but should my cousin die, how can they ever bear to look at you again?'

'But we are not sure that he will die,' broke in Jack Pownal—'let us hope. Hope is a beautiful thing, and at this instant, we cannot dispense with her—therefore let us say to ourselves, "The good parson will recover his health, and all will be well." But for the moment, while all the world is so miserable, what shall the man do who was so unlucky as to break his head ? Madam, I pray you, decide the question.'

Joan hesitated ; then she said :

' I dare not tell Amyot to go now to my uncle, he is so miserable ; go away now, Amyot, and come here to-morrow, if you can, and to-day, if I can, I will tell my grandmother, and what she says, that you must do. She will know what is best.'

' That is most prudent,' said Jack Pownal ; ' you shall be obeyed, Miss Brough. I will charge myself with him, this great villain ; he shall break no more heads before to-morrow, and after that—well, his uncle must speak to the colonel, and have him taught discipline. Come away, you great rogue, you rascal, you murdering wretch, you ——'

' Stop,' said Amyot ; ' hold your tongue, Jack ; I want a word with my sister. Joan, could you not go home now, and find out how Arnold is, and give us some signal from the window of your chamber ? We will watch at the corner of the Square.'

Joan agreed.

' If he is worse, or no better, I will wave, his black ribbon from the window ; if better

I will show this white handkerchief for a minute or two.'

She curtsied to Jack Pownal, and hastened towards home. The young men lingered, anxiously watching until, in a few minutes, the black ribbon floated from the window, and then they turned and walked silently away.

The short winter afternoon was closing in, and the darkness rapidly coming on, before Joan had any chance of seeking counsel from her grandmother, and by that time her misery had so increased by brooding on it, that she had well-nigh persuaded herself that the very worst consequences must ensue if Amyot told his uncle ; and had almost resolved to say nothing to Mrs. Darley about the matter. Almost, but not entirely, for Joan's affection for her grandmother was deep, her confidence in her so sincere, that it was almost impossible for her to keep anything secret from the old lady.

Sitting on a low stool by the parlour fire, she had been debating the question with herself for three long hours, and with no certain result, when the door opened, and Mrs. Darley came in. Joan started to her feet with a smothered exclamation of delight, and hastened to seat the old lady, pale and exhausted with her long watch, in the high-backed chair beside the hearth. Then she brought a footstool for her feet, and a pillow for her head, with the gentle touch so pleasing to the old lady, who murmured :

'Bless thee, my child, art glad the wicked priest is better ?'

'Truly better—is my cousin truly better ? Oh, madam, I am so glad !—I think I never knew what gladness was before. And will he surely recover, do you think ?'

'Did I not say he would last night ? But why so monstrous glad, Joan ? He is naught but thy cousin—nay, not a true cousin either.'

'Nay, I know, but I count him cousin. I love him as such ; but that is not all, dear grandmother. May I tell you a dreadful story ? —and then you will marvel no more that I rejoice that my cousin is like to live.'

'Ay, tell me,' said the old lady wearily. ''Tis the old story, I suppose.'

'What old story, madam ?'

'Nay, never mind—tell me thine. Yes, sit down at my feet, and lay thy head on my knee. I am a silly old woman to-day, and like to have it so ; and now, what is it ?'

'It is about Amyot,' Joan began.

'Oh, Amyot! I thought it had concerned thy cousin. Well, Amyot, what of him?'

Slowly, and with some incoherency, Joan told her tale, to which the old lady listened with more than one exclamation of horror, and with a stifled sigh or two. When she ceased speaking, there was a silence for some minutes; then Mrs. Darley said:

'I fear that Aimée is right, and that the lad was not duly whipped when young. Such ungoverned tempers must prove something wrong; yet Mr. Swinden was no fond fool to spare the rod. Well, sweet one, and to this weighty question, when shall Amyot tell his uncle, I scarce know what to say; I will consider, Joan. I would I knew in what fashion the boy will tell it—much depends on that. Mr. Pomfret is not always the pleasant gentleman that thou hast seen him.' Joan's lips quivered in the glow of the firelight; her grandmother perceived it, and stroked her fair hair. 'Thy brother is a sore pain to thee, child,' she said. 'How say you, shall I see him to-morrow, and school him how to address his uncle, and shall I tell Mr. Pomfret the tale he has to hear, and so prepare his mind beforehand?'

' Oh, grandmother, if you would be so good!'

' Ay, it will be better so ; and now that I can assure thy uncle that his son will live, perchance he will bear it with less anger ; but he is sitting beside the patient now, and may not be disturbed ; and thou, Joan, shouldst be with thy aunt. Leave me, child—I am weary, and intend to take some rest.'

' And, grandmother, may I know what my uncle says ?'

' Thou wilt know all that it concerns thee to know ; and now go. If the lad is to be hanged, I will not fail to tell thee.'

The sight of that black ribbon, and the night of anxious doubt that had followed it, had wrought in Amyot a marvellous degree of self-reproach and contrition ; and when he appeared in his grandmother's presence, it was with no thought of defending himself or explaining away his fault. His passion fairly over, Amyot was ever apt rather to exaggerate than make light of its disastrous effects, and to declare that he was, without exception, the most desperate character in the universe. In just such a mood did he now stand before Mrs. Darley, and the old lady could scarce conceal a smile at the sight of her tall, strongly built grandson, overwhelmed with shame and confusion, listening patiently to her reproof, and entirely acquiescing in its justice.

'What's to be done with thee?' she said, gazing at his blushing face over the top of her spectacles. 'Truly, I think you English people a most stubborn set of beings. It is the roast beef and the strong ale. Thou needest to be kept on bread and water; nought else will exorcise the evil spirits which rule over thee. What! a poor starving wretch wants some money that thou owest him, and thou art so enraged that thou wouldst break his head; and so blind does thy passion make thee, that thou dost not even know the man who has offended thee! Whence got you this mad temper, grandson Amyot, I pray thee?'

'Truly, madam, I know not. Glad would I be to be quit of it.'

'Like enough, like enough; when the mischief is done thou art mighty sorry! But hearken, thou young villain—wouldst have been as grieved had thy iron fist broken thy enemy's skull instead of thy cousin's? Tell me that, and then shall I know how much thy repentance means.'

'Dear madam, I have not thought on that

matter. My cousin's danger has put all other thoughts out of my head.'

' I thought no less. It is a poor brain, thine, Amyot. Well, I set thee this lesson. Wilt thou study it ? Yes, thou sayest. I doubt it. Once out of this scrape, thou wilt forget all thy sorrow and repentance, and plunge straight into another. Nay, make no promises. I know thee. It hath been ever thus.'

' I am in no mood to hope well of myself, madam,' Amyot replied gloomily. ' When passion seizes me, I own I am possessed, and know not what I do.'

' Then I tell thee, grandson, that thou must learn to rout out the demon that possesses thee, or we must seek a lodging for thee in Bedlam ; but if I hear thee speak more in this foolish fashion, I will add another to the many ill-names I give thee in my mind, and call thee coward. Yes, Amyot Brough, if thou canst not war against thyself, I call thee coward. What ! thou canst look at me now !'

' Grandmother, it is not I. When I am in a passion, I don't know what I am doing.'

' Talk not such silly stuff to me. Thou hadst full knowledge of all thine actions on

Friday night ; thou wilt not escape me thus.
And now, what dost thou propose to say to
thine uncle ?'

'Nothing but that I grieve from my heart.
There is nothing else for me to say.'

'Well, doubtless thou wilt be glad to hear
that Mr. Pomfret has no wish to see thee. So
he bade me tell thee. I told him the ugly story
last night, and found that he had guessed the
whole. Art astonished ? Well, so was I. This
was how it came about. Thy cousin revived
much yesterday, towards evening, was quite
himself, and talked cheerfully, and his father—
men will be fools—asked him about his accident—whether he knew who had struck the
blow. Arnold was loath to speak, but at length
confessed that he did. He was sure, he said,
that some mistake was the cause, and he prayed
his father not to urge him further, saying that it
was one known to both, and much discomfort
might arise if the thing were known. Your
uncle had marked your sister's disconsolate
state, and had little difficulty in guessing who
was in fault. To content Arnold, he promised
to keep the secret from thy aunt ; but he bade
me tell thee he had no wish to see thee for the
present.'

'And my cousin—did he say anything of me?'

'What should he say of thee? Send thee his respects and thanks for thy courtesy, maybe! Nay, he named thee not.   It is likely that even as thou preferrest to think thyself mad, so he chooses to think thee drunk.   And now thou hadst best seek thy sister, and bid her farewell; and when thou art far away, and thinkest of thy cross old grandmother, remember that she is ready enough to be proud of thee if thou wilt let her.'

CHAPTER XVII.

Yea or Nay?

MRS. DARLEY'S confident assurances were verified, and in three weeks Arnold was himself again, and ready to return to his work. By common consent the cause of his illness was seldom mentioned. ' It has a vulgar sound to have been wounded in a drunken frolic,' Mrs. Pomfret said, and her step-son smiled and cordially agreed, the more readily that such remarks were wont to bring painful blushes to Joan's face and a gloomy scowl to his father's. The former was oppressed with a constant and ever-recurring burden of self-reproach, in that she had failed again and again to induce her cousin to listen to her timidly expressed regrets that one belonging to her should have done him harm. Arnold always turned the subject whenever she attempted to allude to his illness, though whenever Amyot's name was mentioned by her or anyone else, he was as much interested and as full of kindly sympathy as he had ever been. It seemed to Joan that he was more interested in the one letter she had received from Amyot since his departure for Flanders than anyone else in the house. More than once she asked herself if it was not possible that his memory had been impaired by his illness, though that she knew could scarcely be, since he had told his father all particulars of the accident with perfect clearness.

The day before that fixed for his return to Swynford, he came into the parlour where Joan was engaged in writing a letter. So intent was she on her employment, that she did not look up when he entered the room. For some time he occupied himself with a book; and after a while a lively conversation began between himself and Mrs. Darley, who was knitting near the window; and Joan, amused, laid down her pen and listened.

This her grandmother soon perceived.

'Joan, thou idle child, finish thy letter and get thy seam. Thou hast been long enough busy over that long letter to thy good-for-nothing brother! I would have thee better employed.'

Joan's fair face flushed; she looked up suddenly, and her eyes met Arnold's, who said:

' Have you space, Cousin Joan, for a message from me? It is of no great matter if the paper is full; if not, will you give him his cousin Arnold's loving wishes, and tell him I look to see him at my house when he returns from the wars?'

Joan's pen faithfully recorded the words; then, having sealed her letter, she rose hastily to fetch her sewing: and as she passed Arnold's chair, she said in a low voice:

' Cousin, I thank you with all my heart; and so, I know, will Amyot.'

' Nay, the invitation is scarce worth thanks,' said Arnold lightly, as he opened the door for her; ' if you had seen my house, you would wonder that I should dare to give it.'

' Arnold, you are a base schemer, and I will have none of your evil doings. You are winning the child's heart, and you dare to do it before my face!'

' I dare not do it behind your back, madam; but, to tell the truth, I had not dreamed that as yet she cared for me. Do you truly mean what you say ?'

'Arnold, we had best look into this matter. Tell me what are your own thoughts, and I will tell you mine.'

'Then mine are quickly told : I love my cousin Joan—yes, more than ever I had thought to love anyone—and every time I see her, I am more and more set upon winning her to be my wife. Those are my thoughts, dear madam— bluntly told, but the truth, and nothing but the truth : and now will you tell me your mind, much though I fear to hear it.'

'My good Arnold, I will be tender of your feelings ; and, to begin, I will not scruple to say that I like you moderately well. You will not, I think, ill-use my child ; you will not beat her, swear at her, nor starve her. Nay, laugh me not to scorn, but hear me further. I am not ques- tioning that you love the child, but yet there is such a thing as a selfish love ; and I have no mind that my child shall be your wife merely because you want some one to make your home bright, look after your servants, and mend your linen : there are many homely wenches who can do all that, and are good enough for parsons' wives. I listened to your description of your

house the other night, and I said to myself,
" The child shall not live there ;" so now your
reverence has my mind—but nay, not altogether;
I may have more to say by-and-by.'

Arnold Pomfret was silent for a minute, but
only for a minute.

'I am considering,' he said, 'how best to
prove to you that my love for my cousin is of a
better kind than you deem.   Yet I thought you
knew me better than to judge me likely to
marry merely to improve my bodily comfort.
Yet I would not have you think that I had
purposed to take her to my house as now it is,
and as you heard me describe it.   Much must be
done to the old rectory before it would be fit for
a lady's presence ; and as soon as my church is
made somewhat more fit to be called by such a
name, then I mean to set about the repair of
the house.'

' And why not repair both at once ?'

Arnold hesitated, and began to pace the room
with his eyes fixed on the carpet.   At length he
said:

' You will always have a full confession, dear
madam ; and indeed, were it only my own business, I would conceal nothing from you : but
this much must I say, that of the money which

I had destined for the repair of both church and rectory I have been forced to use a part; and so I must defer the rebuilding of my own house for six months at least. Therefore, madam, you see that my cousin will not be hurried into matrimony, if she be pleased to favour my suit.'

'And this money, you have wasted it, Arnold Pomfret—I know you have! Do you think a careless spendthrift shall have my child? What call can a young priest have to spend such a sum of money, unless it be sinful waste? Ha! I have it! This money has gone to pay Guy's gaming debts—I know it! My daughter Pomfret told me that his father would pay no more, and she lamented her son's hard lot—not so hard, it seems, since he has a soft simpleton of a brother who will come to his aid. Nay, nay, I doubt much whether you are fit to wed my child.'

'Since you but doubt, I must take leave to hope, madam. May I not approach the subject with my cousin herself? I leave London to-morrow in the early morning.'

'You are a bold man to talk thus to me. I tell you my mind is not made up. What says your father of this whim of yours?'

' He is well satisfied with my purpose, and bade me hold fast by it ; not, I trust, that he judged me likely to change, but that he foresaw some difficulties in the way. You, madam, he said, could ill spare your grand-daughter.'

' He said that !' said the old lady, bridling. ' Men judge all others by the measure of their own selfishness. And your mother—what did her wisdom put forth ?'

' I have not spoken to her of the matter, but am well convinced that she loves my cousin well, and will be right pleased to call her daughter.'

' Of course, of course. Well, Arnold Pomfret, listen to me. This forenoon I go a-driving with my daughter Pomfret ; Joan will be at home ; she has writing to do for me, and so you do not take up all her time, I care not if you have some conversation with her. The child has sense, and will not ascribe too much meaning to your words ; and if my good Johnstone should chance to be of your company, it need not inconvenience you, since she has lost her hearing, and seldom comprehends except it be most specially ill-convenient. Nay, don't thank me ; the maiden has not said " Ay " yet, and neither have I.'

'A terrible tedious drive, child, and a fog came up from the river before we reached home. I verily thought the man would lose his way ; but the oil-lamps were lighted and the link-boys out as if it was night. But it's over now and no harm done, but that I am wearied of your aunt's shrieks and the jolting of the chariot. But I have good news for thee, Joan. I called to see Mrs. Wolfe in Old Burlington Street, and she has had tidings from her son James, who is with the army in Flanders ; and he speaks of having met his old schoolfellow, Amyot Brough—" a likely young fellow," he calls him, and that from James Wolfe .. high praise, as thou very well knowest. But how now, Joan ; thou art not attending to my words. Art deaf to the praises of thy beloved Amyot ?'

'Grandmother—madam, something has happened in your absence. I am almost afraid to tell it, lest you should think me to blame ; yet I do not know what else I could have done.'

'What hast thou done, child ?—torn thy slip, or dropped ink on thy new apron, or quarrelled with thy cousin ?'

'Grandmother, would you have me quarrel with him ? Sometimes I think you would.'

'And so thou hast done it just to pleasure me. Thou art a most dutiful grandchild. But what was the matter of thy quarrel, and which began it ?'

Joan dropped her eyes, and tracing with her slender foot the pattern of the carpet, said, while a smile played about her mouth :

' It has not yet begun, madam ; yet it seems to me that we are like to quarrel all our lives long, and that for a most silly purpose. Can you guess my riddle, dear grandmother ?'

The old lady sat down, and taking the girl's two hands in hers, said :

' Thy cousin Arnold has asked thee to be his wife, child—that much I guess ; but if thou wilt have nought to do with such a purpose, it had been better that thou hadst left the matter in my hands. A young girl should not be in haste to wound an honest man.'

' Dear grandmother, I did not wound him. What I said I cannot precisely tell ; but he was not vexed. How could he be ? Surely, he knew that what he wished and you wished, I would gladly do.'

' Then how about the quarrel ?'

' Dear grandmother, I was but joking. My cousin would have me believe that he holds me

most singularly dear. It is his kindly heart
that makes him ever think others so monstrous
excellent. I was too abashed to chide him for
his foolishness, but I told myself that since I,
too, held him good and great beyond all other,
we should for ever quarrel which should love
the other most.'

'Thou silly child, art sure thou lovest that
tall, grave-visaged priest ? What canst thou
find in him to like, I ask thee ?'

But Joan's eloquence had exhausted itself.

'Indeed, madam, I cannot tell ; yet I do know
this : he is quite unlike all others that I have seen.'

'You have seen but few, perhaps scarce
enough to be sure that thou knowest thine
own mind. One day I thought thou hadst a
liking for thy brother's merry friend, Lieutenant
Jack Pownal.'

'Oh, madam, to speak of him beside my
cousin Arnold !'

'Well, well, is it so ? But listen, child ;
there shall be no talk of marriage until I give
thee leave. Thy cousin has a house not fit to
lodge a pig. He has much to do before he
thinks of wedlock.'

'Grandmother, did you think I should be in
haste to leave you ?'

'N'importe. I must seek out another stray child, but this time she shall be ill-favoured enough to stay with me. Naught that is pleasant to gaze on will rest satisfied with my company, and I love not changes.'

Yet as the evening passed, it seemed strange to Joan that what had made so great a change to her personally, had made so little outward difference. Her grandmother and aunt talked of their drive, their visits, the fog, and other trivial matters; her uncle discussed politics with his son, and she, as was her wont, sat silent and listened; and yet it was Arnold's last evening, and to-morrow they would be miles asunder. Was it all a dream? Had she wholly misunderstood his meaning? Joan shuddered at the thought. Surely, when that long dinner was over, they would have more of the converse which had been so sweet in the afternoon. What was that her uncle was saying?

'Come with me to the play to-night, Arnold. Your mother fears the fog, and will not venture abroad. You care not for the play, I know, but you might bear me company this last night of your stay in town.'

'Rather, Mr. Pomfret,' said his wife fretfully.

'should you stay with us, and not deprive me of my son's society, since I cannot go abroad.'

'That would I gladly, since I, too, detest the fog, and have no great esteem for this particular play; but I have promised to meet some friends there, and I choose to abide by my word. But stay with your mother, Arnold, if you will.'

'If you will allow me, sir, I will drive with you to the theatre, and return at once ; I start early to-morrow, and have still some preparations to make.'

And thus it was settled, and Joan breathed freely again.

'My son Arnold *is* a true gentleman,' said Mrs. Pomfret, when the two gentlemen had departed ; 'yet he has an awkward mode of speech—why did he not pay me the compliment which in his heart he intended, instead of speaking as if all his thoughts were set on his baggage ?'

'I, too, feel aggrieved,' Mrs. Darley said, her bright eyes full of merriment. 'I looked for a neatly turned phrase of politeness, and lo, I am forgotten entirely ! Joan, how thinkest thou ?— is not thy cousin a barbarian ?'

'Poor Joan !' remarked Mrs. Pomfret ; 'if she looks for courtesy from her cousin, she must have been monstrously disappointed throughout her sojourn here. In his eyes it is verily a crime for a lady to be young ; he is a mighty strange person. I should have warned you, Joan, of his uncouth manners, and that you must not look for pretty speeches from him.'

'Dear aunt, he is always kind to me,' was Joan's reply, while her fair face and neck flushed rosy red, whereupon Mrs. Pomfret exclaimed impatiently :

'Kind, of course ; but you do not take my meaning, child. Arnold has a fine presence and figure, but he lacks those elegancies in word and pleasant turns of speech which mark a man of good-breeding. Mother, your fair dove is but a wood-pigeon still.'

'Joan, while we poor women are left to entertain ourselves, thou hadst best amuse us by reading aloud. Fetch that book of verse thy uncle commended to thee, and give us something wise for our meditations. Thy aunt will soon improve upon them in her dreams. She loves a short sleep after dinner.'

Joan obeyed, and while Mrs. Pomfret reclining on her couch, soon fell into a doze, her more alert mother sat erect, well pleased to listen to the musical voice that gave forth the pleasant lines with such correct modulations, and to feast her eyes on the graceful figure and fair face before her.

'That will do, child ; it is pleasant verse enough, but thy aunt is in the land of dreams, and here is thy cousin returned to pack his effects ; perhaps he has need of our help—are there any small concerns to be set in order before you return to your wilderness, reverend sir ? We are well persuaded that nought but the care of your worldly affairs brought you home from the play to-night.'

'I will not contradict you, madam, since my worldly affairs comprise other matters beside my clothes and books ;' then, glancing from her to his mother, and perceiving that she had not been aroused by his entrance, he added in a lower tone, as he stooped over the old lady's chair : 'My cousin did not say me nay ; she has been very good to me, but I am not yet entirely content, and thinking over all I said to her, I fear I led her into the error of supposing that the scheme I had so much at heart was wholly to your liking, therefore I pray you, madam, absolve me from the sin of this small deception, and say that you are well content.'

'I never was in all my life—it is not my nature

to be contented ; I am ever hoping for something better to befall, or striving hard to think well of things as they are. Therefore, Arnold Pomfret, it is useless to seek for such professions from me ; you must make yourself happy with having gained your end, which should be enough for any man.'

'But it is not enough for me,' he pleaded earnestly, 'nor for my cousin either, I see it in her face.'

'Then what will you both do ? Do you imagine I shall shower blessings on you just for the sake of adding to your bliss, which seems to me as perfect as needs be. No, I shall hold to my right to grumble, and you must put up with it.'

Arnold withdrew his arm from the back of the resolute old lady's chair, and looking sorely perplexed, placed himself at the opposite side of the hearth, leaning against the chimney-piece, and gazing at Joan's downcast face, in which the colour came and went, as she listened to this conversation.

At last she looked up suddenly as she felt his eyes fixed on her, and said timidly : 'Cousin, you do not know my grandmother, or you would be well satisfied to leave the matter thus.'

'Should I ? Then enlighten me, sweet cousin,
or I feel myself defeated in this combat, and
scarcely know whether you are truly mine or
not.'

'Then my grandmother has gained her object,
and is triumphing over you. She delights to
puzzle people, and now I know she is much
elated. Dear madam,' Joan was now kneeling
at her feet, stroking the white wrinkled hands,
'you force me to let out your secrets : when you
thought for one minute that I was unwilling to
do what my cousin wishes, you were angry
with me, and blamed me that I had wounded
him ; yes, Cousin Arnold, that is the truth, so
now you know that she is well content. No,
grandmother, do not pull your hand away! I
want it, and Aunt Pomfret's dog has carried off
your knitting.'

'Get up, Joan, and cease thy falsehoods, child;
thy aunt is waking, and will be curious to know
what all this turmoil is about. Arnold, we will
make the best of this bad business ; who knows
but you may get your head broken in right
earnest before the wedding-day ? Your roof is
likely to tumble in, I hear, and the staircase
will scarce bear your weight. We will keep up
our spirits, there is hope for us yet!'

CHAPTER XVIII.

Captain Guy.

'I do not love changes,' Mrs. Darley had said in prospect of Joan's betrothal, and as if to prove the sincerity of her words, the months that succeeded that event were passed by her and Joan in the most unbroken regularity and monotony at Westerham.

Returned there, the old lady lost no time in discovering that her grandchild's education was by no means perfect. 'What have I been about?' she said. 'Why, I have been bringing her up to be a fine lady, and she is going to become a parson's drudge, to mend and make, bake and brew, cure and cook, for a parish. We must begin all over again. Dear me! it would have saved a world of trouble if I had settled about the husband before I began the training of the child.'

And to repair her many deficiencies, Joan was set to study the art of housekeeping, and to learn by practice the many duties which would fall to her share as a poor man's wife; for 'though he has an ample income, Arnold Pomfret will always be a poor man,' Mrs. Darley averred, and Joan agreed that it was highly probable.

And while the spring and summer of 1747 were passing away thus monotonously in the quiet Kentish village, Amyot was growing used to his military duties in Flanders, and, not a little to his surprise, discovering that even in time of war it was possible for one day's duties to be much like another, and for events and excitements to be rare.

Fortune did not smile on the British arms in this campaign, and much discontent was the consequence. Amyot, who had scarcely ever thought of the possibility of defeat, was much surprised that French armies did not vanish like smoke before the allies, and much inclined to think somebody ought to be shot or superseded.

'We spend such heaps of time doing nothing,' he complained, as with his comrade, Jack Pownal, he sauntered listlessly along the streets of Maestricht one autumn evening ; they were quartered in the town, and spent much of their time together. 'There's that place they make such a fuss about, Bergen-op-Zoom. Why can't they send us there ?—it will surrender in no time to these beggarly Frenchmen, you see if it doesn't !'

'Yes, all the world knows that ; bι , do you see, mon cher, we are not in their confidence. They have their reasons, our generals, and no doubt they are very good.'

'No doubt they are very bad, I should say. It is the Prince of Orange and the Dutch who keep us doing nothing. It is a bad plan, this partnership business ; our Duke is brave enough, and clever enough—if he had his own way, things would go differently ; but these Dutch are lazy—they're never to the fore when they are wanted.'

'Well, my dear Brough, it may be as you say ; but after our one combat at Laffelt, I am not entirely convinced that it is quite impossible that we shall be beaten. Experience learns us many things. and you know the proverb, " The child that burns himself fears the fire." '

'Then, having been beaten once, are we never to fight again?'

'Softly, mon cher; but assuredly we will fight again—"He that fights and runs himself away, will live and will fight on another day." That is a fine sentiment, truly.'

'You *are* a brave fellow, Jack—you are more than half a Frenchman yourself!'

'But no, my brave fellow, it was not the French that saved themselves at Laffelt.'

'Neither was it the English!'

'Oh no, neither the one nor the other.'

'Well, for my part, I wish I had taken up my father's trade; they *can* fight like Britons at sea.'

'They haven't old Maurice to fight against—he would outwit them if they had.'

'Jack, you make me mad. No Frenchman could beat us if we had but fair play.'

'There you are wrong, altogether and quite entirely wrong. What did your friend James Wolfe tell you the other day, that a soldier must, before all things, be modest? You do not follow his advice. And yet am I much obliged to Messieurs the Admirals Anson and Hawke; if they had not made an end of the French fleets, we should be too entirely ashamed of ourselves.'

Amyot was silent; then, as if desirous of changing the subject, remarked :

'Have you heard that Wolfe has received a wound ?—not a very serious one, yet they say it is likely he will return to England before winter. Some say the Duke goes soon, and that peace will shortly be concluded. We shall not carry much glory home with us.'

'Nay, our shoulders might support a trifle more; but we being nobodies, that will be no great matter. And, for the Duke, everyone can see it is no want of courage. A somebody, I know not precisely who, has said that he has not the talents for to make a great general.'

'Somebodies without names generally talk prodigious folly,' Amyot replied irreverently. 'But how like you the idea of a peace, and nothing to do, Jack ?'

'It is not precisely to my taste, but, in fine, that will not endure.'

'Jack, you must go to school and learn English. Sometimes you talk like a native, and then again there is no sense in what you say.'

'So, then will I try to improve. I will

marry an English wife, and she shall chastise me.'

'No, truly, she shall correct you, you mean.'

' Correct, chastise, it is all the same thing, no difference at all. And you, Amyot, you shall learn French; you have greatly neglected all your good occasions—tiens! it is abominable, shameful to reflect, that you have a friend who speaks the French like a native, and a grand-mother who was lifted up at St. Cyr, and who is Parisienne to the ends of her fingers, and your accent is truly barbarous.'

' Because I hate French—I am a Briton.'

' You are half French, you big John Bull. Allons! you *shall* learn the French, and speak him like a native too.'

' Stop, Jack; do you see that long fellow coming down the street?'

'What, the Captain Guy Pomfret ? I save myself! he puts always his hand into other men's pockets, and mine is inconvenient empty,' and Jack darted off like a shot, while Guy Pomfret, perceiving Amyot, crossed the street, and ac-costed him with the familiarity of a relative and old friend.

' Charmed to meet—haven't seen you for

ever so long— thought you must have fallen at Laffelt. No! what luck—anything to do ? Come along and spend the evening at my quarters— some capital fellows coming. Cards—oh yes; don't play if not convenient, but give us your company.' And Amyot, not quite willingly, agreed.

Jack, from a safe distance, had watched the proceeding, and ejaculating ' Very content you are not my cousin, Monsieur le Capitaine !' departed in an opposite direction.

Three officers were lounging in Captain Guy's quarters when he and Amyot arrived. All were strangers to Amyot, and eyed him somewhat suspiciously, until the words ' My cousin' from their host explained his appearance ; then their manner entirely changed—they greeted him with rapture, courteously begged he would take a hand, while Guy pressed him to make himself at home, and play or not, just as he liked.

'Any news from the old people, Brough ?' asked the merry captain, as Amyot seated himself at the table ; ' they never write to me—have dropped my acquaintance altogether ; shall drop theirs when I go home.'

' Close-fisted, aren't they ?' said one of the

company; 'younger sons are apt to be counted troublesome.'

'Just so,' said Guy; 'ought to be a law against a man having two sons.'

'Your cousin's an only son, I've heard you say.'

'Yes; with a prodigious handsome sister though, going to marry my brother.'

'What, the parson?—mad, isn't he, Pomfret?'

'Not too mad to manage his own affairs, I am sorry to say. What's the matter, Brough?'

'I—I don't understand you,' said Amyot, reddening. 'Is your brother mad?'

'Oh, not what the doctors call mad, only a trifle strange here,' and he touched his forehead.

'Madder than you?' asked Amyot, whereupon the others laughed, and said that was not so bad a hit.

'Oh, we're all mad,' said Guy indifferently, 'but the disease takes different forms—go on, Amyot, fire away.'

The game proceeded more silently, and very much in earnest, and Amyot was beginning to think of the letter he should have to compose to his old lawyer at Penrith, when a heavy step was heard on the stair, which creaked and shook, as a hand fumbled at the door, and a private soldier, put in his head with : ' By your leave, gentlemen ; I was sent hither to search for a certain Lieutenant Brough—do you know such a name ?'

' That's he ; what do you want, man ?'

' I was to give him this here,' said the soldier, ' and to say as I have a horse below.'

Amyot opened the folded paper, and read :

' I am starting for England in a day or two. Can you come and see me for an hour ?   I am detained in my quarters by a trifle of a wound, but would be glad to be the bearer of any messages for your friends.

' J. W.'

Captain Guy read the billet over his shoulder and scowled. ' How did he know where you were ?' he asked.

' I cannot guess ; but it is good-natured of him to make this offer.   I pray you, excuse me, Guy, and you, gentlemen.'

' Nay, stay and finish this rubber,—you must ; hulloa there, you fellow, walk the horse about that he may not catch cold !   Sit down for five minutes, Brough. '

The five minutes had grown to thirty before Amyot made his escape, uncomfortably conscious that his diversion had cost him more than was any way convenient, and inexpressibly glad of the excuse which had enabled him to leave his merry friends so soon. And as he started off in the direction pointed out to him by the soldier who had brought the letter, and felt the cool evening breeze blow on his face, he asked himself how he could have been such a fool as to have been drawn into play with such sharp hands as were always to be found at his cousin's quarters.

'I am an idiot, and nothing less, always doing what I've vowed I won't; but how could Wolfe know where I was, I wonder?'

This question was easily answered when he reached his destination; as he entered the house, the sound of voices reached his ear and in a moment he found himself pounced upon by his lively friend Jack, who exclaimed: 'Arrived—our trick has then succeeded! Were they very ferocious, your cousin and his friends?'— while Wolfe, raising himself from a half reclining attitude, joined in the laugh, and added: 'I warrant you've left a small fortune behind you; how are you, Brough? Will you forgive me for enticing you away from your amiable friends ?'

'I was glad enough to come,' Amyot replied; 'but did Jack tell you where I was, since your messenger said he had no difficulty in tracing me out ?'

'Jack came here a while since, much concerned for you. I railed at him for deserting you in such a faint-hearted fashion; but he alleged that Captain Pomfret being your cousin, he had scruples about interfering between you; but I was less delicate, you see. But now, I pray you be seated. This is but a mean kind of room, and we have neither wine nor cards for your entertainment; but Jack is a merry fellow, and the best of company when he chooses.'

'And when are you going home, captain?' inquired Amyot; 'and how came you by your wound ?'

'At Laffelt, I have but just come here. When am I going home? In a few days, I expect; your regiment may remain here through the winter, or be speedily sent to England; but I shall certainly start before you. What commissions have you for me? I shall make it my business to see your uncle and aunt; and before long I shall hope to go to Westerham, to see my own friends, and yours too.'

Amyot charged him with some few messages, which Wolfe noted down and promised to deliver faithfully, while Jack Pownal paced the room, humming martial airs. At last, impatient at having no share in the conversation, he broke in, exclaiming :

'If you see the good Amyot's fair sister, you may bear her a message from me, captain ; tell her that he does not conduct himself entirely to my taste, that he still loves play, that he still has pleasure in quarrels, and in fine, he is not always " bon garçon." She should write to him and reproach him, for truly there are the moments when he gives me much of pain.'

'I will not forget,' said Wolfe gravely. 'And you, Amyot, have you no defence to make ?'

'My sister knows Jack,' was the reply ; 'but he is wrong when he says I love play. I care very little about it, but I can't always refuse. And as for quarrels—I am the most peaceable fellow in the world when I am not put out.'

' Hear him ! hear him !' cried Jack. ' The most peaceable fellow in the world when he is not put out ! But touch him with the end of your little finger, and he will have your heart's blood ;

that is what you call peaceable, do you? Oh,
you are a vain dog, and there is no mistake!'

'But, Brough, pardon my curiosity,' said
Wolfe, when Jack stopped for breath. 'But
will your estate bear the pull you are making
on it? For I know that it is impossible to be
much in Captain Pomfret's company without
suffering for it. His friends, too, are hard
gamblers.'

'I know,' said Amyot, in a melancholy tone;
'but I don't want to quarrel with my cousin.'

'Listen! listen!' cried Jack. 'He not desire
to quarrel. Why, it is what he loves best in the
world. But, you see, he will only quarrel for a
nothing.'

'But need there be any question of quar-
relling?' said Wolfe.

'It would be difficult to avoid it—terrible
difficult,' Jack said, shaking his head. 'The
captain has a fashion of talking quite extraordinary. I save myself, that is what I do.'

'Run away, you mean—talk English, Jack.
Well, Brough, if you can't fight, let me counsel
you to do the same.'

'I'll keep out of his way whenever I can; but
running away, or refusing his invitations altogether—I cannot well do that.'

'You had better do so—it would be your wisest plan,' Wolfe began, when an unusual bustle outside attracted his attention, and Jack exclaimed :

'What is happening there below ? Shall I go to see ?'

'Some drunken row,' Wolfe remarked. But at that moment a heavy thud was heard outside the door, which was speedily burst open, and Captain Guy and two of his companions rushed into the room. One of them, stumbling on the uneven floor, made a headlong plunge, and lost his footing altogether. The other two, not being altogether steady on their legs, seated themselves without ceremony—one on the table, the other on the bedstead—and burst into a loud roar at the sight of their companion's prostrate figure. Then they looked round the room, and stared at the three friends as if uncertain who they were.

Amyot was the first to speak.

'What do you want, Guy ? The captain here is ill; you might have used a little more ceremony if you wished to see him.'

'Wished to see him ? oh, who ? I forget who we want; my memory is bad. Who was it, Solmes ?'

'The young blade who owes us money.
Don't know who he is—nor care either—but
you should know ; you brought him in, and let
him run off in that mean fashion—one of your
brood, no doubt ; they're all a mean lot.'

' Don't know what you're talking about,' said
Captain Guy, whose intellect was not of the
clearest ; ' why doesn't that fool get up ; somebody put him on his legs, will you ?'

' Look here, Guy,' broke out Amyot hotly,
' if I touch him, I'll pitch him out of window,
and you after him ; get off that table and take
yourself off. If you want me, I'll come with
you.'

' No, you won't,' said Wolfe in a low voice ;
'Captain Pomfret, my friends and I are engaged, particularly engaged, as the man outside
should have told you ; but perhaps you did not
ask him.'

'Can't understand ; don't know who you are,
or what you want. This table is precious un-
steady ; have you never a chair to offer a
gentleman ?'

' Not one,' said Jack. ' Your friend there
seems drowsy, captain,' for the other officer had
sunk back on the low bedstead in a heavy
drunken sleep, ' and your other friend is in still

worse case—he has fallen quite flat on his nose, and smashed him.'

' No ; has he ? Well, he came to get some money. Now it'll go to fee the surgeon, and he owes it to me. Who owed him the money ? Can't make out ; somebody here, I s'pose.'

' Captain Pomfret, allow me a few words in private,' said Jack, approaching with a deferential air ; ' just a little word in the street outside, where these gentlemen shall hear nothing ; I assure you it is vastly important, and much to your advantage.'

' To my advantage ? Then I am your man, to follow you to the ends of the earth,' and Guy rose with such alacrity that, his sight being not of the clearest, he had nearly measured his length over his prostrate friend, when Jack seized him by the arm, and with some difficulty piloted him safely to the door.

There were some loud words, and something like a scuffle in the street below, but in five minutes the young lieutenant returned triumphant, saying :

' I have done his affair: now to be rid of these two insensibles; they are entirely at our mercy. What shall we make of them ?—a bonfire ?—or pitch them out of window, as said Amyot ?'

'Get rid of them,' said Wolfe wearily, 'especially that fellow who is settled where I greatly desire to be. Can't you two take them up tenderly, so as not to disturb their slumbers, and put them out into the street, where they can wake at their leisure? Don't rouse that fellow Solmes—he is apt to be dangerous when in that condition.'

'Come along, Brough; gently, my dear fellow—let him think the mother's arms are still around him, and that he is again an innocent. "Hush, my babe, lie still and slumber"—so, so, my pretty; never lift the little head; but plague you, you are made of lead! Amyot, you boast of your great strength—exert it, I pray you, or I shall fall with fatigue.'

'You ought to be greatly obliged to us, Wolfe,' remarked Jack, when this task was accomplished, 'for having rid you of so much lumber, for verily my arms do ache, and Brough is in still worse case, giant though he is.'

'Rather,' said Amyot, 'ought I to be beholden to you both, for having endured so much annoyance on my behalf. I wish you had let me kick Guy out.'

'Ever the same; he will make himself be

hanged one of these days,' groaned Jack; while Wolfe added cheerily :

'Don't think of that, Amyot : it was my doing, seeing I sent for you from their company. But we are well rid of them ; how can we hope to beat the French with such men as they ? Let me pray you to forswear their company, for the honour of old England, if for no other reason.'

'I will,' said Amyot ; 'that is, when I have discharged my debt to them ; and now, captain, we'll relieve you of our company, of which I should say you must be heartily tired ; but, in truth, I never thought those noisy fellows would follow me, and I am sincerely sorry to have been the cause of such vexation to you.'

'Thanks to Jack here, they didn't trouble us long,' said Wolfe good-humouredly, as they took their departure ; Jack remarking :

'Do not deceive yourself, captain ; he'll be scampering after these rogues again in a day or two, and I, what shall I do ?' and he threw up his hands with a gesture of despair.

Amyot laughed.

'Why should you trouble yourself about me, Jack ?' he said, when they were again in the dark street, groping their way to their own quarters. 'Why not let me go to the bad, if you think I am so set upon it?'

'I did never say that, never; on the contrary, I think you are a brave garçon, real good fellow—like you much, love you with all my heart, but find you big fool, all the same.'

'Strangely contradictory,' said Amyot; 'explain yourself, Jack.'

'No, that is what I never am able to do; why, say you? Because I am an unreasonable being. Why do I like you? In verity, I cannot say, but all the world likes you, so I am in the fashion, only all the world does not tell you frankly you are a big fool.'

'Are you sure it is the case, then?'

'Sure! but yes; I can prove it to you so evidently that you will say, "Jack, my friend, I am a fool—you are right." And see you, this is why: First, you have not more money than you find convenient—you have confessed to me that you wish to spare it for a certain purpose, which purpose is one reason why I love you with all my heart; yet when that unlucky captain comes in your road, you go with him quite amiably, like a lamb, though you know quite well he will put his hand in your pocket; say, are you not a fool? Then you listen like a good child when

that wise Wolfe talks to you like a grandfather; you will do all that he says, you will
be good officer, good gentleman, good Christian; then you meet a man who is no good
officer, no gentleman, and very bad Christian,
and you too are a vaurien, a pagan, an idle
dog; but I tell you truly, that you are my friend,
and I love you with all my heart.'

'You are a queer kind of friend, Jack, if I
may make bold to say so.'

'Do we not say all what we will to each
other? is it not thing understood? Perhaps it is
also true, that when I say these unpleasant-
nesses, I walk a little further off, because I like
not black eyes, nor bumps, nor bruises, but I
am prudent, I—and when you make yourself
hanged, which assuredly you will some day, I
do not think it will be my head that you will
have broken, so am I quite content.'

'Whose will it be, think you?'

'Nay, how can I tell?—that rascal captain will
have blown his brains out before long, so I
do not think it will be his. N'importe! there
are always heads fit only to be broken, provided
you fall on one of these.'

Amyot was silent: a softened mood was on
him. Jack's raillery often wrought this effect,

and he listened humbly. At last his friend spoke again :

'And now will I tell you why you are brave garçon, and I love you de tout mon cœur.'

'No, Jack, you need not tell me that.'

'Yes, but I will. It is because a man can tell you the truth, all short, aim straight, and fire right in the face, and you will bear it.'

'For the simple reason that you aim so straight you shoot me dead—I have never a word to say,' Amyot replied ; 'but enough of that. Stick to me, Jack, if you can.'

'Stick to you! without doubt! You are out of heart to-night, my boy, because of this unlucky money, but we'll find a way out of that scrape —never despair !'

END OF VOL. I.

BILLING AND SONS, PRINTERS, GUILDFORD.